P9-CDV-946

DISCARDED

no place *for* heroes

Also by Laura Restrepo

PUBLISHED IN ENGLISH

Isle of Passion

Leopard in the Sun

The Angel of Galilea

The Dark Bride

A Tale of the Dispossessed

Delirium

no place *for* heroes

no place
for heroes

laura
restrepo

a novel

TRANSLATED FROM THE SPANISH
BY ERNESTO MESTRE-REED

Nan A. Talese • Doubleday *New York London Toronto Sydney Auckland*

This book is a work of fiction. Names, characters, businesses, organizations, places, events, and incidents either are the product of the author's imagination or are used fictitiously. Any resemblance to actual persons, living or dead, events, or locales is entirely coincidental.

www.nanatalese.com

Originally published in Spain as *Demasiados héroes* by Alfaguara, an imprint of Santillana Ediciones Generales, S.L., Madrid, in 2009.

Book design by Maria Carella

Library of Congress Cataloging-in-Publication Data
Restrepo, Laura.
[Demasiados héroes. English]
No place for heroes : a novel / Laura Restrepo ; translated from the Spanish by Ernesto Mestre-Reed. — 1st American ed.
p. cm.
Originally published in Spain as Demasiados héroes in 2009.
1. Mothers and sons—Fiction. 2. Colombians—Argentina—Fiction. 3. Voyages and travels—Fiction. 4. Birthfathers—Fiction. 5. Buenos Aires (Argentina)—Fiction. 6. Argentina—History—Dirty War, 1976–1983—Fiction. I. Mestre-Reed, Ernesto. II. Title.
PQ8180.28.E7255D4713 2010
863'.64—dc22 2009047858

ISBN 978-0-385-51991-5

PRINTED IN THE UNITED STATES OF AMERICA

10 9 8 7 6 5 4 3 2 1

First American Edition

To Payán, by his side

Everyone has the right to
think his father is a good guy.

FÉLIX ROMEO

As for me, right now I'm
not in the mood to listen
to heroics.

ELIAS KHOURY

❧

"I NEED TO know how it happened," Mateo tells his mother. "The dark episode, I need to know exactly how it happened."

"I've already told you a thousand times," she responds.

He was the one who had given it that name, *the dark episode*, partly because it had been so painful but also because it was buried under a mountain of half-truths. The worst part was that he had no memory of it because he had been too young to remember. Blindly stabbing—an expression he had heard. That's how he felt, like a blind man trying to jab his way out of a story that he did not understand, but in which he played a part and which snared him in its net.

"Come on, Lolé," Mateo says, softening his voice and addressing her by the name he had always used when he was a child. Now he prefers to call her by her given name,

Lorenza, and when he is irate with her, simply Mother. "Come on, Lolé, tell me again. Let's begin with the park."

"You were two and a half. It was a Thursday afternoon, and you, your father, and I were in Bogotá. At the Parque de la Independencia."

"And he was wearing a thick wool sweater."

"Perhaps."

"From the pictures I know that he liked to wear thick wool sweaters."

"Not sweaters, pullovers."

"What are pullovers?"

"Sweaters, but that's what he called them. Pullovers. We Colombians call them sweaters; in Argentina they call them pullovers. Ridiculous really, since they are both English words."

"But what I want to know is if he was wearing a thick wool sweater that specific afternoon."

"Who knows? But I do remember his hair was long. In Argentina he always had to keep it short, the dictatorship did not tolerate hippies. But when he got to Colombia, he let it grow. If you want to know what your father looked like then, Mateo, look in the mirror and add a dozen years. That's how he looked."

"Not true, I don't have wide shoulders. Uncle Patrick told me that Ramón's shoulders were wide."

"Soon yours will be just like his."

"Okay, back to the afternoon, in the park."

"Ramón and I stroll, hand in hand with you. The sky is hydrangea-blue, like it is in Bogotá when—"

"I don't care about the color of the sky in Bogotá," Mateo says. "I want to know what happened."

Sometimes Lorenza tells her son that the most horrendous thing about the dark episode is that it happened exactly when she thought the horrors had all but ended. They had left the Argentinean dictatorship behind, and she and Ramón had survived living underground. After five years together in the resistance movement, they had distanced themselves from the party and left Argentina for Colombia, as bewildered as monks who abandon the cloister and poke their noses out into the world. For Lorenza, who was Colombian, the change had not been too difficult; after all, the return to Bogotá had allowed her to be with her people again, in a world that she knew well and that she took to without much drama. But for Ramón, an Argentinean, the move left him in limbo. He grew contemptuous of everything around him. He found her family abominably bourgeois and began to treat her like some unfathomable creature who had little in common with the woman he had fallen in love with in Buenos Aires. Once the complicity that had bound them during their years in the underground was broken, they became strangers to each other.

"In Bogotá, your father became invisible to me," Lorenza confesses to her son.

"What do you mean 'invisible'? Nobody really becomes invisible."

"Maybe I was too busy with you, with my job, with my family, maybe just busy with myself. Besides, this does happen with people who have grown very close during times of danger. The danger passes and they quickly find out that it was the only thing keeping them together. You see, I no longer had a place for your father, like having to wear a thick coat in the middle of summer."

"A woolen pullover in the middle of summer."

"You don't know what to do with such a thing, it doesn't belong on you. But Ramón didn't help either; he began to behave in a manner that, let's just say, was unusual. He couldn't come to grips with life outside the party. But wait, it was worse than that, he couldn't come to terms with how to live outside the dictatorship, without having an enemy right in his face that he had to destroy before it destroyed him. All this made living together an incurable headache, so we separated."

"Stop, Lorenza. *We separated?* You say 'we separated' and that's it, you're free and clear? Who separated? Whose idea was it?"

"Mine."

"You wanted to separate?"

"Yes."

"And my father didn't want to?"

"No. He didn't."

"That's very different than 'we separated,' no?"

"I had gotten a job as a journalist, and when I left him, I took you with me to my mother's. Ramón stayed in the apartment that we rented in the center of the city."

"So we suddenly became upper class, and he remained in near poverty."

"Not exactly. You and I were in a guest room, and he had his own apartment."

"Let's go back to the park."

"We're in the park. Thursday, five in the afternoon. He lifted you up to one of the horses on the carousel, and we stood on either side to hold you and talked. A surprisingly quiet chat, I would say, nothing like the heated arguments we had before the separation. Ramón asks me if I am sure that the separation is what I want. A few days earlier he would have screamed such a thing at me, but now he poses the question in a neutral tone, like a notary clarifying some detail. I tell him yes, I'm sure, that the separation is over and done with, that it doesn't make sense to reopen the discussion. He says he didn't mean he wanted to discuss anything, he only needs to make sure that there's no going back. Yes, I say, there's no going back. He doesn't persist and changes the topic. He says he's going to take you on a trip to a finca for the weekend. He'll pick you up early the next morning, Friday, and bring you back Sunday before seven at night. It's a finca near Villa de Leyva, and your father says that I should bundle you up because it will be cold."

"Don't you ask whose finca it is and where it is exactly? Don't you even ask for the phone number of where I'll be?"

"No. I don't want him to think that I am questioning his life. He is an excellent father, who adores you and cares for you well, and at that moment it seems to me the most natural thing in the world that he wants to spend a few days alone with you. I also remember thinking that if he was already organizing trips, it was because he had grown used to the idea of the separation. We each take you by the hand, and as night falls, the three of us stroll again through the park. At a certain point, you fall and scrape your knee and cry a little, not long though, nothing major. The strange thing is that Ramón and I chat agreeably, but about nothing in particular. For the first time since the quarrels of the separation began, we have a nice time together. I start to feel that perhaps we can function as a separated couple who share a son amicably, and that makes me happy."

"Okay," Mateo says. "And now to the dark episode."

"Friday, I get you up early, bathe you, dress you, and ask your grandmother to make you breakfast."

"You said before that you made me breakfast."

"No, your grandmother does. I pack your suitcase for the cold, a pair of corduroy overalls, a sweater—"

"Pullover."

"A pullover, socks and undershirts, your teddy bear pajamas, which are the warmest, your raincoat and galoshes. At seven thirty, Ramón rings the bell, and I turn over the child—that's you—and the suitcase to him. You're very happy, you enjoy being with your father and are glad to see him. I also give him another bag stuffed with Choco Quick, some apples, powdered milk, a box of Rice Krispies, and two of your toys."

"Do you remember which toys?"

"I remember each detail with a terrifying clarity. I put a green clown in the bag, one we had given you for Christmas, and a pair of long woolen ropes that you loved to drag on the floor. You say that they are serpets, and we can't take them away from you, even to launder them. Serpets? At first we didn't know what you meant or why you were always dragging them on the floor, until we realized the serpets were serpents. Inside the bag, I also put a small bottle of disinfectant for Ramón to put on the scrape you got in the park. This I give to him at the last minute, after he has left the apartment, taken the elevator, and is crossing the lobby that leads to the street. I yell at him to wait, and run after both of you, barefoot and in my robe. I put the small bottle in the bag and I take advantage of the moment to give you a last kiss. You go to throw yourself into my arms, but your father holds you back. I say you are going to enjoy your trip very much, and you ask if there will be cows. You mean horses; you called horses cows. Ramón responds that yes, there will be cows and you will be able to ride them."

"Cows, horses, serpets. Can we move on to that night?" Mateo asks.

"I work in the national politics section of *La Crónica*, a new weekly that has quickly gained some renown. Friday night is the closing deadline and the newsroom is swarming with people. Ministers, lawyers, opposing political leaders, and friends of the house all stop by. Anybody who has a fresh story, or wants to participate in the discussion about what will be published, comes by and joins the conversation. And out of that swarm of activity, the weekly articles emerge, always down to the wire."

"I don't want to hear about your journalism, Mother."

"Fine, but don't call me Mother."

"But you are my mother."

"But you always say it with an attitude. Look, let's not fight. Let's go back to the newsroom at *La Crónica.* At about one thirty in the morning, we put the last touches on the edition, and it is after two when I get back to my mother's. She hears me arrive, gets up, heats a vegetable stew for me, and keeps me company while I eat it in the kitchen. As we're saying good night, she tells me that an envelope arrived for me and that she left it on the bedside table. She goes to her room and I brew some tea and go to the guest room, which has two beds, yours, which is empty, and mine. All I want at that moment before going to bed is to take a long bath in very hot water, to soothe the frenzy that overwhelms me after the closing of each edition. Every day you wake me up before six, but this weekend I will be able to sleep in."

"So do you open the envelope that someone has left for you?"

"No, I don't even look at it. When I go into the bedroom, I don't even turn on the lights. My back hurts, so I throw myself on the bed, in the dark without taking off my clothes, thinking that in a few minutes I will get up and bathe. But I fall asleep. A few hours later, I'm awakened by the cold. In the haze of dawn, I can see the clock, it is almost six. I undress, put on my nightgown, and because I'm thirsty I look for the cup of tea, which is sitting half full on the night table. That's when I see the envelope. I would have ignored it but for one detail that catches my attention, it is scrawled with your father's handwriting. It says, 'Please give to Lorenza.' A note from Ramón? That seems odd, but not entirely. Let's just say that I open it unsuspectingly, and quickly realize that it is not a note, it is a handwritten letter, several pages long, and this does make me grow uneasy. Your father's handwriting, which is small and muddled, makes me reach for my glasses in my purse. I put them on and read."

"What does the note say?"

"It's not a note. It's a long letter. What does it say? It says, 'I am leaving forever and taking the child. You will never see us again.'"

"That's it?"

"No, there are a lot of explanations, pages and pages of explanations, justifications, and accusations. In short, he asks forgiveness for what he is about to do, and then goes on to blame me for everything."

"Tell me exactly what the letter said. I need to know what explanations my father gave."

"I couldn't read any more at that moment. I had just realized that my son had been taken from me, and I was shattered."

"So you read the whole thing later."

"No, I never read it all the way through, I didn't care about his reasons. Only those cruel words: 'I am leaving forever and taking the child.' After I read it the first time, everything went black and I had to hold on to the side of the bed not to tumble over. Then I began to howl, the wild howls of a she wolf whose litter has been taken from her."

"Grandma says they were like the howls of the night during the dictatorship years. She says that when they woke her up, she thought someone was murdering you."

"It was worse than that."

"And then?"

"I don't remember."

"You don't remember, or you don't want to remember? That morning, what do you do?"

"Howl, suffer, die several times over. Your father is an expert at living underground, at counterfeiting passports and tickets, forging signatures. He's used to changing his identity time and again. To hide and disappear, that's your father's talent. And he has just disappeared with you."

⁂

Ramón Iribarren, I am your son, Mateo Iribarren. I have come to Buenos Aires to meet you. If you get this message, you can call the Claridge Hotel, room 506. I am going to be here until the end of the month. Thank you very much. Sincerely, Mateo Iribarren.

On a sheet of notebook paper, in his uneven handwriting, this is what Mateo wrote and signed, years after the dark episode, after his mother had just gone over parts of the tale with him again.

Lorenza read the paragraph and asked herself how it was possible for her son, now an adolescent and taller than her, to have such awful handwriting, long-legged scribbles crowded together, climbing and falling from the line at will. The contrast between the childlike penmanship and the sober and dignified tone of the content made a knot in her heart. "Ramón Iribarren, I am your son, Mateo Iribarren," Mateo read in a loud voice, and asked his mother, "Is it okay, Lorenza?"

She had to go out for a few hours and leave him alone in his trance. She had no choice but to fulfill the obligations that had purportedly brought her to Buenos Aires, although she had truly come for something else. She had come to keep a promise she had made to her son years ago, to be with him when the time came to look for his father. She knew that once she left the hotel room, Mateo would remain seated by the telephone, fiercely focused on what he had written in the notebook, going over it again and again, to memorize it, so that when the time came, the words would not fail him. *Ramón Iribarren, I am your son, Mateo Iribarren. I have come to Buenos Aires to meet you.*

"'I have come to Buenos Aires to meet you'—you think I should say that, Lolé, 'to meet you'?" he asked, when his mother was already at the door.

"Yes, I suppose you can say that."

"But I already know him. He's going to say that we already know each other. Maybe I should say 'to get to know you again.' No, I don't like that, either, it sounds weird. And the 'sincerely,' you think I should say 'sincerely'?"

"You can take that out if you want, or change it to 'a big hug' or something like that?"

" 'A big hug'? Are you crazy, Mother? How can you suggest that? Don't you realize how awful it sounds? If you want, I'll take out 'sincerely,' but don't ask me to send a big hug to a man who has had nothing to do with me. The only thing he has caused us is harm, and now you want me to send him a hug?"

"Forget it, Mateo, don't send him a hug. I only suggested it because you asked."

"Bad suggestion, Lorenza, possibly the worst suggestion ever. I think I'm going to leave it just how it is, 'Sincerely, Mateo Iribarren,' and stop fucking around with it, it stays the way it is."

The boy chose only the words that seemed most precise and discarded the rest, not wanting to overdo it and yet not wanting to leave anything out. His message had to create a certain effect, produce results, and he weighed the possibility that there would be no answer to the telephone call he was about to make, like someone tossing a message in a bottle into the sea.

"What if Ramón doesn't answer, Lolé?" he asked for the tenth time, his voice betraying his fear. "What if his answering machine malfunctions and he can't understand the message? What if something like that happens and then when Ramón wants to call me, he can't, because the message is garbled, or maybe he doesn't even remember me. Lolé, do you think he even remembers me?" He imagined a thousand different scenarios of the doomed encounter, as if on this particular Buenos Aires morning he could undo so many years of absence with the sound of his voice alone, with a mere paragraph that he rehearsed again and again. Yet he was unable to pick up the phone and dial his father, whom he had seen for the last time when he was two and a half years old and his father had taken him away.

They had not heard from Ramón since, not a single phone call, or a letter, or only a few letters at first and then nothing, only the vague and contradictory reports that reached them by luck and through third parties. That Ramón had been imprisoned, that he was bald and had lost a tooth, that he lived with a Bolivian girlfriend and was busy helping Bolivian miners organize, that he was now a labor director in one of the poor sections of Buenos Aires. But they never knew his whereabouts, because he did not try to find them and they did not try to find him. Or to put it exactly, Lorenza did not look for Ramón and he did not look for her and their child. They could not include Mateo in this tangle because he had never been given the opportunity to voice his opinion on the matter, not until the moment of this enraged demand, the sorrowful insistence that had forced Lorenza to fly to Buenos Aires to be with him.

After the dark episode, years had followed filled with

suitcases, roads, and airplanes, but the two of them had never run into Ramón. Never even came close. On the contrary, she had imposed upon herself, as a matter of destiny, the urgent task of pushing the son far away from his father's influence. She warned him that if his father had taken him once, he could easily try it again. But she never spoke ill of him as a person to her son or suggested that he was a bad person. That she would never do.

"Tell me about this man, Lolé," Mateo asked over and over. "Come on, Lorenza, tell me about him."

She told him that he was a moody man, but convinced of his ideals, a vibrant and intelligent man. She assured him that he was courageous and good-looking, and that they had been happy in the years that they lived together. But every time that Mateo asked how he could find him, she made up excuses and found ways to stall him.

"You have to be a little older, Mateo," she said to him. "It's not so easy."

"What's not so easy?"

"Your father, your father is not easy. You have to be a little older and grow strong. And then we'll go looking for him."

Mateo relented willingly, so careful not to hurt her, and determined to accept whatever man was living with them at the moment as his father, and that man's children as his siblings. This is the one, Lolé, he'd say, with this one we can create a family and be happy, and yes, she'd agree, this one will stay forever.

But there was always another one, a new one. And the

routine of everlasting love would begin again, the rented house in some neighborhood in another city, and the illusion of domesticity crafted by taking the bus to school and regular visits to the dentist, the assurance of ordering a favorite dish at the neighborhood restaurant every Sunday, the peace of mind that came from knowing friends' phone numbers by heart, friends who would always be friends. Mateo and Lorenza put up pictures of horses on the walls of his room, planted flowers in pots, adopted a cat, and got hold of a secondhand bicycle, which they painted to look like new, because this was it, here they would settle forever.

"Forever, Lolé?"

"Yes, my love, forever."

And then one day signs would begin to crop up, the long-distance phone calls for Lorenza, the whispered responses, Lorenza in some other world when he tried to show her his drawings or tell her a story. Soon Mateo would realize that it was time to give the cat to the neighbors, abandon the bicycle on the patio, pack the suitcases, and wake up in the house of strangers.

Mateo would take out his colored pencils and concentrate on his drawings during the long airplane flights, desperate to know: Why, Mother? Why did we have to leave if we were fine where we were?

"Switching bicycles was the easy part, Lolé," he would confess to her later. "It was switching cats and fathers that was difficult."

She would have liked to explain why things had to be the

way they were, why they led such a life, which perhaps was later to blame for his infantile, jumbled handwriting. Why such a parade of absences and shocks, of moves from schools and houses and countries, so many fearful nights, partings from friends, having no father or too many fathers, so many whys, which in time cast a pall of confusion over his childhood and prolonged it unnaturally. She wished she could have given him detailed reasons that could be condensed into a paragraph.

"Maybe it's better if you don't tell me," he confessed to her sometimes, because his mother's political tales sounded alien and her love stories just plain bad.

"You have always dragged me through your issues, Lorenza, and I have never known what those issues are."

And then one day he was taller than she was, and he stood before her, committed and defiant, having grown so big and his mother so tiny beside him, and he gave her an ultimatum.

"This is it, Lorenza, I want to meet my father. If you don't take me, I'll go by myself." He rummaged through the things he had stuffed on an upper shelf of his closet and pulled out a Basque beret, which he had been saving for a long time to give to Ramón on the day that he saw him again.

"My father and I are Basque," he always said proudly to whoever might listen. "Well, we're Argentinean, but with Basque roots."

Realizing how Mateo had struggled through his adolescence and with the ongoing tug-of-war he had with his identity, Lorenza had begun to understand the implications of raising a child whose father was no more than a phantom, someone who vanishes after inflicting his harm. She would help him look for Ramón, but first Mateo needed to understand the language of the old story, be brought up-to-date on each episode, to help him create a whole out of the fragments he already knew. They would have to give it some serious thought, talk to each other a lot, and work together as a team so as not to be led astray. They would also have to rely on their own strength alone, for no one else could help them in this search.

So the decision had been made and they were now in Buenos Aires. But how was Lorenza to begin to look for Ramón Iribarren, if when they lived together, they had mastered the art of hiding so as never to be found? How could she search for someone whose daily life with her had been taken up with changing their names, counterfeiting personal identifications, remaining invisible in the places where they lived, and creating jobs that they did not have?

"Tell me, Lorenza, tell me how you found out that my father's real name was Ramón," Mateo asked, although he already knew, because that was a part of the story that she had told him many times, just like the old tales about the cat with raggedy paws, except that this cat had raggedy paws and its head was screwed on backward.

"Do you want to hear it again?"

"Go on, tell it to me again, the story about Ramón's name. Again."

"It was a whole month after living with him that I discovered that your father was named Ramón, and only because an electric bill arrived with his name on it. When I realized what I had stumbled upon, it felt as if the envelope would burn my fingers. It would have been better if I had never read what it said, but there was nothing I could do. The bill fell into my hands and before I could stop it, that 'Ramón' slipped into my vision, which turned out to be his name, and also the last name, which would one day be yours, that 'Iribarren,' which revealed his Basque roots."

"It's all very strange."

"For security reasons. I couldn't know his name for security reasons. That's the way it was in the underground."

"The underground, I don't like that word. That's one of those terms you use. But answer this in your own words. Before you saw the electric bill, what did you think Ramón's name was?"

"I had no idea. I called him Forcás, which was what other party members called him." Lorenza had grown so used to that fake name, that the surprise of coming upon the envelope was almost painful, at first seeming to refer to someone she did not even know, some man with another identity, a Ramón who dwelled in worlds from which she was excluded because they were grounded in his childhood, his family, his past, that is, in everything that was truly him, the history of his private life, a whole swath of it in which she had no part and which she should not pry into. How then should they begin to look for Forcás, so many years later, when she didn't even know the real names of his comrades in the party? Who could she possibly ask about Ramón Iribarren, a name that his old friends in the party likely had never heard, since they all knew each other by their pseudonyms, what in those days they called noms de guerre.

"It's a great name, Forcás," Mateo said. "It sounds like a warrior. I like it better than Ramón. In fact, I don't like Ramón at all. It's the name of some stranger. What about you, Lolé, your nom de guerre? I know, of course: Aurelia. They called you Aurelia. It still sounds so bizarre, all of it."

"A cat with raggedy paws and its head on backward," his mother tells him. "But let's see, kiddo, let's see what we can do to turn it back around."

Everything seemed to indicate that searching for Ramón would be like looking for a needle in a haystack, but in the end it proved quite simple. After years without knowing a thing about him, it took them only a few days to discover his whereabouts.

⁂

Two nights before, Lorenza had returned late to the Claridge Hotel and dashed into the room to tell Mateo that she had seen them, that they had returned to the country. She had found them, their old comrades! But she had to hold her tongue when she found him asleep. He always complained about her insomnia. She not only did not sleep, he claimed, but she didn't let anybody else sleep. So she said nothing and satisfied herself with watching him sleep.

Mateo's sleep was not peaceful. It had never been. He talked in his sleep, was restless, often so entangling himself in the sheets that in the morning the bed would be stripped bare. Lorenza wondered to what distant lands her son journeyed and how lonely he must be in his travels. Of all the languages in the world, it was the language of her son's dreams that she most yearned to understand, but she realized that its jargon derived from the grammar of other worlds, a dialogue in the dark with a stranger, someone she did not even know.

"Who are the Maccabees?" Mateo had asked her once, still completely asleep. "The Maccabees, who are the Maccabees?"

She didn't really know. A people from the Bible, right? That was as far as her expertise went. Fortunately she did not have to elaborate because her son just as suddenly fell back into a deep slumber and the sleep-talking episode ended. But Lorenza remained uneasy. What is he doing in the middle of the night, she remembered thinking, with these Maccabees?

When he was asleep, he looked exactly like Ramón. She remembered being shocked to discover the unmistakable features of a grown man on her son. He was no longer a child, no longer a boy, almost a stranger. This illusion persisted until he awoke, when the mark of his father vanished from his face and those gestures that she recognized as genuinely his livened his face again. He then seemed such a different creature that she could see herself in her son, as if looking at a clone, he as her only son, she as his only mother. Only then was she able to reclaim that son who had always been so exclusively hers and so little Ramón's.

Mateo sensed her presence and half opened his eyes for an instant.

"What's wrong?" he murmured.

"Nothing, kiddo. There's nothing wrong. Go back to sleep."

"You have news for me."

"Later, you're half asleep."

"Not anymore I'm not. Come on, tell me."

Lorenza sat on the edge of the bed and told him about them, their old comrades in the party, how just a few hours ago nine of them had shown up at a reading of her new novel and had searched her out afterward.

"Was Ramón there?" Mateo asked, bolting upright, but when she said no, he threw himself back on the bed and covered his face with the blanket.

"Can you hear me from inside that cave?"

"Barely."

Although he pretended not to listen, she told him about hugging her old comrades in the middle of the street, now at last with nothing to fear, the whole gang raising a ruckus, not having to look over their shoulders to see who was following them, or lower their voices lest someone overhear. She told him that they all went to a pizzeria called the Immortals, its walls covered with photographs of legendary tango artists.

"Quite a name, the Immortals, and all of us there moved by the occasion and teary-eyed, reminiscing about the disappeared; *el negro* César Robles, Pedro Apaza, Eduardo Villabrille, Charles Grossi," Lorenza recited the names. "Imagine that, Mateo, our dead, and there we were remembering them in a place called the Immortals. We shouted over one another trying to catch up on everything that had happened since the fall of the dictatorship. It was very strange to talk of these things out loud and in a public place, given that before we could meet in groups no larger than three, whispering in some bar for no longer than fifteen minutes at a time."

But on that night, so many years later, they had reunited with no need for aliases and nothing to fear, to celebrate the end of the nightmare with pizza and beer—or rather, to celebrate with her, Aurelia, now Lorenza, because they had already celebrated among themselves. They had been a long time in coming out of the hole in their struggle to rejoin the living, adjusting to the light of day, to what had begun to be called a democracy.

"But Mateo, the thing is, I had left Argentina before the end of the dictatorship and have been gone all this time. Do you see? For me those days have long been frozen in time. And then on the very night you decide you don't want to accompany me, look what happens."

"Did you talk to them about Ramón? Did they tell you where he is?" Mateo's voice rose out of his cave.

"Yes, we talked about him, and no, they don't know

where he is, but they gave me some idea. Nothing too exact, but let me tell you the whole story, moment by moment."

She had found it amusing when they had revealed their true names and professions, like Dalton, who had been imprisoned, a skinny towhead, a good guy who had been director of the magistrate and who, he told her at the Immortals, was really called Javier something—a Javier, who would have guessed, that name didn't suit him at all—and taught classes at the university and had three kids; or Tuli, a driven black woman, who during the days of military rule offered support to the Mothers of Plaza de Mayo, and who in reality was Renata Rocamora, a double bassist for a tango quartet, which that very week was performing at the Café Tortoni.

"If you want, we can go," Lorenza proposed, to which Mateo growled like a bear. "What a joy to learn that Tuli is devoted to the tango. I asked her if she had played during the time of the military rule, and she said she did. Strange, because in our group at that time nobody really seemed to care about the tango. The music of the resistance was Argentinean rock, what we called *rock nacional.*"

"Argentinean rock was part of the left?" Mateo seemed suddenly interested. "I thought it was more the music of pothead hippies."

"Potheads? No, what are you saying? That music was ours. Or maybe it belonged to the potheads as well, but it was mostly ours. Case in point, at the Immortals, Dalton told the story of how there came a time when he had hit bottom in prison. He wanted to die. And the only thing that saved him was discovering a phrase that another prisoner had scratched on the cell wall, down low in a corner, almost unnoticeable. It was a line from 'Song for My Death' by Sui Generis, the one that goes, 'There was a time when I was beautiful and truly free,' although Dalton said that the only thing that was legible was 'and truly free.' But with the mere discovery of those three words, he no longer felt alone or wanted to die."

"Like in *Night of the Pencils*," Mateo said. "I've already seen the movie."

"Well yeah, it's nothing new. In such endgames, whatever happens is like the story of the cat with raggedy paws, it's been told time and again. But at the moment it happens, it carries great significance. Anyway, Argentinean rock was the music your father liked. The first time I went to his place, he showed me his records as if they were some kind of treasure. And, of course, when Dalton told the story of the lyric scratched on the wall, we burst into the song in its entirety, and this led to others, the songs of Charly García and Fito Páez, León Gieco, Spinetta. You can't imagine how good it felt to sing like madmen after so many years of silence."

"Very romantic. But I think Spinetta came later, Spinetta is not old enough."

"You're wrong there, kiddo. Bones Spinetta was idolized at that time, with Almendra and Sui Generis! My favorite, the one I adored was Sui Generis's 'Scratch the Stones.' "

"If you put on a record by Sui Generis at a party these days, they'll toss you out on your ass. So don't get any ideas."

"It's so weird, isn't it? So many years later finding out the real names and real lives of people you had been so close to."

"Yeah, as if Batman and Spider-Man got together in a pizzeria and took off their masks and revealed their secret identities to each other," Mateo said. "And to top everything off, they start bellowing ancient songs. Did you talk to your comrades about me?"

"Of course, isn't that why I was with them in the first place?"

"What I don't get is how you found them if you didn't even know their names."

Lorenza explained that the reading for a novel is a public event that is announced in newspapers, so that anyone who wants to attend can come, and that's how they had found out she was in Buenos Aires.

"Yes, I know that. But how did they know that Lorenza So-and-so, who writes books now, was the Aurelia who had been in the resistance with them?"

"One of them figured it out and passed the word along."

In the middle of the reading, the bookstore manager had handed her a piece of paper folded in half. "It's from the audience," he whispered, and she flushed when she read the first word: Aurelia. No one had called her Aurelia in years, nobody even knew that once, in Argentina, that's who she had been. The note said, "Aurelia, do you have time for a coffee with your old comrades?" She couldn't see them from the stage because the houselights were dimmed, but before she finished her presentation she said into the mike, "I know that some of my old friends are here, and I want them to know that yes, I have all the time in the world to have coffee with them."

"But that's not the part I want to talk about, Mateo. I have news."

"Don't tell me: Ramón was there," he asked, almost begging, and she noticed how pale he suddenly grew.

"No, he wasn't there, I told you." But she had asked a lot of questions and gotten some clues. A metallurgist for an auto syndicate, who was called Quico—or who had been known as Quico in the resistance when he lived in Córdoba, and now was called something else, did not live there anymore, and had retired—had confirmed that Forcás had been in prison, not because of politics, for by the time he had been arrested the military junta had already been overthrown some years before, but because of money problems. Quico thought that after a few months in jail, Ramón had been released and had gone to Bolivia. Gabriela had also been at the pizzeria, and Gabriela, the Gabrielita who had been by her side during the commerce protests, her best friend in those days, told her that she had heard that Forcás had returned from Bolivia and had settled down in La Plata, where he had opened a bar.

"A bar?" Mateo asked his mother.

"That's what Gabriela said. Do you know what it felt like to reconnect with Gabriela? We both found out we were pregnant about the same time, and we would go together to El Once barrio, both with bellies like globes, to the meetings of—"

"And where is this bar?" Mateo interrupted.

"According to Gabriela, in La Plata."

"I don't buy it, Lolé, that detail seems off. I am almost sure that Ramón is in Bariloche. He must be wandering those mountains like a Steppenwolf, or at least that's what I think."

"Stop. Let me tell you about La Plata. Gabriela thinks that the bar thing hasn't gone well for Ramón, but that he keeps at it, trying to forge ahead. She doesn't know that much more, but she gave me some leads to a comrade in La Plata who might know."

"Ramón is not in La Plata, Lorenza. Why do you insist on this? It doesn't sound right . . . La Plata. And the bar thing, even less so. Ramón must be in a cabin buried in snow, in Bariloche."

❋

"SPIT, LOLÉ," Mateo ordered his mother the following morning, as she brushed her teeth. "Spit out whatever you have in your mouth, it drives me nuts when you talk with all that foam in your mouth. Besides, Ramón is in Bariloche. I'm sure he is in Bariloche, where I last saw him. He likes the mountains, like me. Do you think I got that from him, the fact that I love the mountains?"

"Don't go loopy on me, kiddo, he is not in Bariloche. Were you listening when I told you that he was in La Plata?"

"Are you going to spit or not?"

"Turn the TV down so we can talk."

"I'll turn the TV down if you spit the foam out."

"All right! There! I spit it out. But from now on everybody brushes their teeth whenever and however they damn well feel like it."

"Good. So no more nagging about yellow teeth and cavities or counting the days since I brushed them last. And so, did you always trust your comrades?"

"Pick up your clothes, kiddo. Room service is bringing breakfast and I don't want the room to be a mess," Lorenza ordered, but it was like speaking to the air. "Come on, Mateo, pick up a little bit. And yes, I did."

"You did what?"

"Trust the comrades in the party. Isn't that what you just asked?"

"Even if they were tortured to get them to name names?"

"Well, I was never denounced. In general, those in the party did not betray each other. There was a high moral standard among the comrades. A high mor-al stan-dard, that seems like such a dated phrase, but it was true, a very high standard."

"Were you ever tortured?"

"No."

"And if you had been tortured? Would you have denounced others?"

"Torture is a pretty fucked-up business. Who knows how much you can take?"

"And what did they ask? The torturers, what did they want to know?"

"Names, addresses . . . sometimes they were after something specific, and sometimes they just asked general questions. Other times they had no idea who they were torturing or why they were torturing him, and then they didn't even know what to ask."

Years later, after she had returned to Colombia and had been writing for *La Crónica* for some time, she interviewed an ex-sergeant who had been a torturer in Argentina during the dictatorship. He told her that they would jot down any information that they ripped from the prisoner on scraps of paper, which they would more often than not misplace.

"Maybe we should just go to La Plata to look for your father," Lorenza said. "I can't tomorrow or the next day, but Thursday I can. I'm free Thursday through Monday, so we can take a bus to La Plata, and if nothing turns up there we'll look for him in Polvaredas, where his grandparents lived."

"Why don't we just look him up in the Buenos Aires phone book?" Mateo grabbed the tome and began to leaf through the pages. "Let's see I . . . I . . . Irigoyen . . . shit I went down too far, here, Iribarren Armanado, Pablo; Iribarren Cirlot, Dolores: Iribarren Darretain, Ramón! Here it is, Lorenza, Iribarren Darretain, Ramón—"

"You're kidding!"

"No, look, Iribarren Darretain, Ramón."

"It can't be, Mateo, let me see. There it is, a Ramón Iribarren. It has to be some other person. It can't be him."

"What other person, Lorenza, with those two surnames? It's him."

"Maybe it's a joke, so prosaic, the enigmatic Forcás easily

reachable and in alphabetical order. I don't buy it, going from the underground resistance to the phone book. Shit, so these are the fruits of democracy?"

"Behold, my father, after so many years of mystery," the young man said, and both broke into laughter because there was nothing else to do.

"Let me see again," Lorenza said, grabbing the phone book.

"Iribarren Darretain, Ramón," Mateo recited. "It's there. Who else can it be?"

"Does it say where he lives?"

"What? Here, in Buenos Aires. It's the Buenos Aires phone book, right? Shit, that's so fucked up, Lolé. Maybe he lives right next door. What a disaster, what a shock. Let go of the phone book, leave it wherever it was. And shut it, I beg you, I don't know what got into me to go looking in it."

"Let me at least write down the number—"

"Come on. Lorenza, let's get out of this room."

"But I just ordered breakfast."

"Cancel it. Let's get out of here. Cancel the order, Lorenza. We can have breakfast downstairs."

"You're still in your pajamas."

"Then hide that phone book. Put it under the bed, wherever, I just don't want to see it. Come, come," he said, going to her, and putting her hand over his tightly shut eyes, like when he was a child and afraid of something, "cover my eyes, Mommy, please, please, cover my eyes."

⁂

When Lorenza returned to the hotel room late that afternoon, she found her son still in his pajamas, his hair tousled, sitting beside the phone.

"Did you call?" she asked.

"No."

"Come on, kiddo, just get it over with," she tried to encourage him. "What are we, heroes or buffoons?" The question was her papa's. Anytime that he had to take a risk he'd said it aloud: Heroes or buffoons?

"I'd rather be a buffoon," Mateo said. "The heroes can all go to hell."

"Then I'll call. Just to confirm that it's his number," she proposed. But he screamed no, not to do it.

"Don't stick your nose in this, Mother. I have to take care of this on my own, by myself." He grabbed the phone from her, but immediately settled down and handed it back. "Fine, call, Lolé. But I forbid you from saying anything. Just see if it's his voice and hang up right away."

She promised that she wouldn't say anything, that he had nothing to worry about, she knew that the words had to come from him, from Mateo, and only him. Then she dialed the number and let it ring a few times, as he obsessively twisted the lock of hair that fell over his brow with his index finger, like he always did when he was nervous.

"No one picks up?"

"Not yet."

"Maybe Ramón doesn't live there anymore," Mateo said, and she realized how badly he was tormented by doubt.

"Maybe he leaves early for work and doesn't come back till late at night."

"We won't know unless we call," his mother said, and waited until a machine picked up, the recording asking for the caller to leave a message because there was no one home at the moment. She listened to the voice and hung up without leaving a message, just as they had agreed.

"It's him," she told him. "It's your father's voice."

"Are you sure?"

"Of course I'm sure."

"Did he say his name? Did the voice say that it was Ramón Iribarren?"

"No, not in so many words, all it said was, I am not here to take your call, or something like that. But I know it was him."

"Well, at least we know that he is alive. That's something, right? Unless, of course, he died after he recorded the message, but no, no, that would be too Gothic. And what exactly did he say: I am not here to take your call, or we are not here? You have to remember, Lorenza." Mateo grew impatient when she claimed that she couldn't really remember, and he shot her an angry glare.

"You're right, wait a second, let me think," she responded. "But don't give me that murderous look."

"So just tell me then. It's very important. If Ramón said, I am not here, then he could live alone. But if he said, we are not here, then he probably has kids, another wife. Do you think that he would speak to his other children about me?"

"If you want, I'll call him."

"That's not the point . . . with that expression."

"What expression?"

"No expression at all, that's the problem. How many years has it been since you heard Ramón's voice? And now you hear it, and it's like nothing, and you answer my questions like a robot. I don't even know if you still love Ramón or despise him."

"I neither love him nor despise him. I keep him in mind."

"I know, so he can never harm me again. Yet you do me more harm, robot face," Mateo said, with an affectionate nudge to his mother's chin that landed a little too rough. He began to shadowbox around the room like Muhammad Ali, dancing like a butterfly and stinging like a bee. "Shit, fuck, shit," he chanted, throwing jabs and uppercuts in the air. "Are you sure, Lorenza?"

"Of what?"

"That it was his voice."

"I could pick it out from a million other voices, that muffled and guttural voice was his. Besides, it's almost exactly like yours, Mateo. You both mumble and speak so low that one can barely understand what you are saying."

"So you're saying that his voice hasn't changed at all."

"Not at all, not even a little bit. It's exactly the same voice of the young man I knew. Yours, on the other hand, changes day by day, and there are times now when you sound just like him."

"I don't think so," Mateo said, continuing to shadowbox

against some invisible foe. "There's nothing about me that resembles Ramón. I don't want to look like him. Shit shit, what a bitch son of a fucking shit," he went on, and his fist assaulted a pillow until it began to spit out its down. It was not rage but a swarm of uncertainty that needed release.

"All right, take it easy, Cassius Clay," she implored and passed him the phone receiver. "Stop monkeying around and make the call."

"No! What if he's come back home and answers? What if the real him answers?"

"Tell him you're in Buenos Aires."

"And then hang up?"

"No, then you talk to him, if you want."

"That's not what I want," he said but dialed the number anyway and listened closely. "You're right, this guy really mumbles, you can barely understand him. Besides he sounds like such an Argentinean . . . he is so Argentinean."

"Relax, Mateo, you're revved up like a squirrel."

"It's true," he laughed, "I must look like a fucking electrocuted squirrel. Do you remember, Lolé, the time that the squirrel crawled up my pants and shirt and perched on my head. I think Ramón was still with us then."

"No, that was much later, at the Parque de Chapultepec. In Mexico."

"Unbelievable, the only thing that I remember about Ramón is not Ramón but a yellow cur that he picked up in the park and named Malvina. I know I played with her, but I can't remember what city it was."

"That was in Bogotá. We lived in an apartment in the Salmona towers. Not the one we live in now, a smaller one we rented with your father."

"I wonder whatever happened to that doggie. You think Ramón took her with him? Or maybe he let her back out on the streets where he found her. Do you know why we didn't keep Malvina with us? Or, I don't want to know," Mateo said, throwing another punch in the air. The memories he had of his father were in truth not his but his mother's, and having to continually ask her was worse than asking to borrow a toothbrush.

He dialed the number again, listened for a moment, and hung up again.

"I just wanted to know if his voice really sounded like mine. It's weird listening to Ramón again after all these years," he murmured, and a cloud of frustration dimmed his gaze.

"And?" Lorenza asked. "What does he say exactly?"

"There's no one here to take your call, that's all, there's no one here."

Mateo fell on the bed. He leaned back against the pillows, turned on the TV with the remote, let the tension escape his body, and was soon engrossed with *Thundercats*, a cartoon that he had loved as a child and that on that afternoon in Buenos Aires, so long afterward, hypnotized him once more. Ten minutes passed, then twenty, and Mateo did not move, not really there, silent, his eyes fixed on the screen, lazily twirling the same lock of hair with his index finger.

"Aren't you going to call again, Mateo?"

He said that he would, but not at the moment, later.

"Then get dressed, and if you want we can go out and grab a bite. You must be starving. Hello? Knock, knock. Is anybody home?"

Lorenza tapped him on the head to see if he had heard her.

"Okay, Lolé, but not now, later."

⁂

THE SCHOOL PSYCHOLOGIST once asked Mateo to write a profile of his father. The title was "Portrait of a Stranger," and this is what he wrote:

My name is Mateo Iribarren and I don't know much about my father. I know his name is Ramón Iribarren and that he is known as Forcás. Sit, Forcás! Stay, Forcás! It is a good name for a dog. Ironically, the dog that we adopted with Forcás, he christened Malvina. Not Lassie or Scooby-Doo, not even Lucky, but Malvina, like the islands that the Argentineans were fighting for, tooth and nail, against the British. That's what interested my parents, political conflict and class struggle.

Ramón Iribarren left when I was two and half years old. My grandmother, my aunt, and my mother explained to me that he's in Argentina.

A year later we received his last letter, and I've never heard anything about him since. My grandmother tells me that after he disappeared, I began to hate vegetables and grew fearful of the dark. I've gotten over this, at least the darkness phobia. But even now, before going to bed, I jam a chair against the closet door, because who knows what can come out of there when everything is black.

To imagine what my father looks like, I think of characters that I have seen on television, like the powerful buck king with enormous antlers who appears at the end of the movie *Bambi*. And why not? We all have a right to think that our father is a good guy. Félix Romero, one of the kids in my class, always said that; maybe because everyone accused his old man of being a mafioso. And if Romero thinks well of his father, I have the right to think that mine is a buck. The problem is that Ramón does not belong to the real world, and talking about him is like trying to paint the portrait of a ghost. I carefully collect the reflections of those who knew him, so as to make a collage of who he may have been. When all this gives me a headache I think again of the king of the deer, which is a lot easier. You are allowed this kind of leeway when your father is an enigma. The only clue he left me was his last letter, a piece of paper in which he drew Smurfs and frogs and squirrels climbing a flowering tree. It looks like something sketched by a preschool teacher. Your father had thick wrists and a very broad back, like a bull, my uncle Patrick, my aunt Guadalupe's husband, often told me, and he threw back his shoulders and puffed his chest to complete the imitation. Every time I asked him about my father, he said the same thing, and always ended it with the same pantomime. My aunt Guadalupe assured me that my father was an intelligent man, always up-to-date with the news. It seemed that he knew what was happening in any part of the world and spent all his time reading history and economics. He was a sweet *papi*, Nina used to say, closing her eyes and sighing. Nina was an ancient nanny who cared for me and my cousins when we were infants. Those details are important, the image of the buck with huge antlers has evolved to a figure who has become a supermacho he-man. According to what everyone has told me, my father was an intelligent, strong, and good-looking man. What more can you ask for?

When I was eight, I asked my mother for the first time to take me to Argentina to meet Ramón. She said no, not for the moment, we needed to wait until I was older. The last thing I knew about him was that he was in jail, and I think he's still there. Someone who knew him back then told me that he had been charged with political offenses.

Lorenza (that's my mother's name) thinks maybe that's why he disappeared from our lives. But there's something about that story that doesn't quite add up. If this was the case, why hasn't Lolé come to his aid? If he's a prisoner, he must need our help. But she insists that we can't go looking for him until I am older—not before that, no matter what. Anyway, the image I have of my father is rather positive. In addition to those qualities allotted to Ramón by my aunts and my grandma is the suggestion that he was some sort of superhero in the war against the dictatorship. And since I am obsessed with the Greek myths, I imagine him chained to a rock like Prometheus, wailing and desperately trying to free himself so that he can come see me. I also see myself much later, already eighteen and equally heroic, in the shape of a bull like him, going to Argentina to rescue him.

Lorenza (I don't know if I already mentioned that she is my mother) and Ramón (that's my father's real name) were in the underground resistance against the gory dictatorship. That word is very much Lorenza's, gory, or I should say very much of her generation, a generation obsessed with repression, another one of their favorite words, and with talking about gore. They say the gory dictatorship, the sanguine dictator, rivers of blood, bloodstained country. When I criticize her for it, she says that I have a point. Today it's not appropriate to talk about blood and gore, unless you're a surgeon or a butcher.

I've never known the date or place of Ramón's birth. In one of Lorenza's old albums I found a picture of him when he was nine years old, dressed like a Prussian soldier for a play at school. In another one, he is already a teenager, playing *fútbol* in a team uniform. It seems as if he might have been the captain, from the vigorous gesturing toward his teammates with his arms. But who knows, it could easily be that Ramón was as big a flop at *fútbol* as I was. When they told me how he had joined the party at twelve, I thought it had something to do with some party thrown by his *fútbol* teammates. Later, I learned that it was a political party and that he was nicknamed Redboy. Who knows when it changed to Forcás. By fifteen, he had left school to dedicate himself to the struggle,

Lorenza says, and I wonder if she would be using the same admiring tone if it was me she was talking about leaving school.

❋

"TELL ME ABOUT the dark episode," Mateo asks Lorenza, and she says that she will, but suddenly she can't, impossible all of a sudden for her to remember, as if the memory of it were a black box lost in the sea after a midair accident, unwilling to give up its information. "What happened that early morning after you had found out that Ramón had kidnapped me?" Mateo presses her.

"Kidnap is a strong word."

"Then what would you call what he did?"

"It doesn't have a name."

"Why do you strip the names from the things that Ramón has done?"

"You mean the Ramónisms?"

"Not funny."

"Yeah, I can tell you don't think so."

That morning Lorenza had plunged into an anguish so all encompassing that it robbed her of the faculty of thought, hence the difficulty in trying to put the moment into words now. Instead of words, echoes were all that remained, resonating within—one in particular, the odious echo of premeditation, the scene in the park, the previous afternoon, when she had had no idea what was about to happen. Naturally Ramón had known the course of events down to its last detail. It was so well planned that he even asked her to pack a suitcase for the boy. Lorenza, oblivious to the misfortune that she was helping to engineer with that macabre ritual, packed everything the boy would need for the journey: his clothes, his food, his clowns, and the serpets.

"During the first hours after the news sank in, the image of each of those objects of yours enlarged and shrunk in my head," she wanted to explain to Mateo. "Enlarging and shrinking like hallucinations, as if I were in the throes of a high fever."

How could she possibly transform that maniacal anxiety into a peaceful memory to put into words? Not only had Lorenza voluntarily given away her son but she had helped set up, step by step, the unimaginable sacrifice of losing him forever. She had relinquished her son as one relinquishes an expiatory victim. It had been a deadly ritual, and she herself had officiated. She had approved it, given her permission, her blessing, right there in the park the day before. When Ramón had asked her if she was sure she wanted to separate, she had said yes, sealing her own misfortune; then, when Ramón had asked her if there was any way around it, she'd replied that there wasn't, that there was no going back. Another ritualistic gesture on Ramón's part, to let her call that sinister coin toss, which she had lost without even knowing it. He forced her to bet, without warning her what she was risking. She had naïvely, stupidly, sentenced herself. She could have stopped everything with a single word, but had failed to do so.

"You didn't know," her mom tried to reason with her on

that miasmic morning. "How could you have known? It's not your fault. You could never have guessed."

"Yes, I could have," she barked back. "I could have known. I should have known."

Everything had been evident from that afternoon in the park. The signs were there, exposed, a warning siren should have gone off in my head. Everything pointed to what Ramón was about to do, even Ramón. All one had to do was look and listen to realize it.

"I wandered from room to room like a madwoman," Lorenza tells Mateo, "convinced there was nothing we could do. My head was a battered mess that repeated one thing over and over: There is nothing to do."

Like a robot, and only because her mother insisted, she made the few phone calls that she could make, knowing beforehand that they would prove futile. She dialed the three or four numbers of the people who knew Forcás, though it was all too clear that he wouldn't be hiding anywhere she could so easily find him. And of course those friends knew nothing. Ramón? The boy? No, they hadn't seen them. They had no idea where they could be. It's no use, Lorenza told her mother, who still pushed her to keep on trying. It was no use.

Ramón's parents didn't have a phone in Polvaredas, but she was able to reach one of the neighbors, who called them over. She heard the voice of Grandpa Pierre on the other end of the line, and could sense the old man's excitement on hearing from his grandson, his son, and his daughter-in-law.

"How are you?" the old man asked. "When are you coming to visit us? Grandma is down in the dumps. It's been a long time since she has seen her grandson. Send some pictures, will you? Let me get Noëlle, the old coot has been complaining that you people don't write, don't keep us up-to-date. Let me get her, she's going to be thrilled."

Obviously, Grandpa Pierre and Grandma Noëlle did not have a clue about Forcás's whereabouts. They could not even begin to suspect the calamity that had just occurred. Of course not. Forcás would have never chosen his parents' house to hide Mateo. Now Lorenza had no one else to call. And because in Argentina they had never known anyone's real name or their phone numbers, she had no way of getting in touch with their friends there.

"Wait, Lorenza, you're skipping over some very important things. Tell me about the conversation with my grandparents. It must have been the last time you heard their voices."

"Right. After that, we never talked again, nor did I hear anything about them."

"So tell me about it, then. That was the last conversation."

"I can't remember, Mateo. After I realized that you weren't with them, I wasn't even listening."

"Did you speak with both of them, or just my grandfather?"

"With both of them, first with him and then with her."

"Did you tell them what had happened?"

"No."

"But they must have asked for me and for Ramón."

"I suppose I told them that you were fine and that Ramón wasn't around, so I couldn't put him on. Something like that."

"And that was your farewell to them?"

"I'm afraid so."

"So then Ramón took me from you, and you took my grandparents from me."

"I didn't know any better."

"Me neither. Don't worry, Lolé, you and I are a team."

She could have prevented it and yet did not. She could have noticed, could have realized, and yet did not. She could have stopped it and yet did not. The mocking refrain haunted Lorenza back then. She could have her son in her arms, and she didn't. Her thoughts got all tripped up on that fact and couldn't move on, a cat with raggedy paws and its head on backward, a cat without a head, without paws. It drove her mad to realize, at such a late point, the devious rituals in which she had been inducted, the trap that Forcás had set for her to make her both responsible and complicit, a trap that only someone like her, who refused to see the obvious, would have fallen into.

At seven, she contacted the publisher of her magazine, an influential man who might be able to help her. She made a great effort detailing to him exactly what had happened in a most coherent manner; and through him they gained access to confidential information from several airlines, which gave them access to the passenger lists of flights that had left Bogotá during the last twenty-four hours. It was a futile task, however, since she knew that Ramón would have used false names.

Flights where? they asked Lorenza. Flights to anywhere. Domestic or international? Domestic and international, it could be any of them, or none of them. It was also possible that he had not left Colombia, or even left Bogotá, although the likeliest scenario was that Ramón had taken Mateo to Argentina, where he knew the land like the back of his hand. It was rather obvious. He wasn't going to take off to France, or Australia, with a small child in tow, almost no money in his pocket, and ignorant of the language. He had probably returned to Argentina, but he also could have gone anywhere else.

The head of security at the airport did not think they had boarded a plane and escaped by air. And he tried to reassure Lorenza that no one, not even the father of a child, could take such child out of the country without the express written permission of the mother, a notarized letter from her authorizing the minor's trip. But nothing was easier for Forcás than falsifying a letter of permission. That would not have been an impediment. The only thing that was evident to Lorenza was that there was so little she could do. There's no going back, she had told Ramón in the park. She herself had uttered her sentence, there's no going back, without understanding the weight of its full meaning. Never again, Ramón's letter said. Never again would Lorenza have her son. Never again. In what corner of the world could she start looking for him, if he and his father could be anywhere at this point? Existing as if in another time, their fingerprints rubbed off, their lives recast.

Her small child was lost in the immense world, out of her reach. Her son, Mateo, had become a droplet in the ocean. Her son had been snatched from her. What the dictatorship's henchmen had not been able to do to her, Forcás had just accomplished.

Since it was Saturday, most of the offices were closed, but hour after hour of that entire day, with her mother perennially at her side, Lorenza was in contact with a lawyer and a government official, the former having the grace to meet her in his own apartment and the latter at his country house. Not that she believed anything would come of her efforts, on the contrary. She knew with certainty that those superficial gestures would yield no results. Ramón must have already gone under and was now moving below the surface.

Her sister and brother-in-law did whatever they could, and the magazine assigned an investigative team to the case. But by that evening, they still were empty-handed. There was no trace of the boy or of Forcás. Hours had passed and they were still right where they had begun. Everyone they had consulted had advised that she should immediately report the kidnapping of her son to the Argentinean authorities, so that they could garner public support for the case. Her family had the contacts to do it, starting with one of her father's old friends who had been ambassador to Argentina and who offered himself to make the gesture before the military junta.

"No," Lorenza said, "no, no, no, no. I will not cross that

line. Those criminals don't find children, they make them disappear. No."

Although the decision might appear incomprehensible and abhorrent: No. Betray Forcás to the dictatorship? No. She couldn't go there. She wasn't going to ally herself with her enemies to chase the man who had once been her closest ally. She would not let the position they had put her in drag her through that degree of depravity. Should she look for her son relying on criminals who had abducted hundreds of kids, children of female prisoners they had executed? Not even the loss of her son would force her to cross that line.

"Very nice, Mother," Mateo said disdainfully, and the resentment trembled in his voice. "Congratulations, very much like you, your political convictions always before anything else."

"Wait a second, Mateo, just wait a second, and listen to what I'm saying."

"I don't want to know any more," he said, leaving the room, walking quickly down the hallway and just reaching the elevator as his mother caught up to him.

"You're not going anywhere," she said, blocking his way. "You're staying right here and listening to me. You wanted to hear the story, right? Now you're going to let me finish. Come on, let's go back to the room. Would you like an ice-cold Coke, to cool off a bit?

Mateo did not reply but followed her, and once inside the room, filled a glass to the rim with ice and poured himself a ginger ale from the minibar.

"Good, now look me in the eyes," his mother told him. "There was also something else to consider, Mateo, something of a very practical nature. Think, Mateo. What could it be?"

Mateo drank his ginger ale sip by sip and then took his time chewing on the ice.

"They would have never found him," he said finally.

"Exactly, that was the practical consideration, it would not have helped us. If the dictator's henchmen had not been able to round up Forcás for all those years, they weren't going to do it then. Asking them for help was not only a repulsive and grotesque thing to do, but in the end it would have been a colossal mistake. I risked everything if I played that hand. I was desperate, but not so blind that I didn't see these things."

⁂

LORENZA WANTED TO take advantage of what was left of the beautiful sunny afternoon. Mateo had not even showered, so content in those pajamas, which almost had a life of their own by now, the same pair of socks that he had nearly worn out on the hotel carpet. He finally went to shower, taking forever, and when he reappeared in the bedroom, amid clouds of steam and cologne, he looked very handsome and dazzling, like new.

He came out crooning the Who's "Pinball Wizard," with razor nicks on his face, minty breath, his hair washed with jojoba shampoo, conditioned and rinsed and slicked with a double dose of gel, a clean shirt, black fitted Levi's, a pair of custom-made Clarks shoes instead of his usual ratty Converses, a confident smile, and a sudden interest to go out and get to know Buenos Aires.

He had been struck by relentless hunger pangs and he wanted to jump into the first diner they passed, but Lorenza convinced him to wait until they reached La Biela, a bar in the heart of the Recoleta neighborhood, next to a splendid park that she knew well from family outings in Buenos Aires when she was a teenager.

They chose a table by the window to watch the passersby, and Mateo, who seemed to have decided to act according to the mores of a man of the world now, pulled the chair back for his mother. Then he put on his best adult voice and in a tone suitable for ordering a double whiskey at the bar, asked the waiter for two glasses of milk.

"Do you want both of them at the same time?"

"Yes, please, if it's not a problem."

"Wow, kiddo, sleek!" Lorenza lauded him.

On the sidewalk, a family passed by with a puppy, a Bernese mountain dog, on a leash, a spongy and irresistible ball of bouncing and nuzzling fur, with a pretty black head and white snout. Mateo, who was a dog lover, got up from the table, went out on the street, and asked the owners the name of such a handsome creature and if he could pet it, and he stayed with them for a while. He returned eager to tell his mother that the puppy was named Bear, but she jumped in first and with a big smile announced that she had ordered two plates of roasted pork loin with pineapple, which had been one of her father's favorite dishes.

"You mean you ordered pork loin with pineapple for you," Mateo said, emphasizing the "for you."

"For both of us, you're going to love it. My papa loved it. What a pleasure it will be to eat the same dish he always ordered when we used to come here."

"But you know I hate pineapple and pork gives me a stomachache." Mateo's disappointment seemed unfathomable.

"No, no, you'll like this dish, I promise. As soon as you taste it you'll agree, just see."

"Don't do that, Mother. I wanted to order something else. When are you going to stop making decisions for me?" The radiant expression had completely disappeared and his confident air had evaporated. He sunk in his chair and began to anxiously twirl a loose lock, forgetting about the great care with which he had fixed his hair. Lorenza tried to apologize but immediately realized that it was too late, that no one could break through the absorbed silence that had overtaken her son. No one except the waiter, who approached the table to hand them the menus again because they had sold out of pork loin.

"Everything else is available," he offered. "But we're out of that."

"Thank God," Lorenza said, and asked for a ham and cheese sandwich, a salad, and tea. Mateo took the menu disinterestedly, but sat up in his chair. He grew more cheerful as he read through the list of pastas, and after considering all the choices, he decided on *fettuccine alla panna*, which he devoured as soon as they put it in front of him and which quickly restored his spirits.

"So you came here with your papa?" he said, suggesting to his mother that he was ready to consider a truce. "Did you ever come with Forcás?"

"We wouldn't have been able to afford it. Besides, the resistance had once attacked this restaurant. They set off a bomb and it was closed for some time."

"Stop, stop, I didn't ask you for stories about attacks or wars. What I wanted you to tell me is how you ended up in Buenos Aires the time you met Ramón."

"Life works in mysterious ways."

"Ah, no, I'm falling asleep already. Can you please not start with such a cliché?"

"You know what, Mateo? I don't want to talk to you anymore. I was wrong to order the pork, all right, but stop being so rude."

"Oh, come on, don't get mad."

"Then stop being such a pain in the butt."

"Fine, I'll stop."

"This is the thing, if you'll listen, you can learn. You've come here searching for your father, and years ago I too came here trying to find mine."

"But your father lived in Bogotá. And wasn't he already dead?"

"He had just died, a few days before."

"So?"

"So I had to go looking for him. We all do it, go searching for our dead."

"You wouldn't cry when he died. You've told me that."

"They say that a death that truly matters to you never makes you cry, instead it defeats you," she told him, and then asked if he wanted some of her salad. He shook his head, but she insisted. When she tried to put a few lettuce leaves on his plate, he grabbed her by the hand and glared at her, enraged.

"Again with this, Mother?"

It was their old war about food, in which they had been engaged for a long time, forever, it seemed. And what she felt at that moment was, in some ways, also rage. It unsettled her that her son refused to eat fruits and vegetables. She felt infuriated, worried, and confused, not understanding how he could feel such an aversion for any food that had more than one color or texture, that strayed too far from the primary flavors.

This predilection for white and soft food, milk, bread, vanilla ice cream, pasta, seemed to her to go against all instincts of survival, decency even, as if he feared bringing anything dark, unfamiliar, or surprising to his mouth, as if his innards only tolerated those first foods from the age before fear set in, the childish pap and puddings that he seemed to yearn for still.

"So what's the story with that, the fact that you couldn't cry for your own father?" he asked, his tone suddenly calm and seeking a quick cease-fire.

"It's not a story, I'm allergic to tears. They burn my skin. They're salty water, after all."

"Maybe your personality is shaped a little too much by that allergy."

"Perhaps. Those who can cry don't flee in the face of some sorrow, they stay put and weep until they learn to tame the tears."

"And you, on the other hand, fled instead of going to your own father's funeral. But I'm not sure I buy this whole tears thing. Tell me why you weren't there, if you loved him so much. Because instead of taking a return flight to Bogotá to bury him, you took another flight, one that brought you to Buenos Aires."

"One morning in Madrid, the phone woke me with the news of Papaíto's death, a massive coronary, his heart had burst into a thousand pieces. I hung up, got up, bathed, dressed, took the train, went into the party's office in Virgen de los Peligros, near the Puerta del Sol, and told them I was ready to fly to Argentina."

"You mean you didn't even tell them your father had just died?"

"No."

"Why?"

"Think of the party as a mosque, and your feelings and all the other personal stuff as your shoes. Before you enter the mosque you take your shoes off. When Papaíto died, I didn't tell anyone, and a few days later, I was on a plane to Buenos Aires."

"This is bizarre, Lorenza, very very bizarre. You need to explain it to me."

"I will, but let me finish my tea in peace first. You know how I love to drink my tea . . . in peace."

There was a brief silence.

"Ready now?"

"Here goes. Every single day since I had left my parents' home, I dreamed about returning. I was doing my duty in Madrid, basically performing supporting tasks for the Argentinean resistance from the outside. I lived my life, followed my passion, worked like crazy. It was fine. Let's just say that I thought I was fulfilling my destiny, or that thing that we each call our destiny, and who knows what it truly is, or why we insist it's got to be one thing and not another. We say 'my true destiny' with such conviction that who knows where it comes from, but it is the crazy cow that we jump on."

She had felt she was fulfilling her destiny, yet deep down what she wanted was to go back home. But she never did it; so perhaps she both wanted to and didn't want to. Although she would have liked it to be different, the truth was that she missed her father too much and every day she told herself the same thing, today I won't go back, but tomorrow I will, this week I can't, but next week I'm out, I can't take it anymore, I'll stay for the summer, but by fall I'll be there, back with my people. And so time passed, and she continued to postpone her return, month after month, year after year. When her father died, a return was no longer possible for her. She had always been able to return to her mother and sister, and in fact often did, but the reunion with her father remained pending. To return for his burial would have been dreadful, that wasn't the kind of return that she had wanted, she would not have been able to get through it.

"I'm going to tell you something I've never told you," she said. "It's about my father, a little story about Papaíto. It's about a present that he sent to me in Madrid a few days before he died. It was a dress that he must have sewn himself at his tailor shop, death looking over his shoulder, although he must not have suspected that, because he was relatively young and the heart attack hit him without warning.

"I never got that parting gift of his. The news of his death arrived first and I took off for Argentina. Months later, I found out through the comrades in Madrid that it had arrived, but I never saw it. I never knew what color it was, or if it came with a letter, or what that letter said. And do you know how much that dress eats at me, Mateo? For years that memory has been seared in me, and it still hurts to think about it."

⁂

THE INCIDENT WITH the pork loin with pineapple had been a replay of a much earlier one, with mango. The same story repeating itself. Mateo must have been eight or nine years old and Lorenza wanted him to eat a mango, whether he wanted to or not. There were things that his mother did not understand: for one that his problem wasn't with fruits and vegetables but with Lorenza herself, especially when she tried to force him to eat fruits and vegetables. He considered himself a tolerant person. If she wanted to eat mangoes, many mangoes, a dozen mangoes, then so be it, he wasn't going to stop her. She could eat a carrot if she felt like it, or a tomato, or spinach, or bite into a raw onion for all he cared. He was a tolerant person. As opposed to Lorenza, who was obsessed with putting whatever atrocious thing that came out of the earth, or the sea, in his mouth. She tried to stuff him with mollusks and squids and other things with claws and spines, animals that God created to live secretly in the depths of the sea, where whatever they might do, they were out of sight. In the great darkness of the ocean is where they belonged, not in his stomach. But she insisted that they would nourish him and make him stronger, and for the life of her, swore they were delicious. Just taste them, she pronounced in a false and honeyed tone. She was a sadist with food. She knew that Mateo would not want to taste anything that came from her plate, or even her fork, but she never relented. You don't know what you're missing, she said, lustily putting a bite into her mouth. When he heard her saying have a taste, Mateo, or worse, have a taste, my child, his tolerance plunged to nearly zero. First of all, he wasn't a child, damn it, so when was she going to stop calling him that? And he felt like retching and spitting as if he were possessed. But she persisted, her tolerance reserved only for her political views. She always pronounced that word in an affected tone, like, "The government should be *tolerant* of the opposition." Couldn't she understand that tolerance also meant not becoming hysterical because Mateo was repulsed by some green tuber or some rotten cheese? It's a French cheese, she would say, as if that would win him over. And it's delicious, a word that soon became hateful to him because she so often repeated it while brandishing a fork. Was he exaggerating? No, it wasn't an exaggeration, the scenes were grotesque, but Lorenza was wholly unaware, she could not look at herself objectively, making those endless speeches and creating such a circus around their meals. From the time he was very young, Mateo closed his eyes, opened his mouth, and chewed. Sometimes he cried and regurgitated a bit, but without opening his mouth so she would not get mad, and then he swallowed that sour filth. Three more little bites, she then said sweetly. But he was older now and he could not stand her "it's delicious" looks anymore; he wanted to slug her in the face. Of course he wouldn't do that. He would never hit Lorenza, but it would be good for her to know that sometimes he wanted to.

Many times before, he had given in and accepted anything just so that she'd remain calm and happy. And she had taken full advantage of this, like the time with the mango. She proclaimed that a mango was joy itself, the passion of the tropics, the fruit of paradise, or something in that vein. But Mateo did not open his mouth, not even when she speared his lips with the end of the fork. It's true, she had tried to spear his mouth open, but not even then did he open his mouth, he was not going to have a second bite, not on his life, or hers. He had spit out the first one as soon as he felt the uneven and fibrous texture of that repulsive bright-orange fruit inside his mouth, something not uniform and which therefore could not be trusted. Lorenza warned him, if you don't have some fiber, your stomach will suffer. And he wanted to scream back, what's making my stomach suffer is that poison you're trying to stuff into me. But they had each gone too far to go back, it was life or death now, mango or catastrophe. Zero tolerance, Mateo sought refuge under the table, feeling that his mother would rather see him dead—choking with a piece of mango lodged in his throat—than accept defeat. Lorenza got down on all fours, closing in on him with a fork in her hand, like a demon with its trident, making him feel like an idiot for not eating a mango—especially since later, at school, he found that almost no kids like mango, so that when it came down to it, he wasn't that unusual.

The weird thing was that she would lose control of herself in such a fashion, how her brain would shut down when she grew angry, so she couldn't think straight. Guadalupe had saved him that time with the mango. She had walked in on the scene and screamed, "Both of you, stop." And her admonition had its effect. In their household, Guadalupe was the head of the sensible and communicative faction and Lorenza of the delirious faction, and more than once Guadalupe had saved him from Lorenza. There were many times when Mateo liked his mother's nature, that frenzied manner in which she accomplished things. But when she overdid it, it was a nightmare, and for the most part, she overdid it with him. As far as he was concerned, her best side came out when she sat down to write because she'd remain still for hours, forgetting that he had to eat right. Mateo took advantage of those lulls to eat spaghetti and drink milk, spaghetti and milk. And since he was at peace, he'd sneak into the kitchen and perhaps taste a grape, without her knowing, of course. Because if she were ever to find out, she would be so thrilled that she would want to celebrate the eaten grape and then begin an educative campaign, buying grapes by the bunches, forcing the issue until Mateo realized that they were delicious and ate them one after another.

He enjoyed the time when she was writing because he knew he wouldn't have to go chasing after her if she decided to travel on a whim, make sudden decisions, or take up new political causes and leave everything else to go to hell, for the sole reason that she was Lolé and Lolé did whatever the fuck she wanted. Hadn't Mateo noticed the murderous fury in her eyes when he refused to eat something? Now that he was tall and robust, no one could force him to do anything, and even if he didn't lift a finger against her, she glared at him as if he were a monstrous abuser of mothers.

When they reminisced about the incident with the mango, Lorenza laughed because she thought it was funny, and maybe Mateo even joined her in her jubilance, but not in earnest, because deep down he hated her for it. And now to the mango incident he could add the incident with the pork and pineapple, which he would likewise never forget. Never. Have a taste, child, I beg you, a little taste. No,

Lorenza. That was it. From that moment on, Mateo would never again taste anything she offered. He just didn't have to anymore.

⁂

GET USED TO not going around asking about what doesn't concern you, her comrades had warned her in Madrid on the eve of her departure for Buenos Aires, where she went after the death of her father. This was their response when she had asked why Forcás was called Forcás, a nickname that made her recall that strange poem by Rubén Darío, "Forcás from the Country." This Argentinean Forcás was one of the leaders of the party inside Argentina itself, a being of mythical proportions—that is, for those who supported the resistance from the outside. Since they didn't know him personally, they considered him a legend: after all, he was the secretary of the organization, the one who controlled the strings for the whole clandestine operation. Secret printing presses, movement of money, safe houses, placement of directors, lists of sympathizers, the forging of passports and other documents so that fugitives could sneak out of the country—all this depended on him. In Madrid they knew him well because they often collaborated with him on things that could only be done from the outside.

"Should we get an ice cream?"

"Maybe some caramel flan instead."

Many Argentineans had sought exile in Madrid and collaborated from there, and comrades from other countries had joined them. She was one of them. They made denouncements, raised funds, and coordinated campaigns all over Europe, hoping to find those who had disappeared still alive somewhere. But the dream that some of them most truly longed for was to return some day to Argentina to join the proper resistance against the dictatorship from the inside.

"We thought we had to lay it all on the line."

"What line?"

"It's just another expression, I guess that's how we put it."

"*We* thought? *We* put it? Why are you speaking in the plural as if you were a crowd? Like the devil in *The Exorcist*, who gives me the chills when he says, 'I am not one, but legions.' So tell me, why did they call Ramón Forcás?"

"That's just what I had asked in Madrid, and since they told me that they had no idea, I recited what I remembered from the Darío poem."

"They called Ramón Forcás because his parents were from the country. Pierre and Noëlle. My grandfather Pierre, my grandmother Noëlle. Pierre Iribarren, Noëlle Darretain. Lolé, do you think Grandma Noëlle loved me?"

"She loved you very much, you were her only grandson. When you were a baby, we dressed you in clothes she knitted for you, wool for the winter and cotton for the summer."

"I wonder what became of them, Lorenza. Do you think they're still alive?"

"We'll know when you work up the nerve to call your father, won't we?"

Lorenza remembered the mordant incident when Mateo was ten and she found by accident a photograph of Alice Hughes Leeward in his wallet. She was an Englishwoman who had lived for a while in Bogotá, a casual friend of her own mother, but aside from that not very closely connected to the family. But nevertheless, the boy had carefully tucked the photo into his billfold—Alice Hughes Leeward. Lorenza had to laugh.

"What is this woman doing in your wallet?" she had asked. "Where did you get this picture?"

"I found it in one of Mamaíta's albums. Don't touch it, Lorenza, it's a picture of Noëlle," he had responded in a very serious tone, grabbing the wallet from her.

"Noëlle? Noëlle who?"

"My grandma Noëlle, Ramón's mother, my grandma."

"Oh, my love!" Lorenza had hugged him. "That's not Grandma Noëlle, no, no, but if you want a picture of her, we'll find one somewhere. And you'll see, Mateo, Grandma Noëlle has beautiful eyes, like yours, you inherited those gray eyes from her."

After this incident, Lorenza made it a point to take Mateo to the French Basque country, so he could discover the birthplace of his paternal grandparents and the origins of the blood in his veins. The opportunity arose when she was invited to participate in a roundtable discussion on literature at the film festival in neighboring Biarritz. So she dragged Mateo along.

From the tiny and beautiful village of Ascain, in the

heart of Euskal Herria, Mateo sent a letter to his aunt Guadalupe.

It seems that this is where my grandparents were born, he wrote. We are on one side of a magnificent black stone, sharp as a blade, that's called La Rhune, the sacred mountain of the Basques. Lorenza says that if my grandparents weren't born in this village, they were born in one just like it. That's exactly the kind of things that she says, convinced that it solves all my problems. Yesterday I watched some men play a game called *frontón*, throwing a ball violently against a wall, and then I bought a black beret, like the one Che Guevara wore. They told me that it was a Basque beret, exactly like the one all the locals wear around here. I had thought that it was only Che Guevara who used it, being who he was. But Grandfather Pierre also used to have one. Lorenza said that he always wore it, so she never saw the top of his head. I asked her if Forcás wore one when he was in the resistance, and she replied that it would have been an idiotic thing to do, that no one in the resistance was stupid enough to go around in a Che Guevara costume.

Before night fell, we went to the cemetery to look for my grandparents' names on the tombstones. But we didn't have any luck, although we looked carefully, tomb by tomb, just because it occurred to Lorenza that they may have wanted to die in their homeland. If they are even dead, which we don't know for sure. We have asked in town about them, but no one knows of them.

I met an old man wearing a Basque beret at a bar who told

me that many people had left for America and never returned. I told him that my grandfather had been a logger. He replied, if your grandfather was a logger, then it probably went very well for him in America. There are trees to spare there because there are no cities and no roads, land is a never-ending forest. I was going to argue with him that there were cities and roads, but it wasn't worth it because Basques are very stubborn, like Forcás, and like me. And Lorenza is more stubborn than any of us, even if she isn't Basque. She brought me to look for my grandparents in France, where it would be a miracle if we find them, but she has never wanted to look for them in Argentina, where they are surely still living. I asked her why, and she said that it was precisely because of that. She says that in Argentina we might run into them, and my father might be with them. It was best if I didn't get mixed up in that mess.

My grandparents immigrated to Polvaredas, a region of Argentina that I don't know. And it's true, my grandfather was a logger. He used a chain saw and they paid him by the felled tree. Lorenza says that she saw very few trees during the times that she visited my grandparents. Maybe my grandfather had cut them all down. He must have been very strong, like Ramón, if he had to work with something as heavy as the chain saw all day.

There was also a story about bunny rabbits. They kept rabbits. Maybe they still do, if they are still alive. My grandparents, not the rabbits. Who knows? Maybe Pierre and Noëlle are still in Polvaredas, maybe they miss me and are looking for me. But that's unlikely. If they had looked for me at all, they would have already found me. When I was a baby, they visited me and brought dead rabbits to make stew. Ramón put them in the freezer and they never came out because my parents didn't know how to make rabbit stew, and besides they thought it was disgusting to handle the reddish, skinned rabbits. My grandparents would call later from Polvaredas and Ramón would tell them that I had eaten the whole rabbit and that I was growing into a giant.

When it grew dark and La Rhune was no longer visible, we walked back to the store with the Basque berets and I bought another one, for Ramón, to give it to him when I see him again.

⁂

WHEN LORENZA ANNOUNCED in Madrid that she was willing to be transferred to Buenos Aires to aid the resistance from within, she was quickly assigned her first mission, to smuggle microfilm, passports of various nationalities, and cash, she didn't remember how much, but a lot, what had seemed to her an enormous sum then. She was to hand it over to him, to Forcás. How do I find him? she had asked, and they told her that he would find her.

"Daaaaamn!!" Mateo said. "My papa, the Indiana Jones of the revolution. What movies have you been watching, Mother?"

She was not to carry lists of contacts or phone numbers. She had to go to a certain hotel and wait until the organization contacted her. They told her that a comrade named Sandrita would pick her up, that she would be her liaison, take her to her lodging, and let her in on what she needed to know to begin work. Forcás would show up later, when she had safely passed through her first days there.

They also told her that she had to come up with a whole minute. When she asked what that was, "a whole minute," they told her that it was any likely story to justify her trip there, in case she was questioned. They decided that at first she would say that she wanted to study literature at the University of Buenos Aires and that she had come to figure out the procedure for enrolling.

"Do you remember the Gila monster?" Mateo changed the subject, like he always did when he was sick of his mother's stories about the resistance. She was more than glad to abandon that minefield, which she always had to cross so vigilantly, because even the slightest misstep ended up making him more vulnerable and he set off the mines. In the wings of all this, they had a gallery of shared memories that did not involve the battlefield. One of them was that Gila monster that they had once seen when they lived on the isolated ranch in the Panamanian jungle. It appeared early one morning in the kitchen, up above, hidden in a corner between the wall and the ceiling. It was a fat, rosy lizard, with little hands. The Panamanian comrades had warned them that it was called the Gila monster, and that its bite was deadly, so they wanted to catch it, but it had escaped.

"It looked like an ugly little baby," she said.

"An ugly little poisonous baby. It bites and doesn't let go, the son of a bitch. And on top of that it chews," Mateo said, "or I should say it breaks the skin so the poison penetrates and drops you dead right there. So many nightmares about imaginary monsters and right there in Panama I found the real one. And do you remember the suicide serpent? That was the most incredible thing I ever saw."

It was at the same ranch in Panama. They were asleep in their hammocks and were awakened by a whistling noise, as if someone were cracking a whip. It was a long, green snake, a meter and half at least, that was flogging itself against the wall; a demented, terrifying creature to be doing such a thing. Mateo and Lorenza watched it with eyes as big as plates, frozen in their hammocks, while a few steps away that mad thing rose above the lower quarter of its body, as if to stand up, and cast itself against the wall with the speed of a whip, as if it wanted to commit suicide. When he was little, Mateo told the story, saying that eventually the comrades had to do hand-to-hand combat with the snake to get it out of there, as if snakes had hands.

"My friends don't believe me when I tell them that I once saw a suicidal snake in my own house. Because we did see it, Lolé. Maybe it was trying to shed its skin. One day, I would like to ask a biologist just what that beast was doing."

⁂

MATEO AND LORENZA left La Biela and headed toward Corrientes, to stroll among booksellers and music vendors and coffeehouses. Lorenza wondered where all the books had been during the time of the dictatorship, she didn't remember seeing them, or buying any, or even stopping to peruse, maybe because she never had any money or because it wasn't safe to do such things, or maybe she had done it, but that was one of the many things that had not been made part of the official register. Her memories of that time were confined to the events of the main plotline. They were simple and directly related to what had happened, no props or scenery, and strangely enough, almost without words.

"Do you smell that, Mateo?" she asked. "It's mold. That's the smell of Buenos Aires."

It was a rancid smell that had an aristocratic whiff. She had experienced it when she had come with her father, and years later when she had lived with Ramón, and now again, here with Mateo. It wasn't ubiquitous or all-pervasive, but engendered in the dark humid corners of the city, the shady parks, the salon hairstyles of the old señoras, the subway trains, the stacks of used books, and diffused through the streets in small whiffs.

There it was . . . coming out from under a railing like steam. There again, clinging to the jacket of a passerby. That old smell. Dictators had come and gone, but Buenos Aires always smelled the same, like a broadtail fur coat stored in a basement. When you are here, it is not very noticeable because the nose gets used to it. But when you leave, it goes with you, and wherever you go and open your suitcase, it jumps out at you so that you can't mistake it. That's when nostalgia hits.

"Put your nose to that book you just bought," she told Mateo. "Do you smell it? It's Buenos Aires. You have in your hands the very essence of the city."

"You sound like a tourist guide, Lolé. Why don't you tell me about the content of those microfilms you were supposed to hand to Forcás, instead?"

"I don't know. I didn't ask. I already told you that it wasn't worth knowing. In any case, we concealed them inside an emptied tube of toothpaste. And I wondered what 'minute' I would have to invent if they discovered such a thing at the airport in Ezeiza. The comrades told me that if it happened, to say an Our Father and hope for the best, because no minute would explain away such a thing."

"Have you ever read *Foundation?*" Mateo asked, and without waiting for a response went on to recount the entire, endless plot, like he always did when he had read something, or had a nightmare or saw a movie. Once he started, he couldn't stop until he reached the grand finale, and this time was no different. He only stopped chattering when his mother told him they were as lost as a Turk in a fog.

"Is that what they say in Argentina, a Turk in a fog?" he asked.

"It's a saying."

Lorenza cursed her poor sense of direction, that hopeless flaw that Trotsky called topographical cretinism, which makes any city into a labyrinth. Unfortunately, Mateo had inherited this trait, a tendency to roam endlessly for lack of an internal compass. The good thing about being so out of it was that you never even realized you were lost. Ayacucho, Riobamba, Hipólito Yrigoyen, they had followed the whim of their feet for hours, and the streets of the city center danced around them. Tucumán? Virrey Cevallos? Sarandí?

They didn't hold hands anymore. It had been a few years since they had last done so. Before that, the boy's hand fit in hers as if they had been made for each other, a big hand and a small hand, and they liked to pretend to fit them together like pieces of Lego. But by the time it was her hand that fit into his, Mateo did not want anything to do with this old game. He peeled away from her indignantly when she tried to hug him and he looked all around to make sure that no one had caught them in such a compromising position. Then Lorenza would restrain herself not to anger him, but she recognized a bit of herself in that distance that her son put between them. As a child, he had always clung to her, the two huddled together like ferrets in their burrow—if it was after midnight, the nightmares chased him to her bed; if they were at the beach, he wanted to fight like sharks; if they were on the street, he zigzagged in front of her, stepping on her with his oversize, thick-soled sneakers. They were like some creature with two heads and eight limbs. And how often had they found themselves in the narrow changing room of a store, as she struggled to try on the clothes and he played with his

Transformers on the floor? Or even at home, as she tried to write while he practiced a jujitsu hold on her arm, or he watched his favorite TV program and she force-fed him spoonfuls of soup, or he tied knots in her hair, or she combed his and he pushed her away? At some point, Mateo became ruthless when it came to delineating his personal space and setting distances. He drew a Maginot Line between them and would not allow her to cross it by even a centimeter. And that's how it should be. Lorenza understood that, as well as the fact that Mateo was no longer her child, no longer a kid, hers or anyone's, and she realized how much it upset him when she ignored this truth. Mateo was justified in his territorial claims, it was only natural. But that hardness made tears well in her eyes, tears which she was allergic to.

"Do you think Ramón has arrived at his house in Buenos Aires," he asked, "or at that cabin in the snowy mountains—"

"Or at his bar in La Plata. If you want, you can call him from the public phone. I have the number in my pocket." He shook his head. Before they realized it, it was past eleven and they found themselves in front of the obelisk, which split in two the red splendor of a giant Coca-Cola billboard and speared upward toward the darkness. How had it become so late? It was something that often happened to them. Although they no longer walked holding hands, their conversation was still as entangling as any embrace and time passed them by unwittingly and the rest of the world remained in the wings. And so they kept on walking, by God's grace, at times entertaining each other and at others simply gazing at the ground, and when she thought she recognized Santa Fe, they had returned to the Avenida de Mayo.

"It's no use, Mateo, we're going around in circles."

"But you lived here, Lorenza, for years. How can you get lost?"

"So what? I still get lost in Bogotá. Wait! Do you smell that? That corner smells like Buenos Aires again."

They ended up in a dirty and crowded street full of theaters and nightclubs, which they found out was Lavalle. Apprehensively, they made their way past the pale neon lights which failed to make the air warm, sidestepping hands that offered passes for the strip shows.

"Let's get out of here, Lorenza. This place is like a frontier. Or look, let's go into this theater, it looks like a horror film."

The movie was terrible, but Mateo didn't care. When his mother suggested that they leave, he said he wanted to see the ending. She thought her son would do anything, even sit through some vile movie, as long as it stalled the return to their hotel room where at some point he had to make that call which he had no idea how to make.

⁂

"RAMÓN MUST THINK I'm weak," Mateo said. "A weakling without any character. He must think that because he didn't raise me, I turned out soft. I need to tell him how I smacked a kid named Joe Ferla in the face in Rome. And when I tell him, you confirm it, tell him he has to believe me because it's the truth."

When they lived in Rome, the rector's secretary from the institute where Mateo studied had called Lorenza one day to tell her that her son had a *scontro di una inammissibile aggressività* with another student, and the rector needed to see his parents. It sounded unbelievable to Lorenza. Ever since he had been a child, her son had known how to defend himself, but he would never set out to purposefully harm anyone, or to go after anybody with his feet or kicking. The years of unmitigated rage would come later, with adolescence, but as a child he had been peaceful and compliant. The institute was the Esposizione Universale Roma, and during the long metro ride from the city center to see the rector, Lorenza thought about the only other incident in Mateo's life where he had revealed a violent side. It had happened years before, at the school he had attended in Mexico City.

"Here it is," the Mexican teacher had told her, indicating a display laid out on a table, all the drawings that Mateo had done during the semester. "There isn't one without weapons, wars, aggression, and blood . . ."

The drawings made an impression on Lorenza, but mostly because of their vibrant colors and beauty, and she said so: "He's a good artist, my Mateo . . ."

But the teacher wasn't interested in aesthetic judgments, what alarmed her were the violent impulses that flowered in the pieces, indicating the urgent need for a psychological evaluation. She said that Mateo must have been affected by some very grim events, those were her words, which perhaps he had lived through in Colombia. Lorenza did not respond. She gathered the drawings, one by one, with the devotion of any mother handling the artwork of her child, as if it belonged in a museum.

That same night, she spread the drawings on the floor of the living room to look at them again with Mateo, who at that time must have been around seven.

"Your teacher says that they are violent," she said. "What do you think?"

"Violent, what do you mean?"

"Well, she says that these figures here are attacking—"

"They're not attacking, Lolé, they are defending themselves. That's very different."

It was a reasonable interpretation. There was definitely a war being played out in those drawings, a bloody one at that, this much at least she had to concede to the teacher. But it was also true that all the figures were indeed in defensive stances, which also worried Lorenza. She couldn't sleep that night thinking about what it was that her son had to defend himself against with such zeal. The following morning she asked him about it at breakfast.

"Why so many defenses and armaments, Mateo? I mean, in your drawings . . . all those shields and helmets."

"You never know what will happen. It's always good to be prepared." His reply was rather vague, so she decided to broach the subject from another angle.

"And do you think that your characters know how to defend themselves? I mean, will their protections work?"

"Don't worry, Lolé, they are im-pen-e-tra-ble," Mateo said, careful not to skip any of the syllables of that difficult word, and he took off toward the bus that he rode to school every morning.

The director of the Rome institute told Lorenza that he had hit a classmate named Joe Ferla. She knew who he was, more than once Mateo had returned from school discombobulated because Ferla had put a cigarette inside his desk and almost burned all his notebooks, or had stabbed him with a pencil.

"What about my son?" she asked the rector. "What happened to him in the fight?"

"Not much, *signora*. He took a few blows and has some bruised ribs."

"My Mateo is a good boy, *signor direttore*, and I understand that this Joe Ferla is a *malandrino*." The word *malandrino* was perhaps excessive for the occasion, but it was the closest to bully that Lorenza could come up with from her limited Italian vocabulary.

"*Malandrino*, no," the rector corrected her affably. "To be precise, let's just say that Ferla is a boy with certain behavioral issues. And as such, he is on probation for repeated acts of aggression against other students. For Mateo, on the other hand, this is the first time he has ever been involved in this type of mischief."

"There you are. So it doesn't surprise me that a good boy like Mateo could end up losing his patience with Ferla's . . . behavioral problems."

"The fact that he hit Ferla is not what gives us serious concern here, but the brutality with which he did so. Please, if you may, read the medical report."

Fractured clavicle, hematomas on the face, a cut two centimeters long over the left eyebrow. In other words, Mateo had given Ferla a first-class beating.

Lorenza tried to justify. "He has spurted up physically in the last few months. He went in a flash from being a child to being a grown-up. I don't think he understands yet how strong he is."

"That could be the case, *signora*, but that wasn't even the worst part, perhaps our most serious concern is over the callous way he reacted when I tried to apprehend him."

"I'm very sorry, *signor direttore*, but can you tell me what Mateo said?"

"When I told him that I would have to call his father to tell him what had happened, he replied in an insolent tone, '*Se vuol lamentarsi con mio padre, dovrá andare a cercarlo in carcere.*' "

"Mateo wasn't trying to offend you, *signor direttore*, he was simply stating the truth. We don't know where his father is, but we suspect he is in prison. Still, I apologize for anything my son might have said or done that was disrespectful."

"Before you leave, *signora*," the rector said, when she was almost out the door, "I want you to know that there was something good in all this. Mateo has just barely started to learn Italian, but he spoke that phrase with a proper accent and perfect syntax."

❋

"I LIKE THAT part of the story, Lolé, at the airport in Ezeiza, when your comrades tell you that you might as well recite an Our Father because there isn't a story that will save you now. I like that, the formality of 'recite' is very Argentinean. It's a line from a movie. And now tell me about the newspapers again."

"What newspapers?"

"How they warned you not to read newspapers on the airplane, and later in the café and on the metro, because any woman who read a newspaper was immediately suspicious. And so what happened, in the end, at the airport, with the microfilms and all that?"

For the length of the flight, Lorenza had put off thoughts of her father's death by wrapping herself in a kind of stupor, as if her mind had shut off during those hours suspended in the clouds. She was cradled in her lethargy, like before the onset of a migraine, when she remained quiet and still, almost invisible, waiting for the enemy to forget her and pass her by. But when they landed, the lurch of the plane on touching the ground jolted her awake. They were in Argentina. It was only then that she grew concerned and asked herself what the hell she was doing there, realizing how stupid she had been to get involved in such a mess. Suddenly her role in the entire drama seemed unreal, as if someone were playing a joke on her, and fear paralyzed her. One of the last missions that she had helped organize in Madrid was demanding to know the whereabouts of a couple and their two daughters, removed from a plane by force just before it was about to take off for Sweden.

Morituri te salutant, she was saying in her head as the plane taxied into the wolf's mouth. *Nevermore*, here's where the current has dragged you, *this is the end, my beautiful friend.*

"Fear paralyzes, Mateo. Have you ever seen it?" she asked him. "It's not a metaphor, it can really happen."

She felt as if she could not move her legs. Her head, which was more decisive, ordered her to go on, to do what had to be done. But her legs had a different idea. They wanted to stay just where they were, in that airplane seat, and they began to search for accomplices in their mutinous mission. They coaxed the hands not to undo the seat belt, and tried to win over the rest of the body, sending out specious messages. This plane is your final protective capsule, they warned, much better to stay here, don't move from this seat. She must have lingered in this state for a few minutes, like someone at the edge of a diving board searching for the courage to jump.

She soon got herself together and when she went through customs she was calm again, surrendering to the lethargy. She didn't grow agitated, even when they searched her, which they did only perfunctorily, nor when they questioned her, which also was nothing beyond the routine.

"It was all thanks to Papaíto's death. It had blindsided

me. And I arrived in Argentina convinced that nothing worse could happen to me after what I had gone through."

Her first days there had been like that, she did things as if she were gliding from one to the other and it wasn't exactly she who was involved in such things. She felt as if she were an actress onstage, and that strange feeling of playacting stayed with her for the first few months.

"Aurelia, me? Aurelia in the underground resistance in Buenos Aires? The whole thing seemed too theatrical." The first time she felt the presence and hold of the dictatorship, it was a physical thing, like a slap. The first time she confirmed that behind all the pomp and ceremony the monster's breath poisoned the air was not because she saw the military police flattening a house, or taking someone in, or firing their weapons. It was rather an ordinary afternoon in a run-of-the-mill café about a week after she had arrived, when she noticed the disapproval and rage with which some older folk glared at a young couple kissing at a nearby table. Not long afterward, she was strolling down a street during a late-fall afternoon, and since it was hot, she wore a light cotton skirt that must have been somewhat see-through, outlining her legs, though just barely. The moment she stepped onto a bus she heard the insult from a man across the street. Sharp-tongued, brimming with indignation, he yelled: "Get dressed, you whore. Why don't you go to some strip club to show off those hams?" She then knew that the dictatorship was not only enforced by the military but also by citizen upon citizen, and that it was not only political oppression but also moral, like putrid water that slowly seeped into everything, even the most private folds of life.

❄

"So WHAT WAS Ramón doing in Bariloche, I mean, before you met him?" Mateo asked.

"He had worked there as a mountain guide, seasonal work, I imagine. I think that it was the only job he had done his whole life, aside from the resistance."

Ramón had rocked the newborn Mateo to sleep with stories of the mountains of Bariloche. His lullabies were about his time there. He told tales of giant boulders of ice that came loose from Tronador peak with a thunderous noise, and of a tavern at the peak of the Cerro Otto from which you could contemplate the whole world, everything covered in snow, while enjoying hot chocolate beside the fireplace. He told the child about a natural cave where a group of Slavic nuns had sought refuge from an avalanche, emerging with their lives four days later.

"But I couldn't have understood those stories," Mateo said.

"No, how could you have? You were a baby. But he would tell them to you still. And I heard them and later retold them to you when you were old enough to understand. I think that aside from his nostalgia for the mountains of Bariloche, your father was a man without memory."

He had said next to nothing to her about the town where he was born, the friends of his childhood, his teenage girlfriends. He either did not remember or had chosen not to tell her. Or he did tell her, and it was she who had forgotten. And maybe that was why it now proved so difficult to tell her son what his father was like. By that point, she didn't even know, or perhaps she had never known. At the end of the day, it was not so unusual that Forcás had no memories. It was a thing that a lot of them had in common. It wasn't a time for remembrances; too much anxiety to be tending to those interior gardens.

"I have come up with a story, or I should say made up a memory about Ramón. A memory I like," Mateo said. "Maybe it's real, I don't know. There is a very prominent figure with big hands who must be him and he puts me down in a crib made of snow. But I am not cold, but rather toasty. The large figure gives me a pacifier and I notice the many bright lights."

"That happened just as you remember it. Your memory is real. When the three of us were in Bariloche, you were already two and a half. He always carried you on his shoulders on our long walks through the mountainside. There was snow, not a lot, but also sun, and when we climbed a tall peak, he liked to dig a hole in the snow and make a crib, using his wool coat and mine to line it, to lay you there so you could drink your milk and sleep awhile. And I have another image engraved in my mind of you and your father in Bariloche, both wearing wool caps and leather boots, and in the background the splendor of the aurora borealis."

"There you go again with your exaggerations. I have one

nice memory, just one, and off you go dressing up the story with blazing lights. Even a loser like my father lights up, as if he had a saint's halo. You just make shit up, Lorenza. You can't even see the aurora borealis in Bariloche. The lights that you see near the south pole are the aurora australis."

Mateo then grew quiet, looking anywhere but at her. He had grown disgusted with his mother, as usually happened when they talked about Ramón. It always started out fine, continued fine for a while, but things soon heated up and continued to heat up until he exploded, which was followed by long periods of silence.

"All right, no more auroras or blazing lights," she said, after letting a prudent amount of time pass.

"You just don't want to admit to yourself that my stories about my father are not happy ones. There's a lot of pain there, and you are not allowing me any pain—and that in itself is very painful." Mateo's angst got him all tangled up in tongue twisters.

"And there's another thing that doesn't exist at the south pole," he said after some time had passed. "Polar bears."

"Is that right?"

"Yes, I would swear on it. No polar bears and no aurora borealis. Although I don't think Ramón would be out this late, considering how cold it gets there. He is probably already inside his house with a fire going in the fireplace. The little house that he rented that time in Bariloche had a fireplace, right?"

"It did, and we had to keep the fire going all night because there was no other heat source. Sometimes it went out while we slept, and the freezing air would wake us. If the living have to suffer through this sort of cold, what must it be for the dead, your father said. Who knows where such thoughts came from, but he said it every time it was cold."

"If the living have to suffer through this sort of cold, what must it be like for the dead," Mateo repeated, now cheery. "Is that really what my father said, Lolé? And in Bariloche we split wood for a new fire when the old one had gone out. Maybe at this exact moment, Ramón has run out of firewood and has gone out into the woods to look for a supply that will last him the night."

"But what about if he is in La Plata, you crazy kiddo? Or if he's here in Buenos Aires like the phone book says?"

⁂

Lorenza took Mateo out to Puerto Madero on the shores of the river, a popular place, resplendently lit, full of people, cafés, and restaurants. She told him that it had once been the main port of Buenos Aires, and that she'd had secret meetings there with stevedores.

"Who were the stevedores?"

"They were the ones in charge of loading and unloading cargo from ships, well, the ships that still came in, every once in a while. Right here where we are standing now, right around here. Back then the port had been mostly abandoned, a haunted place, all the docks half empty."

She explained that the redbrick structures that were everywhere were called docks, or warehouses, now all transformed into huge restaurants. The dock where she had met up with others was nothing more than a graveyard for cranes, useless hulks and empty wooden boxes scattered everywhere, the remnants of the rich Argentina that with its exports called itself the world's granary. She would meet up there with the stevedores, amid the rusted iron and the whitecaps. Generally there were six or seven of them, unemployed and rusty themselves. They waited for her bundled in their thick, black coats, their hands buried in their pockets. And they had their meetings right there.

"And if anyone saw you meeting and denounced you, wouldn't you end up disappeared or something?"

"Something like that. But so that we wouldn't be noticed we had our cover story, the grill. Whoever passed by there and saw us, all we were doing was roasting, we were just grilling some meat."

"You pretended to eat?"

"We did eat. We set up some coals, put a grill over it, and threw some chorizos on, which we would eat with bread and cheap wine. Meanwhile we would talk in low voices about what was happening, what the press wasn't saying. They would tell us their troubles and we would tell them ours. We would be conspiring, in other words."

"So that's what conspiring is like? What possible harm could you bring to the military junta, hidden there, eating chorizos and speaking ill of the regime?"

"A lot of harm, though you may not believe it. The dictatorship needed silence like you need air. The very act of getting together and talking about things was a way to resist."

"What did you talk about?"

"We told them about the *chupaderos*, for instance, makeshift morgues where the military tortured and killed detainees out of the public eye. Or we brought them up-to-date on the insurrection against Somoza in Nicaragua. The press would say nothing about that, and it was the news that the stevedores liked best. They'd ask us, Comrade, are the Sandinistas on the move? They found it unbelievable that it was possible to get rid of the tyrants, that in another part of the world people had risen against tyranny and defeated it. Some of them would even give me money. They would say, Make sure this gets to them, the ones fighting in Nicaragua."

"Yes, yes, Lolé, but it still doesn't sound like it was accomplishing anything."

"It's hard to say how much we did accomplish. But aside from being a foreigner, I was just a low-ranking militant, you have to remember that. Fucking low-rank, like we said. I moved in the trenches, while those in charge moved in wider circles. Besides, we had labor leaders who were in the thick of it, in the very mouth of the wolf, trying to saw off the legs of the dictatorship from within the syndicates. The matter was infinitely complex and infinitely infinitesimal.

"Every month, the party put out an underground newspaper, taking great risks and facing a whole range of difficulties. They distributed it one by one, a task that took a few hours.

They'd remove the wrapping from a box of cigars, empty it from the bottom, then roll up each of the eight pages of the newspaper until it was the size of a cigarillo. Then they'd fill half of the box with fake cigarillos and half with real ones, and wrap it back up. It was an old trick that marijuana dealers used and they adopted it to mock the regime. One newspaper at a time, to one contact, often having to go all the way across town to deliver it.

"There were a lot of words in those eight pages, Mateo, do you understand, words which were in such short supply. Imagine that we were pizza delivery boys. Ring, ring, yes, with mozzarella and anchovies, and off we would go with the newspaper, rain, thunder, or lightning. And sometimes it didn't say anything new and it arrived wet and cold, but we would be there to deliver it."

"The newspaper story sounds like it was true, but that thing about the whitecaps, the stevedores waiting for you in the fog, you made that up."

"No, there was fog. There still is. You'll see it for yourself in a bit."

⁂

ON SUNDAY, forty-eight hours after the dark episode, Lorenza was still wrapped in the straitjacket of her own anxiety.

"You're going to go crazy if you don't look for help," Mamaíta told her. Lorenza didn't hear her or respond, but paced the house back and forth like a caged lion, her heart beating a thousand times a minute, her blood pressure rising, and her hands like ice. She hadn't been able to sleep, not even to lie down for a moment. She could not eat because it felt as if she were choking. In a picture taken a week afterward for her travel documents, she has the fiendish eyes of a caged animal and sharpened features due to the half a kilo she was losing daily. Although she refused to see a psychiatrist, Mamaíta and Guadalupe persisted and somehow they got her into the office of the well-respected Dr. Haddad, who specialized in treating family members of those who had been kidnapped. Although it was a Sunday, he had agreed to see her right away.

Lorenza walked into the office at eleven in the morning, her eyes darting everywhere but resting nowhere. She wouldn't even sit down, and let her mother relate to the doctor what had happened.

"I don't want to tell you my story or listen to your theories. I just want to find my son," was the only thing Lorenza said.

"Why were you being so obnoxious, Lolé?" Mateo asked. "What had that man done to you?"

"Nothing, I didn't even know him. But it was like I was possessed. It was either that afternoon, or the next day, that I slugged your uncle Patrick."

"Shit, really? Why?"

"Because he said something or didn't say something; because he did something, or didn't do something. Who knows?"

"Did he slug you back?"

"No, of course not. He was there trying to help, and everybody coped as well as they could. I was hypersensitive, a vulnerable and unhinged thing. But I didn't even want to go see that psychiatrist or psychoanalyst, or whatever the hell he was. Not that one or any of them, not then or ever; to this day, I won't sit still on a divan. Not that I sat on one then, I remained standing, trying to keep myself together so I wouldn't explode with impatience, so I wouldn't scream at that doctor that I thought talking to him was a waste of precious minutes."

Dr. Haddad made them return to the waiting room for a moment. When they went back in, ten or fifteen minutes later, he had his glasses on and in his hands were the pages of Forcás's farewell letter, which apparently he had been reading in the interlude.

"You had given it to him?" Mateo asked.

"No, no, I told you I was not all there. I imagine my mother had given it to him, or Guadalupe."

"So what did he say?"

"He said the weirdest thing. I don't know what stopped me from jumping him and slugging him as well, because what he said was like a kick to the kidneys."

This is a love letter, he said.

⁂

AURELIA HAD BEEN in Buenos Aires twelve days, sharing an apartment on Deán Funes with Sandrita, the bundle of dollars still in her suitcase, the microfilm in the toothpaste tube, and the passports under the mattress. Sandrita was growing restless; she said that all it took was one raid and they were dead.

"Forcás was nowhere to be seen. I was starting to doubt his existence, like in that play by Ionesco where the characters yearn for the arrival of the Maestro and the Maestro doesn't show." When the Maestro finally arrives, the others realize that he has no head. Maybe Forcás had no head.

"That would explain a lot," Mateo said. "Forcás has no head."

Through an agent, he told Sandrita to tell Aurelia that soon, very soon. But another week passed and nothing. And then one Saturday, Sandrita came home with two boxes of ravioli, and when Aurelia asked her why two when one was enough for both of them, she said that they weren't for eating, but to hide what she was turning over to Forcás the following day. That is, at noon on Sunday, Aurelia finally had an appointment with him. And they had to set things up. They emptied the boxes and repacked them, first a layer of ravioli and on top a pair of passports, another layer of ravioli, another two passports, a double layer of ravioli, and the top. And a string to make it look good. Sandrita told her to relax, no one would notice a thing.

"But I also have to give him the dollars," Aurelia confessed.

"Why didn't you tell me, we'll have to put them in the box."

"There are too many bills."

"How many?"

"A lot."

The meeting was at the confectioner Las Violetas, on the corner of Rivadavia and Medrano. So that Lorenza had to go to a spot on the map called Rivadavia and Medrano, and Lorenza who had no idea how to get anywhere. Sandrita took her that afternoon, on Saturday, as if they were scouting out the territory, so that Aurelia could find it the next day without problems.

"And what about Forcás? How do I recognize him?" she asked.

"Right before noon, you go into Las Violetas and sit at a table. But not with your back to the door. Never sit with your back to the door, always with your eyes on the door, in case the *cana* show up. You don't want them to grab you unexpectedly. You sit at a table in a spot where he can see you. You put the boxes of ravioli on the table, and you wait for him to come to you."

"And how will he know who I am?"

"Don't worry about him. He'll know what you look like, and if he is not sure, the boxes will tip him off; he knows that you're bringing him ravioli."

Second rule for those types of meetings, the margin of error is ten minutes. If at twelve ten one of you is not there, the other one will suppose that you have been taken and will go, to prevent from being grabbed as well. Third rule, after a meeting, never go straight home or to another meeting before taking a subway or walking a few blocks heading in an opposite direction, to make sure that you're not being followed. Fourth rule, always carry identification. Always. Never go anywhere without an ID, not even to buy some bread next door.

"All right, I got it. Now tell me, what's he like?" Aurelia asked.

"What's who like?"

"Forcás. What's he like?"

"He's good-looking, if that's what you're asking."

"All Argentinean men are good-looking."

"But this one is twentysomething, eyes and hair the color of honey, wide shoulders. Good-looking guy, I'm telling you."

"Any specific details? Defects?"

"No one's perfect. He's not very tall and he's bowlegged, as if he just jumped off a horse."

Las Violetas, a confectionery from the turn of the century, seemed to Aurelia a little too romantic a spot for a political rendezvous. It was truly an art-nouveau jewel, as delicate and ornate as a box of fine chocolates. She felt nervous, and attributed it to what she had to do the following day, or to the lit stained-glass windows of Las Violetas, or to the realization that night was falling at that moment over Buenos Aires. Or maybe because of Forcás, whom she was finally going to meet after so much waiting.

After they had tea in Las Violetas, Aurelia and Sandrita walked a few blocks and went into a café where they had some more tea, during a short informatory meeting with a comrade from the regional directive. He told them about the rumors spreading of the fiasco that had befallen the head of the military junta, General Jorge Rafael Videla, during a trip to Italy. The gossip around Buenos Aires was that the pope had thrown the forced disappearances of hundreds of persons in Videla's face, and that the Italian press had greeted him by divulging the existence of *chupaderos*.

On their way back home, meandering to fulfill the rigorous regulations for vigilance, Sandrita and Aurelia took deep breaths of the night air. It was an unforgettable evening when the silence that had always sheltered the dictatorship began to melt, drop by drop, like the snows on top of Monte Tronador.

At a certain point they separated, and Aurelia took a cab to Belgrano R, one of the wealthier neighborhoods in the city. She rang the bell of a Colombian couple who were friends of her mother, to whom her mother had mailed from Bogotá some papers that Lorenza had to sign and return as soon as possible by certified mail. They were inheritance documents relating to the finca that her father had left her in the countryside outside Bogotá.

"A finca called San Jacinto that you never got to see," Lorenza told her son. "It was a lovely place, a little valley covered in mist in between two blue mountain ranges."

Along with the documents, Mamaíta had sent money and a letter in her clear and beautiful handwriting, words made uncertain by grief. She had also sent a pair of high-heeled Bally shoes, made of grape-colored suede, which so many years later Lorenza still remembered as if she were holding them in her hands. Ever loving Mamaíta, to think about presents at such a time. And Bally shoes at that, how crazy, who would think of such an extravagance? Of course, in the Argentinean party the women had to dress up, not like in Bogotá or in Madrid, where they all went with the complete identikit: faded jeans, military vest, native backpack, and lace-up boots with thick rubber soles, like those of a construction worker, what her father had called her little communist boots. In Argentina, one had to adopt almost the opposite type of disguise: comb your hair neatly, wear perfume, put on stockings and other feminine accessories. They even wore nail polish, which Lorenza applied with great care. But no Ballys. The Ballys didn't fit the profile, they were too much.

"That's funny, so now you were a landlord with this property in San Jacinto," Mateo teased her.

"I would have done anything for the comrades not to look at me as some well-off girl playing at revolution. But that's probably how they did see me."

"And the Colombians?"

"What Colombians?"

"The husband and wife who gave you the shoes you didn't like."

"I did like them, they were divine, but I wasn't going to risk wearing them."

The Colombian couple wanted Lorenza to have dinner with them, a simple meal, they warned her, just family, and they served a cheese and mushroom omelet. Of course, they knew nothing of her activities in Buenos Aires. They thought she was in school because that's what Mamaíta had told them. During dinner, as they chatted about nothing in particular, dogs and horses, the wife mentioned in passing that Videla was a great horseman, an outstanding example, and that she admired him because of his role in restoring Argentinean values. A piece of omelet got stuck in Lorenza's throat, but she remained quiet, and bit by bit the conversation returned to the safe territory of animals and Colombian soap operas, and the icy rain that fell over the Bogotá savannah. The husband seemed to be somewhere else, dozing off, but suddenly he would jolt up and interrupt his wife.

"We Argentineans are right and human." He kept repeating this because the saying was so catchy, he said. It was the first time that Lorenza had heard that slogan, coined by the reactionaries as a response to the denunciations against human rights violations in Argentina that had begun to spread all over the world. "What ingenious nonsense—right and human!" the husband went on. "You have to admit that whoever came up with it had a stroke of genius. With a little phrase they shut up all the government detractors. Damn, what valuable nonsense!"

"Those Argentinean generals are top-notch," the wife assured, "very white and well-heeled. Not like ours, those chubby little darkies. But they are selfless, our poor military men, how well I know about their selflessness and capacity for sacrifice. And these Argentinean generals, what model men, with such refined educations, fluent in French and English, with perfect accents, just between us, they're divine, from the best families. I never imagined that a military man could speak perfect French. How could I have? In Colombia they can't even speak Spanish well." Lorenza listened to all this feeling as if the blood was going to burst from her veins. Please, Papaíto, she prayed, don't let a word escape my lips, don't let me utter some insult now that I'll pay for dearly later, and she swallowed those toads, responding only with, "You don't say."

So Videla speaks perfect French? You don't say. And he is a good horseman, so right and so human? You don't say. You don't say, that phrase so common in Bogotá, used by the speaker when it is he who doesn't want to say something. But before long, Aurelia couldn't take it anymore. She made up something about having to attend a conference at the university, and grabbed her letter, shoes, money, and inheritance documents, expressed her gratitude, and got up from the table. But the hosts, ever courteous and warm, asked her to stay for dessert, homemade *île flottante*, following the recipe in *L'Art Culinaire* step by step, she shouldn't miss out on that. They relented when she insisted that she had to go right away, and told her that there would be a car waiting for her.

"Oh, thank you, thank you, but no. I'll take a taxi. You're very sweet, but you don't have to do that, I'll take a taxi."

"What do you mean, you're taking a taxi this late? Let the driver take you, that's what he's here for. His name is Humberto and he is quite a character. And tell us, what is this conference about? Very intriguing. Where do you say it is, at what school?"

"The one in Buenos Aires."

"A conference this late on a Saturday night? It's ten o'clock, what kind of conference starts this late?"

"Well, it's technically a debate," she stammered, her shortened breath making her flush. "But you're right. What a disaster. It's already too late. I've missed it."

"Then what's the hurry? Eat your *île flottante* in peace and then have some coffee, which is Colombian, of course, one hundred percent Colombian. Because these people may have their beef, but coffee, coffee is our specialty. And if you want, you'll join us for a little cognac afterward. I promise, Humberto will drive you to your house afterward; and wait until you go inside, so we can all sleep soundly, so your mother can't say that we have not taken care of her little girl."

Lorenza finally made it out of that house in the Mercedes owned by the husband and wife, Humberto driving. She had to mislead him so that he wouldn't find out where she lived on Deán Funes. Let's head toward Recoleta, Humberto. It was the first thing that came into her head, but she regretted it immediately. Shit, why had she said that? Recoleta is like the cemetery. Or I should say, Recoleta was the name of the most traditional cemetery in Buenos Aires, but also of the neighborhood that surrounded it. Humberto put her at ease when he said, So the señorita lives in Recoleta. Congratulations, it's a very beautiful place. Very beautiful, yes, thank you, Humberto.

They had been on the way for a while, who knew where, when Lorenza asked, playing the foreigner, Are we in Recoleta yet, Humberto? And since the chauffeur said yes, she replied straightaway, Here, here, Humberto, drop me off on this block, I live nearby, so don't worry about me, Humberto. I can walk from here. It's a beautiful night, maybe a brisk walk will refresh me. Right? The best thing after the meal to settle you down.

But Humberto wasn't buying it. She did not have to worry. He had received an order from his *patrones*, and he was the type who would fulfill his duty. There was nothing to do but summon Papaíto's help, because even if it meant paying for it with his life, Humberto was going to drop her off at her door and wait until she went inside. How was she going to get into any of the houses, since none of them were hers?

It wasn't even her neighborhood. She had never set foot in it. How would she open the door, what key would she use. She was in a bind, when, oh miracle, a couple coming out of a building. This is it, she told herself, help Papaíto, heroes and buffoons. It's over there, Humberto, that building in the corner. Thanks, Humberto, here, that's fine, stop. Thanks, Humberto. Stop! Kisses to everyone, ciao, Humberto, ciao. She jumped out of the car trying to reach the door of the building before it closed behind the couple, and she made it. She was inside. She tried to catch her breath. Thanks, Papaíto, I owe you, half a second more and I wouldn't have made it.

When the driver saw that she was inside, he was content

and drove off. Great, we're free of Saint Humberto. We're safe, Papaíto, you were stupendous. But maybe not so stupendous, the couple who had just left was locking the door from the outside. What a nightmare. They had locked her in.

Coño, it was really dark, she couldn't see a thing. Where was the light? Here, here, the light switch. And now where is the button, the one you pressed from inside to open the door. Pawing the walls, she found the damn button and pressed it, but she realized that there were two locks and it had opened only one of them. The second one remained locked at night for security purposes. There was nothing to do, she was locked in.

In other words, a prisoner of this run-of-the-mill building at about one in the morning, hoping that the couple who had left would return, reasoning that if they had keys it was because they lived there, and if they lived there, they would have to return at some point. The light would shut off after a minute and a half and she would turn it back on, not because there was anything to look at but because of how depressing it was to wait in the dark, like Audrey Hepburn, she thought, blind and with her short hairstyle, hiding in the dark from the murderer.

She sat on one of the marble steps and her kidneys must have grown cold because she suddenly needed to pee, adding to her torment, since she had told Sandrita that she would be back by eleven at the latest, and it was almost two. Sandrita probably thought that they were torturing her this very minute. She imagined Sandrita getting the word out—the foreigner has been nabbed, everyone for themselves—or leaping from the balcony in fear of what was to come. Aurelia had to return to the apartment on Deán Funes immediately, but she didn't dare knock at any of the apartments of her prison building so that they would open the front door. It was unthinkable to do such a thing at that hour. So there she was, with her box of grape-colored Ballys, her inheritance documents, and the letter from Mamaíta, with its beautiful and distraught words.

"Did you get out?" Mateo asked.

"If I hadn't, you never would've been born. Don't you see that I was going to meet your father the following day? I finally got out around two in the morning when a young man went out and I snuck through right behind him." That night, at the apartment on Deán Funes, Aurelia couldn't sleep, mulling over everything in her head. The dinner with that pair of toadies of the military junta had left a sharp thorn lodged within, so white and cultured, the sons of bitches generals, such wonderful horsemen, such steeds. Argentinean values? Right and human? Motherfuckers, they were a bunch of butchers is what they were. And it doesn't matter how she looked at it, tossing around on the bed, she couldn't sleep, out of shame for not having said anything. She should have pulled off that tablecloth, embroidered in neat cross-stitching, splattering the omelet and *île flottante* against the wall. Instead she didn't say a peep, eating her food bite by bite, at that table, listening to all their perversions and playing the chickenshit, and now how it came back at her, nausea and upset stomach, as if she had swallowed poison.

On top of that there was Sandrita, who as expected had been waiting for her with her hackles up and had torn her to pieces with quite the lecture for arriving at such an hour, that she had frightened the shit out of her and she had been about to flee the house and sound the alarm, that she was a flake, a lightweight, a shitty petit bourgeois. She went on and on, with good reason, and with that obscene fervor that is characteristic of Argentineans when they begin cussing and losing their shit.

"Did Ramón curse?"

"Yes, a lot. He was a real machine gun with four-letter words."

Aurelia had calmed down somewhat when Sandrita knocked on her bedroom door. She had forgotten to tell her that the meeting with Forcás had been postponed until the following Monday, at six in the afternoon. The leader, Aurelia thought. She muttered that Forcás was definitely headless, and Sandrita took it to mean something else, saying, you have to understand he has a thousand other things to worry about, he's not here just to attend to you, it's not that he doesn't have a head on his shoulders.

"Let's go to sleep," Aurelia implored. "It's almost three in the morning."

"You're going to tell me what time it is?"

"I'm sorry. It won't happen again."

All this and Sandrita didn't even know yet that Aurelia had left the shawl she had borrowed at the Colombians' place . . . Aurelia realized she didn't have it way too late, not until she went to bed just before the damn reprimand. Shit, she thought suddenly, the shawl, I left the shawl at that house. Her pulse quickened and the blood beat against her temples. Did I leave it there with Mamaíta's friends, or had it fallen off while I was imprisoned in the building? If it was in the building, it was gone, but if it was with Mr. and Mrs. Right and Human, they might send Humberto to return it to my supposed apartment in Recoleta, and then they would discover the pile of bullshit that I'd been feeding them, and they would call Bogotá to pass on the rumors, you'll never guess who has become a subversive.

They were such toadies that they would probably whisper her name to the Argentinean authorities. Such things were not unheard of, such was the state of panic, even with those in the right, meaning they would do anything to kiss the military's ass. Lorenza would never go there again. She had to tell Mamaíta not to send anything else there. And what if she had left the shawl in the Mercedes, and Humberto found it?

"She was a little anal, that Sandrita, look at the state she had you in," Mateo suggested.

"Not anal, disciplined. And she was right, if I remained so flighty, I was going to get us both killed. You had to learn how to move, Mateo, and it wasn't easy. You spent your time trying not to get caught in the web of deceit that you had to weave around you."

Finally alone and shuttered in her room, she decided to get Aurelia out of her head for a while, that beast Aurelia, that is, her fiery nom de guerre, that brave warrior who did nothing but screw up and ignore all the warnings. So she decided to think about the land that Papaíto had left her, beautiful San Jacinto, and she closed her eyes to summon giant purple flowers that appeared on the artichokes if they were not harvested on time, of the manna grass that sprouted on the hills and had to be cared for like an open eye so that it doesn't dry, the adobe bread oven that Papaíto had built behind the kitchen. She thought for a long time about that oven and the breads that came out of it, which generally ended up, according to Papaíto, soused. And who knows what he meant by that word, because he used it when the breads came out not fully cooked, but also when they were overcooked, when they stuck to one another and when the dough collapsed. What do you think, Papaíto? And he always responded: A disaster, soused again—which must have meant any of these categories: uncooked, burned, stuck together, or deflated. The truth was, they had never mastered the secrets of the adobe oven.

"If you're talking about good bread, we never quite got there, Mateo. But the faint aroma escaping from that oven on cold mornings was always gratifying. Come to think of it, I suspect that it wasn't really the bread that interested Papaíto but that aroma. And the slow, milky air that flooded the fields of San Jacinto at night. Did it come down from the hills, or was it more likely the hot breath of the cattle mingling with the freezing air?" Alone in her bedroom of the apartment on Deán Funes, Lorenza continued to dwell on these memories: Papaíto lighting the coal stove, removing bits of iron and blowing on them with the bellows; Mamaíta, who stirred the hot chocolate, wearing a poncho over her nightgown; the old copper water tank, which began to rattle as soon as the water got hot; her sister Guadalupe and herself still under the blankets, testing the harshness of the cold that awaited them outside with the tips of their noses; the times when they would lay down a foundation of bricks to add another bedroom to the house, or crawl about on all fours weeding the garden.

"And they were also the years of the literary boom. In San Jacinto, we devoured novels by Carpentier, Vargas Llosa, Juan Rulfo, and Carlos Fuentes. Cortázar's short stories and Gabo's *Autumn of the Patriarch.* We had barely finished reading one when they would be already coming out with another, a new prodigy."

Lorenza also thought about, or should have thought about, the ass they kept, woolly and purplish like the hairy leaves of the *espeletia* and the flowers of the *sietecueros* that flourished up above, in the icy air of the *páramo*. Papaíto had christened the ass the Philanthropist because he was affectionate and spoiled and followed them around everywhere, even sneaking into the house if they left the doors open. He was fascinated with animals, Papaíto was. Lorenza had never met such an animal lover. And it had been that way since he was a child; all you had to do was look at the pictures from that time to prove it. When he wasn't hugging a goose, he was riding a dog or a horse, not a regular riding horse but a scrawny one, picked at by cattle tyrants, from the breeds used to frighten foxes.

That night on Deán Funes, Lorenza couldn't stop thinking about those days, especially about the purebred Aberdeen Angus cattle that her father had imported from the United States and put out to graze in the fields of San Jacinto, in hopes of going into the beef business. They were tiny and squarish, looking more like bovine ponies, with dreamy eyelashes and resplendent black hair. Needless to say, in no time at all, they were no different than the Philanthropist, eating sugar cubes from human hands. Papaíto, who knew each of them by name and spent hours brushing their hair, was of course incapable of sending them off to the slaughterhouse when the time came, so the only thing that perished was his beef business, and the Aberdeen all lived to an old age after a long life as unproductive as it was peaceful.

She thought and thought, about these and other things, until she fell asleep when it was almost dawn, perhaps dreaming about Papaíto, because during that early time in Buenos Aires she dreamed about him a lot, maybe because his death was so recent, or because she refused to accept it. In one of those dreams he was working on a jigsaw puzzle, something that in real life they often did together at night in San Jacinto by the fire. But the jigsaw puzzle of the dream, whose subject was a blue lake, was so big that it fell off the table.

"It was difficult to piece together, Mateo, rather impossible since the whole of the picture was blue, only blue, different hues of blue, the water blue and the sky also blue, so that in my dream, Papaíto was very still, perhaps flabbergasted, looking first at the nascent puzzle and then at the pieces piled on the side, without even trying to put a piece in place because they were all the same, all of them blue, any of them could have fit anywhere in that realm that was blue from beginning to end."

So she was now the inheritor of San Jacinto? That's what it looked like. The papers that certified this were on her night table. And yet she awoke thinking that if Papaíto wasn't there with his soused breads, his overindulged ass and cattle, then she wasn't quite sure what it was that she had inherited. A bit of fog, nothing more, another lost piece of blue in the middle of the jigsaw puzzle.

⁂

"FORTUNATELY, I DIDN'T inherit my father's legs," Mateo said, and asked his mother if it was true that Ramón was bowlegged. But he didn't let her reply. Tired of walking and suddenly irritated that he didn't know where they were going, he hailed a taxi. Once they got in, he opened the window and then claimed it was cold.

"Roll up the window," Lorenza proposed, but he ignored her. "Roll it up just a little bit then."

"Ramón never said goodbye to me before he left, right, Lolé? I don't remember him saying goodbye. The last time I saw him was on the lake in Bariloche. There were red mountains all around. The mountains reflected on the lake seemed real, and the ones that were real were so far away that they seemed fake. Ramón was there with us and then he was lost, lost like the Turk in the fog," Mateo said. And Lorenza thought, but did not say aloud, that the scene he was describing was not so much from memory but from a photograph, the last one she had taken with Ramón, on the shores of Lago Nahuel Huapi. "Or maybe what I remember is only from a picture," Mateo realized on his own. "But I am definitely sure that he never said goodbye. It was only much later that I began to suspect that he was not coming back. With you it was different. I think that when I was little I would cry sometimes when you went to work or traveled. I remember I hated your hair dryer and I used to hide it from you, because if you dried your hair, it meant you would be going out for the night. But the next day you would be there when I woke up. But I didn't miss Ramón at first. Maybe I didn't even realize he was missing for years, or I realized it for a moment and forgot it just as quickly, until one day I discovered how much I had needed him without even realizing it. If he had said goodbye, everything would have been much clearer. I would like to know, Lolé, why do you think he was imprisoned?"

"Who knows what mischief he got into?"

"You say mischief and it sounds almost charming. My charming father and his mischief. Oh, Lorenza, you chose the bastard and I covered up for him," Mateo said, and they both laughed. In spite of everything, there was some comedy in it.

⁂

SANDRITA AND AURELIA kept the apartment on Deán Funes clean and orderly, completely unlike the pigsty apartment in Madrid, or the "war sty" as they had called it, where a whole gang of people lived, all of them Latin American—a Chilean woman, three Argentineans, and Lorenza. When a Brazilian couple moved in above, they christened it *the* war sty.

All of them, except Aurelia, had been fleeing one dictatorship or another, for at that time the Southern Cone was infested with dictatorships and that apartment was a refuge for exiles. People came and went. The living room functioned as a backstage of sorts, with a lot of romance and episodes in the beds, the kitchen became a deposit box for flyers and newspapers, and the ashtrays were always replete with butts. Those butts were the most difficult part for her; and waiting for your turn to use the bathroom, or walking into your room and realizing you no longer had a blanket because it had been allotted to someone else.

In Buenos Aires, on the other hand, they had to keep up appearances, and so they tried to eat at proper hours and keep the refrigerator stocked. Not like in Madrid, where there was never anything in the fridge but a dried-up onion and few cans of beer. Things in Buenos Aires were strange as well because other people in the party never set foot inside your home. For security reasons they didn't even know where it was. Also, you had to keep your windows and door wide open for the neighbors, so they would take no interest in you. Step right up, lady from 4B; come on in, renter from 2A. Would they like some coffee while they went on about the leak that was soaking their carpet? Of course, señora, of course, señor. Let them look all they wanted, let them sniff out and discard any suspicions. Let them walk away with the best of impressions, so they would have nothing to rat to the *cana* about. Let me help you with those grocery bags, señora from 4B. Do you want to borrow an umbrella, señor from 2A, it's drizzling?

"Then how would you meet up with other party members to conspire?" Mateo asked.

"Only in public places, in cafés mostly, meetings which were never arranged by phone. Using phones was playing with fire, so meetings had to be arranged by intermediaries who sometimes took weeks to deliver a message. At least three-quarters of our time was taken up with these details."

"Tell me about the day that you met Ramón."

"If you want, we can go to Las Violetas tomorrow and I'll tell you there."

Las Violetas didn't exist anymore, the receptionist of the hotel would inform them the following day. It was a shame that she could not take her son, Lorenza thought. How precisely she remembered the languid air of that place, the rhombus designs in the marble floor, the lilac-and-mauve rosettes in the stained-glass windows, and even the golden hue of the tea they served in white porcelain cups. And yet how deceitful the memory of that girl she once was, who Monday afternoon waited for a young man she did not yet know, a man who in a couple of years would become Mateo's father. Lorenza tried to envision Aurelia seated there in Las Violetas, checking her watch obsessively, restless, looking up at the door and then again at her watch, self-conscious that the three boxes she had with her were too conspicuous.

"Three boxes? I thought there were two," Mateo asked.

"Two raviolis and one from the Bally shoes." Since everything hadn't fit in between the layers of ravioli, they had decided to build a false bottom in the box with the Bally shoes, with her Mamaíta's pardon, where she hid the dollars and put the Ballys back on top. It was finally six o'clock. Six? Was that really the time of their first meeting? Suddenly Lorenza wasn't so sure. She was sure it had been a Monday, there was no doubt about that, and Mateo would soon see why there was no doubt. She arrived a few minutes early and had a furtive look around. There were about thirty or forty people there, no more than that, so the place was not full, a lot of ladies, a few older men, some girls, and a couple of young men, one to her right and another in front of her, much farther away. Either one of them could have been Forcás. But neither of them was alone: the one on the right was with what appeared to be his girlfriend and the other one with a woman whose face Aurelia could not see. And if they were coupled off they couldn't be Forcás. Although, come to think of it, no one had told her that he would come alone to meet her. In the end, all he had to do was pick up a package. She shouldn't forget that this was not a blind date but the perpetration of a tiny act of war. She should also not ignore the fact that if they had set up the meeting there and not in some other place, it was solely because a busy confectionery would arouse less suspicion, and because the location, on the corner, had two exits, one to the avenue, which would make an escape easier if things got ugly. That is, it had nothing at all to do with her, or with the encounter of the two people fast approaching, or with the small napkins with violets embroidered in the corners, or the Bavarian creams and éclairs that whizzed by on trays to various tables, or with the pretty white tablecloths with the stained-glass reflections. What a shame, this elegance is not for me at all. Being in the resistance still felt like a game to her, or being onstage. Bit by bit she would come to terms with what it meant to live one's whole existence completely in secret, alienated from the day-to-day routine, on the margins of everyone else's normal life. Although who knows, who can say that anybody else's life is so normal, or what strange things they're up to. Even right there in Las Violetas, there was likely someone else with a plan similar to hers, somebody about to whisper some banned information in another's ear, or slip a mimeographed sheet under the table, or perhaps an informant who feigned ignorance while jotting notes about everything.

In any case, it bothered her that she had built all these false hopes around Forcás, although truly, she had no idea what sort of hopes they were, maybe the hopes of good conversation over a cup of tea, or even more to fulfill the need to confess to someone that her father had died recently and she felt terrible about it, or the longing for some affection that would ground her in this city that was so beautiful and so full of spies. And besides, why shouldn't she build up her hopes about meeting a man whom she considered more or less a hero.

"A *hero*, Lorenza? That's ridiculous, to call somebody made of flesh and bone that."

"A little bit yes, but a little bit no."

"A little bit hero and a little bit buffoon."

"Like all of us."

At eight minutes after six, she began to think that she shouldn't linger too much longer. She would ask for the check, wait two more minutes, and if no one arrived she'd be off. Then she focused more intently on one of the two young men who were sitting there, the one whose reflection she could see in the mirror in the back, and realized that he was looking at her as well, also dissemblingly through the mirror, as his girlfriend continued talking to him.

He was rather good-looking, or at least better-looking than the one on the right, who was ugly, plain and simple. The one in the mirror could be Forcás, must be Forcás, although his hair and eyes weren't really honey-colored, and Sandrita had been emphatic about those traits. Well, as for the eyes, who knew what color they were. It was impossible to tell from far away. And the hair? The hair did not have a trace of honey, but was more or less dark, you could say black. And until he stood up, who knew if he was bowlegged. But if it was Forcás, why didn't he come up to her? If he wasn't Forcás, why was he looking at her? Maybe the poor man had nothing else to look at, and was rattled that she was looking at him so much. Aurelia shifted her eyes to the door because she sensed that now someone was walking in, and her instincts told her it was him; but no, not so, it was a group of señoras, so Lorenza decided she would stand up now, because the period of waiting had expired. She would take her boxes, drop them off at home, and go to the control meeting to warn them that something must have happened to Forcás.

"You brought me that *vaina?*" he asked from behind her, almost brushing her nape, a hoarse voice that of course was his, you didn't have to be a magician to figure that out. She jumped. She hadn't expected it to happen like this, that he would surprise her from behind, and she must have grown suddenly, because when she said hello, her voice sounded like an impostor's, like theater parley. He, on the other hand, was very calm as he sat beside her. He was, in fact, grinning.

"A pretty smile," Lorenza told Mateo. "Your father had a pretty smile."

"He hadn't lost the tooth yet," Mateo cut in. "He used the word *vaina*? You're saying Forcás told you *vaina*? He used that exact expression, *You brought me that vaina*? It's so Colombian."

"That's what he said. He must have already known where I was from." Aurelia knew right away that the man beside her smoked, it was the first thing that her nose registered when she met a person. But she noticed another smell as well, one that she liked, the smell of raw wool from the heavy pullover he wore.

"His famous thick wool pullovers."

"This one seemed woven by hand, and it emitted an aroma that inspired confidence, a pleasant animal smell."

"A pleasant animal smell or the smell of a pleasant animal?"

"A smell like sheep. I'm just trying to tell you that he was wearing sheep's wool. But your father also smelled like a third thing. He radiated energy and youth, and that smells too. It smells strong and is alluring."

"It's called testosterone, Lolé."

"I wouldn't have called it that. But now that you've said it, he was a hunk of a man, your father. Of course he exuded testosterone."

"If anybody questions us, let's just say that we met in your country, last year," Forcás proposed, to get their minute straight.

"Got it," she responded. "And what were you doing there?"

"I have an export business."

"What do you export?"

"Leather goods: When we parted there, you said you would call me as soon as you arrived in Buenos Aires, so that I could show you the city."

"Nice. And who introduced us in Colombia?"

"Someone in your family. You tell me who."

"My brother-in-law?"

"Your brother-in-law was my contact for the sale. Give him a name."

"Patrick."

"Patrick what?"

"Patrick Ferguson. Let's say he's an Australian."

"If they ask you anything else, say we're just getting to know each other and don't know a lot about each other."

"Not even names?"

"You'll say my name is Mario."

The place was loud, and Forcás spoke very softly and with a pronounced Buenos Aires accent, so she had trouble understanding everything and had to lean in closer. Maybe it was because of this that at first she smelled him more than watched him. A little bit later, when she leaned back and adjusted her angle of vision, she noticed that indeed his shoulders were wide and his hair was pretty, not exactly the color of honey, more a light chestnut, but it was the same, it was still handsome, everything about him was handsome, Sandrita had not lied about a thing.

"So then it's true, my father has wide shoulders like Patrick always said. But you didn't tell me what happened with the *chat*."

"What *chat*?"

"The one you left in Humberto's Mercedes."

"*Shawl*, kiddo, *shawl*, the scarf."

"Right, right, shawl."

"I never found out. Since I never saw them again, I never knew what became of the *chat*."

"And the boxes?" Mateo asked.

"The boxes?"

"The ravioli, Lorenza, the ravioli."

"That's exactly what your father asked on the day we met at the table in Las Violetas. He asked me what was in the boxes, and it surprised me that he was surprised."

"Oh, I just brought you this *vaina*. It's ravioli," Aurelia told Forcás.

"Ravioli? Are you nuts? Who would be stupid enough to walk around with boxes of ravioli on a Monday?"

"You see, Mateo, why I was so sure that our first meeting was on a Monday?"

"What was wrong with ravioli on Monday?"

"Very bad. When Forcás threw it in my face like that, I started blubbering, embarrassed that I had screwed up again. 'But she told me,' I tried to explain, 'yesterday my contact told me . . .' "

"Listen, yesterday was Sunday, *nena*," Forcás whispered in her ear. "The ravioli would have been good yesterday, but not today. The pasta makers are closed on Mondays. It's suicide to walk around with that on Monday. Except for you, there's no other retard walking around Buenos Aires with boxes of ravioli. No one eats ravioli on Mondays here."

"You're the one who switched Sunday to Monday, how was I supposed to know? How should I know what they eat here on Mondays, as far as I am concerned they eat shit," she exploded. Sandrita had already lectured her and now this Forcás was copping an attitude from the start. "Besides, I'm warning you," she told him, "don't start calling me stupid, or petit bourgeois, and definitely not retard or *nena*, because I am not a *nena*, and will not put up with this shower of insults, I'm up to here with all of it."

"Did the comrades harass you too much?" Forcás asked, softening his voice to placate her and unleashing his seductive smile.

"That's all they've done lately."

"There must have been other fuckups like this one. It's stuffed, this one with the ravioli. What about the other box?" Forcás asked, half mocking.

She turned red again because she knew he was right, she had to be more careful or there would be a catastrophe. By then he would have lit one of the green-label Particulares 30, which he sucked on willfully, as if eager for cancer.

"Okay, so now tell me why they called my father Forcás. Aside from the sheep smell, what else made him seem like he was from the country?"

"Just that, the sheep smell. I learned later that your grandmother Noëlle knitted those pullovers for him, using wool from the different types of sheep they raised at the farm in Polvaredas."

Maybe if she had observed Forcás with a more prophetic eye, she would have even then picked up on how aggressive he was, which was evident in the violence of his movements and his intransigent opinions. Although it had to be that way, more so because he was a soldier than because he was from the country. The truth was that on that first day, Aurelia didn't see him as someone from the country, perhaps because all she noticed was that he was the most attractive man she had ever met. She never found out what time he had arrived at Las Violetas, or if he had already been there when she arrived, watching her and waiting until the last minute to appear. The thing was that he was there now, seated beside her, gazing at her with those presumptuous eyes and quizzing her on why she had brought so many boxes.

"There are a lot of boxes because there are a lot of *vainas*," she replied.

Forcás wanted to know what else there was aside from the passports, and she explained that there was microfilm and money, dollars.

"I thought it was only passports," he said. "I had no idea about the rest. Why would they send all that with one messenger? It's crazy."

"I did what I was told without asking questions. In fact, I was told not to ask questions."

"You're right, it's not your fault."

"That would be the icing on the cake, if it were my fault."

"True, true, the noose is tight around our necks. But what balls, those sons of bitches comrades in Madrid, they were making you walk the plank, sending you with all that."

"Are you sure that's how my father spoke?" Mateo asked. "With that accent and those exact words."

"Yeah, well, something like that. I don't know how to do the Argentinean accent."

"It's all right, go on. But maybe just do his part in a normal accent. It sounds a little forced the way you're doing it."

"I'll do it however I want, kiddo, don't pressure me. Besides, it's almost over. Or do you want to leave the story there?"

"I want you to finish, but without an accent."

Aurelia asked Forcás if they had not told him that she would be bringing all this and he said that they had talked over the phone with Europe but that he hadn't quite understood everything—there were so many codes to throw off the enemy that they were themselves thrown off.

"And that's how the first story ends, Mateo. Nothing else happened," his mother said. "We couldn't linger there because of all the ravioli and dollars in our possession. We had to go. The best thing was for each of us to go our own way as soon as possible. But it was evident that both of us wanted to stay, we felt good together, more than good, I imagine we were both already half in love."

"Already?"

"Well, let's just say we were hooked. Chemistry, they call it. Chemistry, what else? Because when it comes down to it, we had barely talked. Some flirtatious gestures, a tap on the shoulder, a graze of the knees, a goodbye kiss, a few minutes chatting about contraband, goodbye again, a kiss again, ciao, ciao again, ciao, for real this time."

"You go first," Forcás suggested when it was no longer possible to prolong their goodbyes, and she went for her wallet to pay for her tea and his coffee.

"Don't even think about it. Put that away, *nena*." There

he went with the *nena* again, but this time it didn't irk her as much. "You evince yourself if you pay, sorry. You have to let the man pay at these meetings."

"Evince?"

"Make evident, betray yourself."

Aurelia was almost at the door leading out to Rivadavia when she turned around and walked back toward the table where Forcás was still seated.

"I forgot to tell you that the microfilm is in the bottom of the shoe box," she whispered in his ear, taking a last whiff of that rich sheep smell, and he grabbed her by the arm as she was about to go. "Can I see you next week?"

"All right, stop, Lolé," Mateo said. "I want you to explain to me why you fell in love with Forcás. Was it his pretty hair, his wide shoulders, the wool smell?"

"What a question! Let's see. First, because he was a party member. At that time, I would have never fallen in love with someone who wasn't."

"So you liked him because he was a laborer?"

"He wasn't a laborer."

"From the country, then."

"Originally from the country. But that wasn't a social class that we cared much about, we favored the industrial laborers. As you know, the muzhiks betrayed the October Revolution."

"What?"

"Nothing, never mind. Second, I liked that he was the

complete opposite of any boyfriend that Papaíto would have wanted for me. And third, pure old-fashioned attraction, I guess."

"Sexual?"

"Yes, but he also seemed like a very interesting guy."

"Did he seem like he would be a good father?" Mateo aimed the question point-blank and it caught his mother off guard. She felt embarrassed to have gone on about such trivialities, such dreadful tomfoolery. She remained silent for a moment because she did not know how to respond, anything she said would have been inadequate.

"A good father? No, Mateo, I didn't think to ask myself that. I didn't even ask myself if he was a good man."

※

It's a love letter, Dr. Haddad had said after reading the pages that Ramón left her at the beginning of the dark episode. A love letter? Lorenza was enraged. How the fuck is that a love letter? He took away my son, that's not a love letter. She would not even bother to discuss the matter with this Dr. Heart. They commit the vilest imaginable act against you, the most treacherous, and that's a love letter? It announces that you will never see your son again, your two-year-old baby, that creature from your entrails, and that's a love letter? He steals a child using false papers, forging your own signature, even having tricked you into packing his suitcase, and that's a love letter? All the psychiatrists in the world were famous for dishing mountains of shit and this Dr. Heart was the worst of all. Lorenza turned to scram out of there, leaving Mamaíta to say goodbye and thank the man for his time.

"Did you read it, Lorenza?" She came to a complete standstill. For a moment she couldn't move from the door, as if she were making up her mind whether to leave or come back in, and apparently she opted for the second option because she turned around, found a chair in front of the doctor, and sat down. She thought he looked like a cricket, and the cricket was challenging her with his gaze.

"No. Not the whole thing," she replied. "The first paragraph, that's all. I am not going to read the rest of it."

"That's fine," Haddad said, and there was an imperceptible triumphant shift of tone in his voice, as if the fish had bitten and all he had to do was hook it. "It's better that way. Don't read it. But I have read it, in between the lines."

"In the actual lines it says that I will never see my child again. What does it say in between the lines?"

"This man doesn't want to take your son from you, Lorenza. This man just wants you back."

She did not have to ask him to repeat himself to realize that he had just inspired her to have a revelation. Finally something concrete, something to hold on to! A trail, a light, a possibility. The haze of anguish that had dulled her thoughts day and night lifted in one swoop. After speaking with so many people who had offered nothing, someone had said something worth listening to. Lorenza took a deep breath. She was being offered a path that would lead her to her son.

She straightened up in the chair, like a marionette whose strings are pulled, and examined the doctor at length. He was a small man with big hands. Bald. Thin. Prominent nose. Definitely Arab, even in his Western clothes. Although it was a Sunday, he was not dressed informally. On the contrary, his suit, his tie, and white shirt were strictly formal, one could say impeccable. But there was something in his demeanor that was plain, dry, and angular, and it was that, plus the big dark eyes and the bald head, that reminded her of a cricket. Lorenza's voice was very different when she asked Haddad to please repeat and elaborate on what he had said.

"The man who wrote this letter is in love, and he does not want to take your child from you, he wants to win you back. So be ready, Lorenza, because he will call. Do everything you have to, so that when that call comes, you are ready. You know best what you have to do. But he will call you, you can count on that. When? I don't know. In a week, two weeks, a month. When he feels that he is in a safe place, at that moment, he will call you."

Lorenza, who knew that Dr. Haddad had years of experience dealing with kidnapping cases, had meticulously studied his appearance and now looked all around, scrutinizing his office.

"I studied it with such intensity," she told Mateo, "that although I never returned there, to this day I remember every detail."

Boxy furniture upholstered in gray, wood floors, white walls, and on the walls three posters from art exhibitions. On one of them was a bronze sculpture by Archipenko, *Woman Combing Her Hair*, according to the description beneath. On another one, an abstract figure in blue, gray, and black by Malevich. On the third, a series of lines in plum and brown by Rothko.

"Don't tell me that at that critical moment you started looking at posters," Mateo objected.

"I wanted some sign. I was looking for clues, something that would allow me to take that decisive step: to trust him. To be able to act I needed to believe in that man, it was a matter of life and death, to trust him, and I was searching for some confirmation. For instance, a copy of a Renoir would have been an unfavorable clue."

There was something syrupy about reproductions of Renoir. The art displayed in the office, however, was in keeping with the message that the doctor wanted to get across, intentionally or not: clarity, conceptual rigor, simple forms, and mechanical precision. Everything was good then, but it was also impersonal. Something else was necessary for Lorenza to lower her guard resolutely, something that would allow her to make contact, that would engage her emotions, and she saw it on the doctor's desk: a framed photograph. It was not of his wife or their kids, that would have been equivalent to a Renoir, or of Freud or Jung, that would have just been clearly offensive. It wasn't a postcard, either, or a piece of art. It was a plain black-and-white photograph of an olive tree in the middle of a rocky field. Presumably the doctor himself had taken it, in his land of origin. It was just what Lorenza needed.

"Why? What did that have to do with anything?" Mateo asked.

"It had nothing to do with anything. Don't ask me why, but I interpreted it as a green light. I could trust that man, I was going to trust that man. I was going to prepare for that call he had talked about. When Ramón's call came, because it would come, I would be ready to take it."

"Wait a second, Lolé, wouldn't it have been better to read the letter yourself?" Mateo asked.

"No. Listen to what you're saying. Reading Ramón's letter would have just caused anger, or contempt, or guilt, and in the best imaginable scenario, compassion or sorrow, and it was essential that I feel nothing. Nothing at all. This doctor was a third party, an outsider to the case, who had read it coldly and had given, let's say, a diagnosis. Or maybe he had smacked me in the head. Or a sort of prophecy? He had told me, he will call you, and all of a sudden, everything made sense, the pieces of the puzzle interlocked in an unexpected but logical procession, and I found it important to believe his every word.

"From that moment on, that phrase, he will call you, would become my certainty and my compass. I was too emotional to make judgments on my own without becoming delirious, too involved in the drama to be even moderately objective. So I would let the cricket set the guidelines, and from those directions I would devise a plan of action for the only thing I cared about, to get you back."

"Like a robot," Mateo said.

"Yes, like a robot," Lorenza replied. "But you don't even know what kind of robot. Thanks to Dr. Haddad I emerged from my paralysis and became Tranzor Z."

⁂

AROUND THE TIME that Aurelia met Forcás, she also met Lucia, a comrade in the party who still bore the scars of a recent tragedy. A few years before, four days after the military coup, they had disappeared her husband, who was also in the resistance, but only obliquely, since politics wasn't really his thing. His name was Horacio Rasmilovich, and he was known as Pipermín, or Piper, and although Aurelia never got to meet him, little by little, from what she learned from Lucia, she felt she got to know him. Piper was a translator from Portuguese to Spanish, so he was never very busy with work, which was fine by him, because he could devote himself to his true passion, reading history books, especially those about World War I. Lucia was never entirely sure if her husband had been kidnapped because they confused him with someone else, or because they had their eyes on him, or because they had really been after her, and on not finding her grabbed him.

This last scenario tormented her. She couldn't help obsessing over the possibility of such a fatal swap, taking him in place of her.

"That's part of the torment." Lorenza wanted to explain to Mateo that because tyrants and torturers don't show their faces, the victims end up blaming themselves. It was useless to warn Lucia not to get trapped in the cruelty of that cycle, that the pain of the loss itself was enough without adding the burden of guilt.

The only thing that Lucia knew for sure, because a neighbor who had witnessed the scene from her window told her, was that they had taken Piper out of the house blindfolded, his hands tied behind his back, and his head bathed in blood. And that he was screaming something, something he wanted heard, even as they struck him to silence him. The neighbor had *seen* him scream, but she couldn't tell Lucia what words, she apologized, explaining that her window had been shut, that fear seals the ears, and that at that moment some road workers were drilling on the asphalt. From then on, Lucia never stopped wondering what Piper's last words had been, which the noise from the street had swallowed. What message had he wanted to deliver, maybe some clue that would make the effort to find him possible.

"What do you think Piper was screaming, Lolé?" Mateo said. "I want to know as well."

"Generally those who were sequestered screamed their names at the last moment, so that at least there would be witnesses, somebody in the street to hear what was going on and could report the disappearance."

"So you mean Piper came out screaming, *I am Piper! I am Piper, they are kidnapping me!*"

"Probably more like, *I am Horacio Rasmilovich*, his real name."

After that Lucia learned nothing more about him, as if the

earth had swallowed him, and both she and her mother-in-law devoted all their days and hours to looking for him, to reporting his kidnapping to whatever international organizations they could reach, to asking about him in the military tribunals, the general staff of the army, and the Government House. They went together to the archbishopric and to the newsrooms of the dailies, not parting from each other day or night, so that Lucia eventually moved in with her mother-in-law. They consoled each other and conducted a one-topic relationship, talking about Piper at all hours, remembering him, crying for him, plotting strategies to find him, and so on year after year, not letting the passage of time weaken their resolve, on the contrary, each day growing more stubborn, more defiant, marching every Thursday with the Mothers of Plaza de Mayo.

"This exact plaza, Mateo. I wanted you to see it for yourself," Lorenza said, the two of them standing next to the obelisk that had been erected in the plaza's center. "Here is where dictatorship began to fall, because of the shove the Mothers gave it. Every Thursday, right here where we are standing, women wearing white handkerchiefs on their heads would gather and march around this obelisk, demanding the return of their sons alive.

"Can you imagine what courage it must have taken, Mateo? In those terrible times, they were the ones who dared. And they did it here, right in front of the Government House, across the square. They marched with the eyes of the murderers on them and in the face of the fear and indifference of most of the rest of the populace."

Among the Mothers were Lucia and her mother-in-law, carrying, come rain or shine, a picture of Piper on a placard, his friendly face and thick glasses, so fitting his occupation as a translator, but so incongruent with the bold red letters on the placard that announced how he had disappeared. There they headed, lining up one by one, getting up at dawn to march in front of the government offices, Lucia and her mother-in-law, enveloped in their grief, separated from the world, the only inhabitants of a lost planet called Piper.

Every time that Aurelia ended up with Lucia, because of shared party activities, she listened to her talk about her husband with a love and devotion that was gripping. It seemed as if their married life had been a joyful one. She described him as a shy and reserved man, but affectionate, with a sophisticated sense of humor and vibrant inner life. Lucia was very pretty, tall and willowy with an exceptional angular face. And Aurelia knew, because plenty of others confided in her, that more than one comrade would have liked to approach her, invite her to the movies, become friends with her, keep her company in her calamity. But no one had dared. Given her unconditional loyalty to the memory of Piper, any such attempt would have been a transgression. It was all but certain that Piper was dead by that point, there were even some clues that this was the case, like the testimony of another prisoner who had seen him horribly tortured in solitary confinement and who did not think he could have survived. Of course, that likelihood could not be mentioned to Lucia, who was absolutely convinced that Piper was still alive, and that if she persevered in her efforts to find him, sooner or later, she would be successful. Lorenza confessed to Mateo that despite the enormous respect she had for Lucia and the sympathy she felt for her situation, she had not failed to pick up on the hint of madness in her obsession, which, plainly, affected her mother-in-law as well. They kept his things intact, his favorite armchair, his history book, open to the page that he had been reading when they seized him, his clothes laundered and folded in the armoire. Aurelia knew all this because Lucia herself had told her. She told Aurelia that it had to be that way, because any day now Piper would return. Faithful to such convictions, neither of them ever left the city, not on weekends, not on holidays, not on vacations, because what if just at that time they handed him over, what if he reappeared, or if someone showed up who could offer them a clue, someone who might know something, who, careless, might let some hint escape, even the slightest.

"All very understandable," Lorenza commented. "The death of a loved one is a terrible thing, but in the end there is some closure, it's done for, no going backward or forward. But a disappearance is an open door to eternal hope, toward questions without answers, uncertainty, the hallucinatory, and there's no human head or heart that could suffer through it without, at least to some degree, facing madness."

"I know," said Mateo. "You invent things, start coming up with explanations that grow crazier and crazier. It happens to me with Ramón. Ramón is my ghost. If the dictators had disappeared him like Piper, I would have had someone to blame at least."

The whole thing was atrocious, starting with the very phrase "the disappeared"; instead of "kidnapped," or "tortured," or "murdered," they christened them "the disappeared," as if they had vanished on their own, no one's doing, or maybe their own doing because of their volatile nature.

The dictatorship disappeared people and then denied that there were disappeared ones, and so disappeared even the disappeared. Like some cruel magic trick.

"Now you see it, now you don't. Now it's here, now it's disappeared," Mateo said.

That was Piper's state when Aurelia stopped seeing Lucia. Since the compartmentalization of the party was so strict, once you lost contact with someone, that person was gone, like a ring in the sea. And that's what had happened with Lucia. Time passed. Lorenza left Argentina and went on with her life, the military junta fell, and a few years afterward, at a dinner in New York, someone introduced her to an Argentinean oncologist who had been a Montoneros sympathizer. Chatting with him, quizzing him about his experience during the dictatorship, she found out that Piper's mother had been one of his patients and an old family friend. Lorenza immediately wanted to know about Lucia. Was she still waiting for Piper?

"Yes, she's still looking for him," the oncologist told her. "With less conviction than before, but she still lives in her mother-in-law's house—the señora passed away. And as far as

I know, she's never had another romantic relationship. Deep down in her soul, she goes on waiting for him."

Then Lorenza said something about how happy their marriage had been, and the doctor gave her a surprised look. "You mean you don't know?" he asked.

"What?"

"Lucia and Piper were separated when he was kidnapped," he explained. "They had been separated for at least a year and a half. He was already with someone else and so was she. By the time he was kidnapped, their relationship was a thing of the past."

⁂

A WEEK AFTER their first meeting in Las Violetas, Aurelia met with Forcás again, picking up things just as they had left them. The same café, the same minute, but the situation was a little more tense the second time, perhaps charged with premeditated expectations on each of their parts. It was also nighttime and the nocturnal mise-en-scène made for an awkward setup. Let's just say that Aurelia was too dressed up, let's say she had chosen her outfit very purposefully, and that she had blow-dried her hair, and that he for his part was recently bathed and emitted an odor of cologne, one of those virile dark ones that go for the kill, Drakkar Noir or something just as withering, in all truth, to Aurelia's disappointment, who all week had yearned for the stable smell of his wool sweater. Now on the same note, Aurelia was no better off; in those days when she went out at night, she put on a double dose of Anaïs Anaïs, a frenziedly floral perfume. She must have strolled into Las Violetas like Botticelli's spring, trailing a wake of lilac and jasmine. So the reason for the tension was simply that unlike the first time, this time there was a motive. The whole thing had been reduced to its common denominator, a bold flirting where conversation could not flourish. If they had met in Bogotá or Madrid, they would have broken the ice talking about Trotskyite matters, like the antagonism in Angola among the MPLA, UNITA, and FNLA, or the denunciation of the Spanish Socialist Party by the Popular Front for the Liberation of Saguia el-Hamra, or the foreseeable split of the Sandinistas in Nicaragua. But in Buenos Aires, they could not talk of such things. In public places they had to avoid those topics—their topics, their passions—and the nervousness was leading them into a series of phony questions and cutting replies. But the seduction was already having an effect on Aurelia, the pretty hair and the broad shoulders, so much so that she didn't seem to mind the smoke from the Particulares 30. And just when his Drakkar Noir and her Anaïs Anaïs stopped repelling each other and began to mingle, a group of men in dark outfits and buzzed skulls burst through the door, five or six in all.

"It's like I'm reliving that entrance into Las Violetas, which was like elephants stomping into a fine glass shop," Lorenza told Mateo. "Another Argentinean saying: Elephant in a glass shop."

Everybody froze right where they were, even the waiters, as if it were the palace of Sleeping Beauty and the only thing awake was Aurelia's own heart, which began to beat like mad.

"Just keep to our story and nothing will happen," Forcás said, trying to soothe her nerves.

They could see in the mirror in the back that the men forced two señores who shared a table to get up from their seats. They shoved the taller one to a corner of the room and the other one to an opposite corner. A few minutes later, three of the *cana* approached Aurelia and Forcás, who had attracted them like iron shavings to magnets. They asked for their identification papers. Around them, everybody else camouflaged themselves in a stillness that they hoped made them invisible, guiltless. If I've seen you, I don't remember, and if I remember, I'll forget. No one dared to turn and look, but they did look, if not with their eyes. Two of the men took Forcás to the door leading out to Medrano and the other one took Aurelia by the arm and pushed her toward the back, to the staircase leading to the bathrooms. That's how they did it, they would interrogate one in one corner, who are you with, where did you meet him, what were you talking about; and the other person in the opposite corner, who introduced you, what were you talking about, when did you see each other last. Oh, there was a contradiction? Well, you're fucked, you sons of bitches, that means you are subversives and are conspiring, we're going to bust you open.

The *cana* knew that a lot went on in the cafés and that's

how they exerted control, techniques learned at the School of the Americas, or tricks learned from the gringo military in Panama.

"And they were right, kiddo," Lorenza told Mateo. "The cafés of Buenos Aires were the epicenter of the conspiracy; one day they will have to build a monument to them."

One of the *cana* wore a tiny medal on his lapel, a likeness of the Virgin of Luján. He cornered Aurelia against the wall, and since he was tall, his coat scrubbed against her cheeks, so she had a perfect view, the Virgin of Luján: she wore a mantle and crown emitting rays, a half moon under one foot. She was no different than most Virgins, but the one from Luján had the national coat of arms at her feet. Except for that medal he was a typical *cana*. Lorenza remembered his heavy breath on her face, the dark glasses concealing the eyes, and the coarse leather of his black coat.

"It was actually funny the way that they liked to disguise themselves," she told Mateo. "Bastards dressed as bastards."

The first thing he asked her was who she was with. And she told him about Mario, whom she had met a few weeks before in her own country, and she did it with confidence, because she knew that in the opposite corner of the confectionery, Forcás would also respond that he was with a girl he had met in Colombia. Then the *cana* asked her what Mario was doing in Colombia, and while she responded that he had a leather business, she knew that Forcás was saying that exact thing. It was like a symphonic game between them, between Aurelia and Forcás, tossing the ball from one corner of the confectionery to the other, softly, with precision, not tripping up, not missing each other, he in his corner, she in hers, each in the other's hands, each answering questions with the certainty that the other would back it up. Who introduced you? My brother-in-law. What is his name? Patrick. Patrick what? Would Forcás remember that it was Ferguson? Aurelia had chosen it, but it could have been any other name just as well. And yet now their lives depended on the fact that both he and she would say exactly that, Ferguson, and no other. They had agreed on it last week during their first meeting, but had not gone over it this time, all they said was, "Same story? Yes, of course, same one." So of course he would remember. Aurelia was sure he would remember and that over there in his corner, he would be calmly responding, the brother-in-law's last name is Ferguson. And what are you doing here? We are going to go hear some tangos, she said. I am taking her to go see the city, to hear some tangos, foreigners love that, he said. And what had he been doing in Colombia? I told you, he has a leather business with my brother-in-law. And way on the other corner, like an echo, Aurelia couldn't hear but she guessed: I traveled to Colombia to set up the export of some leather goods with her brother-in-law. The *cana* who was questioning Aurelia lifted his sunglasses and fixed them on the crown of his head. They were common eyes, nondescript, maybe coffee-colored, undoubtedly myopic, and while he scrutinized her, she tried to look over his shoulder to find Forcás. At first she couldn't see him, he was hidden behind the thick granite columns, but then she spotted him, he too was looking for her and he smiled as if nothing was happening. Everything is good, he said with his smile, and she smiled back, yes, yes, everything is good.

The incident with the *cana* had been nothing, a little confrontation, routine, but it had been the ceremony that sealed the alliance between Aurelia and Forcás. She had committed herself to a pact of complicity with that man who went by the name of Forcás, and from then on she knew that her fate would be entwined with his, whatever happened. The *cana* ordered her to stay where she was. He put her passport in his pocket and zipped up his coat, then went to look for his buddies, obviously to compare stories, and he returned less worked up, apparently because they had passed the test. With a tone somewhere between cloying and paternal, he warned her not to mingle with strangers, you are a foreigner, he said, there are a lot of bums who will try to woo you with their stories so you take off with them, and instead of listening to tangos, you end up in a mess with some undesirable. Just go home, you seem like a good girl, go home.

"So the one who questioned you had a leather coat?" Mateo asked.

"I seem to remember that he pulled up the zipper of his coat, yes. But who knows. The only thing I know is that he was wearing something with lapels, the little medal was hanging from a hook on the lapel."

"Did he keep your passport?"

"No, before he left he gave it back."

"Then why didn't you say that?"

"What?"

"That he gave it back. That soon afterward he came back in, walked up to your table, and handed you your passport."

"Sorry, kiddo, I forgot that detail."

"You are also forgetting to tell me what happened with those two other guys they interrogated."

"When the *cana* left, I began to sweat. I felt as if a wave of heat fell over me and soaked my shirt, as if I could no longer hold back whatever involuntary physical reaction. And then your father told me that they had taken the two men, and I saw that indeed their table was now empty."

"What happened to them?" Mateo asked, yawning.

"They took them in a patrol car. But go to sleep. I'll tell you about it tomorrow."

"Just tell me now."

"That's it. They took them. We never found out who they were."

"They didn't scream their names, like Piper? I am So-and-so, I am being kidnapped, help me!"

"No, they didn't scream anything. Maybe they figured that the Virgin of Luján would help them—"

"Stop joking around, Lorenza, tell me what you think happened."

"That's it, kiddo, go to sleep."

"Another day and I still haven't called Ramón."

"You'll call him tomorrow."

"Do you really think the Virgin of Luján saved those two?"

"No, Mateo, I don't really think so."

⁂

"It's now or never. I'm going to call him," Mateo announced as soon as he awoke, and Lorenza thought that this time he was really going through with it. "Where is it!" he screamed, suddenly giving his mother a horrified look.

"Where is what, for God's sake? Why do you get all worked up like this?"

"The notebook, Lorenza," Mateo declared in a lugubrious tone. "The notebook where I wrote down what I was going to say." He fell back on the sofa, defeated, and she started to look for it. In a few minutes, she discovered it, mixed up with some magazines.

"You found it?" he asked surprised, as if a miracle had just occurred. "Ramón Iribarren, I am your son, Mateo Iribarren. I have come to Buenos Aires to meet you," he read in a loud voice for the thousandth time since they had arrived. He knew the passage by heart, but kept repeating it nevertheless, like a mantra, like a spell. Lorenza had been watching him closely. Her son was readying himself for the encounter with his father as if it were a ceremony. Or a duel.

"Now or never," Mateo repeated and stared at the phone like a viper hypnotizing its prey before pouncing. But instead of picking up the receiver, he opted for the remote and turned on the television.

"I'll call in a little while. I swear," he assured his mother, as if he owed her anything. "Shit, the Rolling Stones! A concert right here in Buenos Aires. I can't believe it. Look, look, they're going to be at the River Plate Stadium. Let's go, Lorenza. Can we go? Are you even watching? This is historic, the chance of a lifetime. Damn, I love the Stones! I'd rather see the Stones a thousand times more than Ramón. Fuck Ramón, Lolé, let's go see the Stones. That would be enough for me. I swear that if I get to see them I'll return in peace to Bogotá and I'll stop bugging you about my father and Buenos Aires. It'll be a lot cooler to tell my friends how I saw the Stones than bore them with how I met some bald guy who's my father."

So they went to the stadium in the Belgrano District to see the Stones, who were touring with Bob Dylan. Aurelia had to settle for very expensive tickets from the hotel's concierge, the only ones left on the planet because the concert was sold out. When they arrived, Mateo bought himself a *Bridges to Babylon* T-shirt and on the way out couldn't stop talking, he was so excited.

"Spectacular, truly genius," he repeated as they tried to move through the crowd, which was leaving the stadium in droves. "Not to lessen the experience, but it's pretty strange to go to a Stones concert with your own mother, for how can you get all worked up and crazy with your own mother right there? Although, if you think about it, the Stones are probably more from your generation than from mine, Lolé. It's funny how you knew all the lyrics better than I did. And what a drag, they didn't play 'Paint It Black,' even though we yelled, they pretended not to hear, but Dylan did play 'Like a Rolling Stone,' he wrote that, that song, he wrote it, and then the Stones took the name, I think that's how it was, and then they had a falling-out with Dylan and that's why tonight's reunion is historic, Lorenza, once in a lifetime, the Stones and Dylan are friends again and I got to see it! Do you understand? Me, Mateo Iribarren! But you're a geek, Mother, how can you have liked the small stage better; what a loser, you showed your age there, you're definitely ancient, liking that little retro stage because it was more like the ones from your era, but the fucking real show was on the big stage, pulling out all the technological stops, blasted with light, and you ecstatic over that pathetic little stage. The best part was the blue hoop, exploding during the fireworks while they played 'Satisfaction,' and everything else turned blue. Didn't you love that blue hoop of light? Unbelievable . . . you know what I'm talking about, right, Lorenza? The blue splendor when they sang 'Satisfaction,' or didn't you notice? What could you possibly have been thinking about, Mother, it was impossible not to notice that blue light, I don't know why I brought you, waste of money there. Don't laugh, it's not funny, at my age it's a complete mistake to go to a concert with your mother. You don't notice these things, but right next to me there was a pretty girl, a very, very pretty Argentinean girl, and she kept looking at me and I was horrified, trying very hard for her not to notice that I was with my mother, or for her not to think you were my girlfriend, my older girlfriend, that would have been even worse. But why the hell should I care if she thought I was some loser who went to concerts with his mother? Everything got screwed up, so what, I was never going to see her again anyway. It was cold as a bitch, right, Lolé? But inside it wasn't so bad, and once I got jumping and screaming, I was sweating like a horse. Shit, I think I ruined my *Bridges to Babylon* shirt, it's drenched, it probably stinks. You think it'll be all right if I wash it in the hotel? Or maybe I can send it to the dry cleaners. Yeah, maybe I'll just send it to the dry cleaners to be safe. You know inside we were all warm and bunched together, but now I'm freezing to death. Are you? What did Forcás say? If this is how cold it gets for the living, how must it be for the dead? I already told you, Lorenza, I'm not zipping up my coat. If I zip it up, you can't see my new shirt, so what's the point? Thank you, thank you, thank you for inviting me tonight, it was the best, Lolé. The bad thing is how much money we spent. But it was worth it, right? Everything was worth it, a thousand times worth it, a million times, and thanks for my T-shirt, too, this has been the best part about coming to Buenos Aires, the Stones. Bob Dylan is so tiny, right? He looks like a gnome, right? But he's a giant. A little old, but still a giant. What, you don't like my T-shirt? So the fabric is a little sticky, so what? Only a mother could find fault with a *Bridges to Babylon* T-shirt because the fabric is a little sticky. Stiff? The fabric is stiff? Yeah, a little bit, but it doesn't matter. Does Ramón like the Rolling Stones, Lolé? I think he likes them. I think if he liked Argentinean rock, the Rolling Stones are up his alley, they're from his era. And to think we were in the stadium of the Río team, the archrivals of Boca Juniors, the team Ramón is crazy about. You told me that

Ramón was a Boca fan and that he went to *fútbol* games at La Bombonera. You didn't make that up, did you? What would Ramón say if he knew we went to the River Plate Stadium?"

⁂

"YOUR FATHER USED to say that when he had a son he was going to name him César, in memory of *el negro* César Robles, a friend and classmate whom he cared for very much, and who had been murdered by the Triple A during the time of Isabel Perón. So César, and Cesárea if it was a girl, I used to tell him, but I thought it was nonsense, this wanting children in a life so full of danger."

"Ma-te-o Cé-sar I-ri-ba-rren," Mateo said. "What a name I got, César for *el negro* César, and Mateo for what?"

"I picked it."

"I would have liked to have met César, tell him I have his name. Or at least have gone to his grave."

"I don't know where he's buried, but we can find out. We can also look for his children. He was a tough man, a union director in Córdoba, he led the strike in—"

"I just want to know if he was really black," Mateo interrupted.

"He was dark-skinned, dark-skinned people are affectionately called negro, like calling white people white, even though they're rosy, or Asians yellow, though they're really white."

"All these years I thought that Father gave me the name

of his best friend who was black and now he was just dark-skinned? Those kinds of things shake me up inside."

"Shake you up inside?" Lorenza laughed.

"They confuse me. I don't know anything about my father, and the little I do know is wrong. I'd like to visit the grave of *el negro* César, Lolé."

"Let's find out where it is. Although it's possible that it's nowhere."

"It has to be somewhere."

"No. It's possible that they never returned his body."

"And so the children of *el negro* César may still be looking for their father. Like I am with mine."

"The difference being that yours is somewhere out there, alive and kicking."

"Alive and kicking, and he's completely forgotten me."

❋

THE LORENZA WHO came out of the doctor's office was a completely different person than the one who had gone in just an hour before. He's going to call you, he had assured her. And those words, which translated into the possibility of getting her son back, were enough to regain her trust in the human condition, giving her a backbone with which to stand tall, a head to decide and to act, and a heart not only for anguish but now also for courage. Her mother, her sister, and her brother-in-law took turns waiting by the telephone, which nevertheless did not ring that afternoon, nor that night, nor the following day or the one after that. Meanwhile there were a thousand tasks to perform. Lorenza accomplished them, one by one, following a list she had written up with the help of her sister. She worked on it coldly, systematically, analyzing and calculating, giving herself the order not to falter, and keeping her hopes focused on the conviction that sooner or later the telephone would offer up an Ariadne ball of thread that would lead her out of the labyrinth and to Mateo. Once she knew his whereabouts, she'd have to go get him alone. If Haddad was right, this was one of those battles you had to fight on your own. If Ramón's weakness was his love for her, that would be the flank she would attack.

"The first thing I needed was money," she told Mateo, "a lot of money, for the tickets, hotels, travel documents, contacts. And for other things, but basically those. Mamaíta was an angel. Strong and supportive, as she was anytime there was a crisis in the family. I told her how much money I was going to need and she found it right away and handed it to me. Then I had to take care of a bunch of legal matters that would help me if there was to be a custody fight. It was likely to happen, and being a foreigner, the law was not going to be on my side. I also had to get passports. My legal one and a fake one for you, in case Ramón decided to keep yours, plus two other sets of pictures of you, of me, names and nationalities changed and with all the necessary seals. Your father was an expert at falsifying papers and I wasn't. But in Colombia it is as easy as pie to buy a passport. So all that on one end. Ah, and the suitcase. I found one with a double compartment. You should have seen this suitcase, Mateo, this was no toy, but a thing for professionals. So there, ready and sitting by the bed, I kept a suitcase with my clothes and extra clothes for you, because I knew you'd need them. And to top off our grand scheme, Guadalupe and I racked our brains for alternative escape routes out of Argentina, not only by air but also by land. Across the border into Chile or Uruguay, and finally across the border into Brazil. That, plus the contacts at different points, friends who were willing to help. It was a well-planned operation. I had learned something from my clandestine meanderings in the resistance."

All this would only work if Mateo was indeed in Argentina, which was only a guess. But the signs pointing to it were plenty. First of all, it was obvious that Ramón would want to return to his own country, where he would be the local and she the foreigner. Second, Ramón had asked her to pack cold-weather clothes for the boy, and though many parts of the world were getting ready for summer, in Argentina it was the start of winter. Third, Haddad thought that if Ramón's goal was to win her back, he was going to do it on his own territory. In Colombia, things had gone so badly for them that the relationship had shattered. But in Argentina, they had been in love. It was likely that he would want to lead her to the place where they had been happy.

"Smart guy, that Haddad," Mateo said.

"Yes, but another assumption came into play there, that Ramón's letter was a love letter."

"And if it was a love letter, why set up such a Mission Impossible to save me?"

"That's the thing, kiddo, his letter might have been about love, but his actions were acts of war."

"Great way to put it, Lolé, I'm really liking this movie."

"Wait, now is when it gets ugly."

⁂

Soon after the incident with the police in Las Violetas, Aurelia began to meet Forcás at El Molino Azul, a telo in Buenos Aires—tel-ho: ho-tel backward, a hotel by the hour for couples. What a whimsical contraption memory is! She remembered the exterior details of the building, a cement bunker, a kind of eternal monument to momentary love. But inside? Completely a blank. She strained to remember a single object, however insignificant, which would bring back the atmosphere of those afternoons. A blanket, say, a stiff blanket cold to the touch, the color of a dark sea. Or like red wine? Why not. It could well have been a satiny old thing the color of wine, or fading raspberry. A depressing thing under any other circumstance. And the plastic curtain in the shower. It should be yellow or a yellowed white. Or was it green? Pistachio green with printed bubbles, that's what it was. How tenaciously that green curtain had lurked in the dark corners of her memory. But Lorenza was able to snatch it out and she kept casting her line to see what else she could catch in that miraculous fishing expedition, until the pair of teacups appeared, delivered by room service through a gyrating window, pale lukewarm water barely darkened by the musty tea bags and sugar cubes. But not that much else.

Her curiosity about that Molino Azul of her memory had made her, years before, place a call from Bogotá to Felicitas Otamendi, one of her best Argentinean friends, at her law offices in Buenos Aires, to ask for a strange favor. When she had a second, would she drop by that telo named El Molino Azul to tell her what it looked like? Could it still exist? No, Lorenza did not remember what street it was on, she just said that it was an ugly, gray cement building, five or six stories high.

Felicitas agreed to go right away and sent Lorenza her first fax: "This is too juicy, my dear! I have found not only that El Molino Azul still exists but that they offer different types of rooms. Do you want the cheapest one? Or deluxe? A Scottish shower or a Roman bath? It's on Salguero Street and yesterday I passed by to check it out from the outside. It's definitely still there, but the façade isn't gray like you remember, but a milky mulberry color. I'm going back on Thursday, this time to go in the rooms, with a friend who has agreed to come just to play along. Ciao, Felicitas."

So the façade was not gray. Maybe they'd painted it. Or was it those rainy afternoons that were gray? Definitely the first time they had met up in the telo it had been raining buckets, Lorenza could at least swear to that. Buenos Aires had disappeared under the downpour.

Less than a week later, Felicitas was sending a detailed report: "The front door is discreet," it said. "There are no signs or anything else that would identify the place as a transitory lodging. But on one of the outside walls, there's the painting of a great windmill, obviously blue. You first go into a small room with the cash register on the left, behind a mirrored glass which hides the cashier." Right, right, now that Felicitas mentioned it, it was as if Lorenza were watching the anonymous hand that would slip them the key through a slot in the smoked glass. The key to happiness? For a while anyway, because after a couple of hours the noise of a bell would startle them: either they left the room or they would have to pay double. Felicitas described a plaster fountain with a tiny angel, somewhat metaphorical, holding an amphora that poured out a stream of froth over a seashell. Felicitas and her friend had paid the cashier the equivalent of ten dollars, which had secured them one of the deluxe rooms for an hour. "It smelled like cheap and cloying air freshener, a mixture of marmalade and disinfectant, a smell characteristic of all the telos in the world, as I know from experience," she had written.

Yes, that must have been the smell. But the angel, the froth, the seashell? They must not have been there back then, or she didn't remember. "The room is about five meters by five meters wide and is decorated in shoddy art deco." Once they were inside, Felicitas and her friend had amused themselves taking pictures that they eventually sent to Lorenza. They posed in front of the painted cardboard faux-stone, both very tall and very marvelous in their coats, boots, and scarves, on the bed, in the bathroom and facing the mirrors, specifically a huge, hexagonal mirror, with uneven sides, that by all accounts was the pièce de résistance of the set. Those afternoons in El Molino Azul, in the Buenos Aires of the dictatorship. The memory of a long line of couples slowly returned to Lorenza, very young men and women, just as they themselves must have been. They waited for their rooms embracing each other or holding hands, chatting in low voices, not betraying any shame, or need for secrecy, or modesty, as if they were waiting in line at the movies. During the week it wasn't very crowded, but Fridays and Saturdays there was a long wait. In general, they didn't see too many bosses with their secretaries, or prostitutes with their johns, or adulterous affairs; what they saw was mostly students, the type who still lived with his parents and saved up during the week to take his girl to a refuge as far removed from parental control as possible. There was no one there who would insult them, who would point an accusing finger or create a stir. That telo with its wine-dark satin blankets, its cups of cold tea, its disinfectant smells, had been for them a liberated land amid the demoralizing violence of those times. Because of the occupational hazards of the resistance, Aurelia and Forcás could not know where the other lived, and so for many afternoons, El Molino Azul took them in as if it were their home.

Two details of Felicitas's report made Lorenza uneasy: for one, "the bathtub is discreetly hidden behind a frame of frosted glass," and "the bedspread is a plush peach with assorted pillows." Plush peach bedspread and frosted glass? Could her most detailed memories be trusted, the satin sheets and the shower curtain? She had to admit it, the room in Felicitas's photo was not the same as the one from her nostalgia. It was disheartening to have one's memories modernized, she thought, but what could she do, she had to accept the fact that El Molino Azul had opted for an upgrade and undergone a furious renovation. And why not, for even the seediest hotels update their decor now and then. So let them do what they wanted, Lorenza would keep what she had: a pair of young lovers, a green plastic shower curtain, and wine-colored satin sheets.

⁂

GOYENECHE ARRIVED at the café on Florida Street, where Lorenza had agreed to meet him. They had seen each other every day during the time that they had been party comrades on the front lines, but during that hour that they shared in the café, Lorenza found out more about him than she had ever known from the years in the resistance.

He was wearing a dark shirt, a black leather coat, his hair was already graying and balding, but smoothed and gelled back like a tango singer's, just like it had been during the years of the dictatorship. He told Lorenza that his real name was Luis Antonio Méndez, the brother of the Arturo Méndez who had been disappeared in '74, that he wasn't Argentinean but Uruguayan, and that after the fall of the dictatorship he had finished medical school and specialized in gynecology. Who would have thought it? Goye, a gynecologist!

"Even though Goye is not your name anymore," she told him, "you still look like a tango singer."

"A very old one who never knew how to sing." He smiled.

In the old times, Goye played the flute and now, in the café, they laughed remembering the mess he had caused for doing just that, the day he hadn't shown up to a meeting, and had spread panic everywhere because he had been so absorbed with this sweet flute that he forgot the time.

"Damn it, Goye," Lorenza said. "You scared the hell out of us. You dispersed us to such an extent that it took us a month to round up everybody. Do you still play the flute?"

"After what happened, are you crazy? The flute for me was like it was for the czar's musicians," he said. And he told her how if they played well, the czar ordered that the instruments be stuffed with gold, and the flautists ended up fucked, and that if they played badly, the czar ordered them to stuff their instruments up their asses, and the flautists ended up fucked.

Lorenza had sought out Goye for a specific reason; apparently he knew about Ramón's time in prison. And not through the political grapevine but through a chance circumstance: his wife was the first cousin of Forcás's girlfriend at the time he was detained.

Mateo had not wanted to go with her to the meeting at the café. He had decided instead to go shopping in the stores on Florida. A present for a friend, a girl, he told his mother. But he refused to tell her who the girl was.

Goyeneche, or Luis Antonio Méndez, told Aurelia, now Lorenza, that his wife's cousin, a girl named Marisa, who worked as a professional makeup artist, had suffered tremendously when Ramón had been arrested. At first, they had accused her of being complicit, since they had a stable relationship, but later they found her innocent. Goye had already left when Mateo returned from his shopping trip and showed his mother the cherry-colored leather change purse that he had bought for his nameless friend.

"Do you like it?" he asked. "I also bought another one, a green one."

"For another girlfriend?"

"No, for you. Or would you rather have the red one?"

Lorenza took the green change purse and planted a loud kiss on it, which she would rather have planted on Mateo, but he would have resisted. Then she told him what she had learned from Goyeneche.

The prison incident had nothing to do with politics but with some shady scheme, for which Ramón was the brains, along with his only brother, Uncle Miche, who had come up with the idea and was the main player. It involved a good deal of cash transferred monthly from a bank in the provinces to Buenos Aires by a moving company. The money would arrive at its destination in the middle of the night and would be placed in a high-security deposit safe until it was picked up the following morning. But it wasn't the only delivery that arrived, since the moving company had other clients aside from the bank. So Ramón sent, from some town in the interior, a huge wooden box addressed to himself that was scheduled to arrive on the same day as the bank's money.

"So wait . . . my father sent himself a big wooden box," Mateo said. "This is getting interesting."

"Yes, he was both the sender and the recipient."

"I bet it wasn't an empty box."

"Right. But see if you can guess what was in it. Believe it or not, your uncle Miche."

"Uncle Miche? Inside the box?" Mateo laughed. "You're telling me that my uncle Miche was the merchandise? And what shit was he up to inside that wooden box?"

"Your uncle Miche was to arrive sealed in the box to the deposit safe. He'd come out of his hiding pace in the middle of the night, switch the bags of money for fake ones, keep the real ones with him inside the wooden box, which he would reseal and wait . . . for your father to claim him the following day."

"Brilliant! But where did it go wrong?"

"Goye says that according to his wife's cousin they had done a practice run of the whole thing, in a different shipment, not the one with the money, and everything had gone without a hitch. Uncle Miche had spent the night in the deposit safe without being noticed and on the following day Ramón had successfully claimed him. So far, so good."

"What a bitch of a life!"

"I know, it's unbelievable. They repeated the operation, this time for real, on the day the money was sent. But because Uncle Miche is no taller than five feet three inches or so, the box he was in was very heavy, and this time the movers dropped it. Your uncle Miche suffered a tremendous blow to the head and lost consciousness. It seems that he was out when he arrived at the deposit company, and that he only started to come to the following morning, and he groaned."

"Of course, they heard him. The weird case of the groaning wooden box."

"They heard him and figured out what was going on, but they didn't say anything at first. They waited for the recipient to come and claim him and they snatched your father as well."

"It's like an episode of the Three Stooges."

"The two stooges."

"Typical Ramónism!"

"The moral of the story: don't hit your head while you're heading a heist," she said, and the two broke into fits of uncontrollable laughter.

Ramón and Uncle Miche spent a few months behind bars. Nothing serious, since Miche had never gotten his hands on the money, they couldn't prove much. Don't hit your head while you're heading a heist, Mateo repeated on the way back to the hotel, amused. But when they arrived he suddenly grew morose.

"Don't laugh anymore, Lorenza. It's not funny. I would have preferred if Ramón had been a real criminal," he said. "And that the sentence had been many years. At least that way I could have believed that he never looked for me because he couldn't, because he was in prison and they wouldn't let him. A great thug, or a famous underground political leader, someone sentenced to high-security solitary confinement for many years, thinking about me every day, like I think about him. Someone who was sure that as soon as he was let go, the first thing he would do is look for that son he had lost. I swear, Lolé. I had held out such hopes until today. I think I'd rather he was dead. So that I could forgive him. Do you understand? But no, now it seems that he is alive, jailed for some buffoonery."

⁂

WHY HADN'T RAMÓN ever looked for Mateo? The question kept Lorenza awake that night. In her insomnia, near dawn, she wanted to put these thoughts to rest and started reading the novel by Bernhard Schlink that she had bought a few days earlier on Avenida Corrientes. And by chance she came upon a passage that perhaps held the only answer to that impossible question. Why hadn't Ramon looked for Mateo all those years? "There are some things you do just because," Schlink wrote, "because the conscience dozes, becomes anesthetized, not because we make this or that decision, but because what we decide is precisely not to decide, as if our will is overwhelmed by the impossibility of finding a way out and decides to stop pedaling and idles while it can." Perhaps the reason Ramón did not look for Mateo was simply because he did not look for him. Perhaps there was no other answer but that, leaving a void where the boy so much wanted answers.

Lorenza read Schlink's passage several times, thinking that she would have to read it to Mateo. Or maybe not, it would be too difficult for him. She had always tried to protect her son from the pain of the past, as if she could suppress it by simply not naming it. Silencing words had been her main tool, and perhaps it was for that, more than the acts themselves, that Mateo could not forgive her. He couldn't forgive her for minimizing the past, making it seem unimportant, trying to neutralize it, avoiding the topic, not reacting to it. It was possible that Mateo felt that when she came between him and the raging bull of his abandonment, she prevented him from seeing it fully, and left him defenseless against its charge. It was possible that Mateo believed that by denying the loneliness of abandonment, instead of exorcising it, she helped to multiply it, leaving him even more alone. Or was it her own fault, her role in everything which she tried to camouflage with euphemisms?

At breakfast the following morning, all these questions had been reduced to the phantoms of her sleeplessness, truths intuited but not fully integrated. The insomniac night once again constrained her to futile gestures and truncated language, because how could she name such things without deepening the wound, where could she find rhyme or reason? There are never good enough reasons for a father's abandonment, and that made it unnamable. *Idling,* the Schlink passage said, how well it applied to Lorenza.

⁂

LORENZA AND MATEO had a couple of bad days following that, dejected and keeping their distance from each other in reverse, the boy holed up in his dark mood and not coming out of his room, and Lorenza sleepless at night and struggling to work while dozing off during the day. On returning to the hotel, all she had to do was see the PLEASE DON'T DISTURB sign hanging on the door to guess that inside the beds would be unmade, towels would be strewn on the floor, the drapes drawn, and in the middle of the shipwreck her son, in his pajamas still, hair uncombed, subsisting on chocolates, potato chips, and Coca-Colas from the minibar, and in a catatonic state in front of his PlayStation, which would be spitting smoke from hour after hour of continual use. She had always been afraid of the PlayStation. It sounded ridiculous, the idea of fearing such an object, a toy. But that's how it was. The way that Mateo allowed himself to be devoured by the thing made her anxious. It put her on edge—the repetitive little electronic music that invaded him and transported him to a distant world, hyperkinetic and overpopulated with kicking and punching cartoons, who fired machine guns, jumped over barrels, climbed towers, fell over dead, came back to life, crossed through labyrinths, drowned in a moat, and tossed grenades, always at an unsustainable ultrahuman rhythm that was in stark contrast with the statuesque stillness that was Mateo, because aside from his dancing pupils and his thumbs, which punched at buttons in sync with the frenzy on the screen, everything else about him was stillness, absence, hypnosis. And of course, the frightening thing wasn't the game but what Mateo did not say, what he avoided, what he denied when he sat down in a lotus position, like a boy Buddha, in front of that strange illuminated altar. After Mateo learned about the circumstances surrounding his father's prison sentence, he decided to close his ears and mouth and wanted to know nothing more about him, about Buenos Aires, but also nothing more about his mother.

He announced that he would return to Bogotá as soon as they could get a plane reservation, and she could find no arguments to dissuade him. There was no way she could get him to allow them more time to find a less disheartening finale to the trip that they had undertaken with such great hopes.

"Do you want to talk, Mateo?" Lorenza asked him, but her son was so absorbed in the game that he did not even respond.

"Son, don't you think we should talk?" she insisted.

"No, Lolé, anything you say will make me feel like shit. I don't like the way you talk to me."

"I'm doing what I can, kiddo, telling you about things as they happened—"

"That's the problem, you are Wonder Woman and the whole story is like a screenplay for an action film. Your Ramón is a comic-book hero. He does this thing here. Zap! Wap! Does that thing there. Boom! Shoom! He falls, he gets up. Krak! Crock! He's arrested, released, fights against the villains, against the good guys. It doesn't make sense, Lorenza, do you understand? That fiction has nothing to do with the Ramón who is my father. My father is a weirdo, a shitty crook, a frustrated one at that, who doesn't have the balls to show his face, to come offer me some explanations. What does your wide-shouldered warrior have to do with that bastard who erases himself, who disappears? Riiiiiiiing . . . Riiiiiing . . . Hello? Who is it? No one, nobody, no response, I don't know, wrong number, who gives a shit."

"Couldn't you wait for me a few days, Mateo, until I finish my duties here in Buenos Aires, and then we can return together to Bogotá?" she asked. "Or if you want, you can go tomorrow morning to Bariloche, and do some skiing until I come pick you up."

But Mateo refused outright. The only thing he wanted was to be left alone and in peace, submerged in his PlayStation, lost to the world.

❋

ON THE THIRD day of Mateo's isolation, Lorenza decided to cancel all her appointments and stay in the hotel with him, playing with him on the PlayStation, to see if she could reestablish some sort of contact in this manner. If Muhammad can't go to the mountain, the mountain is going to have to sit down at the PlayStation.

"Can I play with you?" she asked.

"No, you don't know how."

"You can teach me."

"You're too old, you don't have the reflexes."

"So try me."

"All right, but let's play Dynasty Warriors."

"Whatever you want."

"Lock the door and hang up the sign, so no one interrupts."

"Who's going to interrupt?"

"Just hang the sign, will you? Dynasty Warriors is my favorite of all the PlayStation games. You play in steps, and the more you advance, the more skilled Wei-Wulong becomes and the more powers he acquires," he explained, suddenly very talkative. Speaking of Wei-Wulong filled him with pride, as if he himself were the one who possessed those powers. Lorenza hung the sign on the doorknob and they entered, Wu, Shu, and Wei, the three kingdoms of Dynasty Warriors, where everything was brutal and luminous. Here there was no resting, but also no fatigue; the battles were ferocious but devoid of blood and bodies, because when an enemy was eliminated, all it did was flash and disappear right away. Mateo barely blinked, everything about him was concentration, tension, and alert reflexes, his vision good only for the vertiginous slashes of the swords. Lorenza noticed how amid those brilliant, sparkling colors, the room vanished and the other world slowly shut off, a slow and boring thing. At this moment, Mateo does not exist, she thought. Wei-Wulong has taken possession of my son.

"Didn't you say you were going to show me?" she asked, and her voice startled Mateo, who had completely forgotten she was there.

He replied that he would, and began to explain the game to her, not handing over the controls yet, telling her when she should bring out the catapults, when she should use the drawbridges, how to score points. Finally, she got him to turn over the controls, but because she played horribly he quickly grew impatient, upset with her and with her incompetence, and made her turns shorter and shorter as he made his longer. His explanations, at first very enthusiastic, became more sporadic and succinct, until he again immersed himself fully in what seemed like a religious silence.

Lorenza soon opened the door and left the room, and Mateo did not even notice.

⁂

"EXACTLY FIFTEEN DAYS afterward Ramón left with you," Lorenza begins to tell him.

"He didn't leave with me, Mother. He kidnapped me."

"Fifteen days after that—"

"It's not called 'that,' it's called disappearing a kid. You, who tell the story of the disappeared in Argentina so often, are afraid of the word when it deals with your own son."

"It's not the same, Mateo, you know that."

"It's not the same, but it's very similar."

"Similar, perhaps, but not really. Let me go on. Fifteen days later I found out that just as I had expected, he had fled with you to Argentina. It was confirmed by a very unexpected source."

"Slow down, Lorenza. Slow down, you've never told me this part."

"So be patient and you'll hear it."

That whole week passed without a call from Ramón. They called her, however, from *La Crónica*. The director of the magazine, who had given her as much time off as she needed, and who did anything he could to help her, told her that a very serious-looking man had shown up in the newsroom asking for her and saying he had news about her husband. A funny word, husband, which Lorenza never used to refer to Ramón, and that those who knew them well would not have used either.

She was there in less than an hour to meet a man who gave her a business card that said he was Joaquín Alberio Pinilla, Attorney. But clearly not just any attorney, his smile shone revealing gold fillings and extremely white porcelain implants, his extremely black curls were just beginning to go gray, and in front of the building he had parked an exceedingly silver Toyota, of the kind that narco traffickers owned. When she had investigated and written about organized crime, Lorenza interviewed some of these lawyers, who acted as spokespersons and representatives for the Mafia.

"If I am not mistaken, you signed this," the man said, pulling out of his pocket a check for one hundred and fifty thousand pesos, a very large sum for her then, considering that her salary was twenty-eight thousand a month. The check was signed in her handwriting and had come from her checkbook. It was dated the day before. "Your husband, the Argentinean señor, gave it to my boss a month ago, post-dated, shall we say. Yesterday the date came up and my boss sent me to cash it, and I'm sorry, it was returned for lack of funds. I understand that your husband is no longer in Colombia, so with all due respect, you are going to have to answer for this." The man fanned himself with the check while he proffered smiles and variant courtesies.

He told her that he respected her and simultaneously disrespected her by addressing her using the familiar Lorencita, a little verbal manhandling that she decided to allow faced as she was with that compromising check and no funds.

"My boss reads *La Crónica* and admires you very much. He recognizes that you are a top-class journalist, and precisely because of that does not want to proceed with a court case, shall we say. The amount of the check is not the problem, but we're talking about principles here. My boss doesn't like to be . . . toyed with. Do you understand?"

"I do understand, Mr. Pinilla, but tell me, what was my husband's check for?" asked Lorenza, already guessing.

"The equivalent in dollars, ma'am."

"There you are, Lorenza, you've told me about his wide shoulders a thousand times," Mateo jumped in. "But you never told me that he swindled a drug cartel leader."

"I'm telling you now."

"But why not till now?"

"Do you want me to go on or not?"

That lawyer, without knowing it, had just offered her another piece of the jigsaw puzzle that she was putting together. And now Lorenza knew what money Ramón was using to survive. The check must have been one of the many blank ones that she'd signed for him while they lived together, to pay the rent or other services. Lorenza made a mental calculation. If after getting Mateo back she kept on living with her mother and turned over her entire salary to this guy, she could pay the debt in four or five months. And it would be much better to give up her salary for a short while than to postpone such a debt.

"Look, Mr. Pinilla, please tell your boss that I am going on a trip very soon, but that as soon as I return I will pay him the money, as long as I can do it in a few installments."

"But he's not going to like that, miss. My boss is not going to like that you too will be taking off for Argentina—"

"Argentina?" Lorenza's heart jumped. "Did you say Argentina?"

"Well, that's where your husband went, Señora Lorenza, and you must understand that my boss—"

"I do understand, Mr. Pinilla, but you must trust that I will pay the full amount. But tell me why you said Argentina?"

"Argentina, that's where your husband went, as you well know."

"I guarantee you that you know a lot more than I do. Tell your boss that my husband stole money from him, but he stole my son from me. Tell him to trust me, because we are actually on the same side."

Pinilla accepted this and sent his regards to Lorencita's mother, asking if she still lived on Ninety-fourth below Ninth.

"You mean Pinilla knew Mamaíta?" Mateo asked.

"No, kiddo, of course not. He was threatening me, just in case I decided not to pay back the debt."

But before the lawyer had left, cordially saying his farewells, Lorenza pulled him to the side.

"Just one more thing, Mr. Pinilla. How do you know that my husband went to Argentina?"

"You're a journalist and you have your sources, right? We have ours." Pinilla smiled from ear to ear. "We are also similar in that way, how about that!"

"So once again, my father the crook, with his little swindles," Mateo said. "He grabs the boy, grabs the money, and leaves you in the lurch, owing those animals."

"That wasn't his plan. Before Pinilla said goodbye, I knew for sure that Ramón would call sometime soon."

"It doesn't make sense."

"It says a lot about who your father is. He had fled from the mafioso, and must have had everything in place so that I too could flee."

"Okay, that makes sense, then you must have run home to take his call."

"Not yet. If the game was so dirty, then I had one round left to play. And now the minutes were ticking down."

When it had been suggested to Lorenza that she report Ramón to the Argentinean military, she made a decision—not that. Now she had just made another decision: except for that, anything.

At the magazine was a worker named Botero, known as Botas, a judicial investigator with whom she got along well. It always paid off to team up with Botas, who knew how to infiltrate even the worst dens of iniquity, in order to find out some detail. There were no hot spots, hidden spots, or whorehouses that escaped Botas. Lorenza thought, this is my man, and went to his desk. Botas made a few phone calls and fifteen minutes later the two were in a taxi, headed toward a lower-middle-class neighborhood west of the city. They rang the bell at a yellow house with a front yard, a metallic fence, and three enraged dogs, those who kill and then eat their kill. A little old woman who came to the door in sandals screamed at the dogs to shut the fuck up and chained them so that they couldn't bite anyone, but still remained ready to attack, in the little living room where they sat to wait. The old woman brought them some coffee in miniature cups and after a brief wait made them follow her toward one of the rooms on the second floor, where they were greeted by a man in a white robe.

"A doctor?" Mateo asked.

"I never knew if he was a doctor, or a chemist, or a secret abortionist. I never knew, never asked. In any case, he wore a white lab coat and was very pleasant. When Botas told him why I needed what I needed, he refused to take money from me."

"You bought a gun. Is there a gunfight with my father that no one has ever told me about? Confess it now, you killed Ramón."

"Hush, *loquito*. You'll never guess what he gave me."

"A . . . murderous knife."

"No."

"A bulletproof vest."

"No."

"An ax, a stick of Acme dynamite, like Wile E. Coyote uses against Road Runner? I don't know, Lorenza, I give up. What did he give you?"

A coffee-colored eyeliner kit, made by Revlon. You pulled off a clear cap that protected the end, like any eyeliner, but you could also unscrew it and pull off the end, to reveal a needle, much shorter than a syringe's needle but just as thin. In the body of the pencil there was a small tube with a thick liquid.

"A few drops will knock him out, a lot of drops will kill him," the man in the white robe had told her.

"Oh, shiiiiiiiit, Lolé," Mateo said. "And you hid that *vaina* in the false bottom of the professional suitcase?"

"That wasn't necessary, I put it in with my other makeup."

⁂

EVENTUALLY, MATEO shut off the PlayStation and sat down to write a letter to Ramón.

"You can give it to him after I leave for Bogotá," he told his mother when he was finished. "If you see him, that is, or see someone who can give it to him." On the desk he left a folded piece of paper inside a hotel envelope, and announced that he was going to take a long bath.

"Can I use all the hot water?" he asked before locking himself in.

"The only thing that is infinite in this world is the hot water in hotels," she replied.

"If you want, you can read it," her son's voice said from the other side of the door, drowned out by the running water. She opened the envelope.

Ramón: This trip to Buenos Aires has confirmed what I already knew. That you have never been anything to me, and that you are not now, the letter said. You have grown in me like a ghost, like a fear of darkness and hatred of vegetables. I recognize your absence in the insecurity of my adolescence and in this arrogant shyness that isolates me from others. But fortunately it is not only that. You have also grown in me like a passion for mountains, and rivers and snow and mist. Every time that I climb a mountain, I seem to remember that I once had a father. I'll stay with the memory and stop searching for you. I no longer expect anything from you.

That's what Mateo had written, but he was still expecting. In the back of the envelope, making an effort to write clearly, he had jotted down his phone number and address in Bogotá, specifying the name of the neighborhood, the apartment number, and the postal code. And if that weren't enough, below he had drawn a little rudimentary map, indicating with arrows how to get there.

Lorenza had another busy workday ahead of her, and was very worried about leaving her son alone, given over to Wei-Wulong and the Dynasty Warriors. Fortunately, the phone rang just then, she picked it up to hear the sweet voice of a girl, asking for Mateo.

"Mateo, it's Andrea Robles, the daughter of *el negro* Robles. She says that they told her you were looking for her and wants to know if you want to go out for a bit," she screamed past the bathroom door, covering the speaker so that she wouldn't hear the categorical no her son would come back with. But to her surprise, Mateo agreed to see her.

⁂

"SHE'S VERY PRETTY, Andrea Robles," Mateo told his mother that night. "An elongated face, thin body, curly hair, and eyes like this. She took me to the Botanical Gardens, which was full of cats, but there we talked. Who knows what all those cats in the gardens eat, Lolé. You think people bring them food? Or maybe the government feeds them. Or they eat plants, botanical stuff, like cows do. It's not just a few, there's an army of cats. I've never seen so many in my life. That is not a botanical garden, it's a feline garden.

"She's older than me, Andrea Robles. Like four years, or ten. At least six, yes six, or seven, that's what I figured, although she sometimes seems like she could be my age, depending on how you look at her, and she talks about revolution, about commitments, about the injustices of this world. Andrea believes in those things, Lolé; she says she inherited it from her father. She told me that for many years she thought he had died in a car accident, that's what they'd told her, her mother I guess, since it sounds like the loving lie of a mother. A lie from a mother afraid that in school her daughter would repeat the true story and get the whole family in trouble.

"In their house, there had always been mystery surrounding the work of her father," Mateo went on. "I mean, even when *el negro* Robles was still alive, they had this problem. Can you imagine? When they asked Andrea what her father did, she didn't know how to reply, so she started making up jobs for him, inspired by things she saw around the house. She always saw papers, piles of papers, typewriters, mimeograph machines, and that's why she started to tell everyone that her father was an office worker. Or if not that, a pilot, because they always traveled for free. Of course, in truth it wasn't free, the tickets were bought by the party, but she didn't know that. What she knew was that airlines gave pilots and their families free tickets, so she decided that her father was a pilot. She also said that he was in the military, or so she told me, that she told people her father was in the military, or was a militant. Funny, right, Lolé? The two things sounded the same to Andrea Robles, the military and militant. She had heard both words in her house and she thought they were the same thing.

"Andrea Robles told me that one morning around seven they were having breakfast as always, and some friends of her mother arrived, who were not really friends but party comrades, but Andrea did not know that until much later. Her mother attended to them in the kitchen. Andrea did not know what they were doing there so early, and they wouldn't leave to let them have their breakfast, and when they finally did leave, her mother sat her and her brother at the table, but instead of giving them breakfast, she told them that their father had died in an accident.

"It had already been some time since Andrea Robles's father had separated from her mother and gone to live in another city, so that Andrea did not see him that much anyway, not every day, not even every month, only once in a while. So that when he was killed, Andrea didn't feel the change much, and pretty soon forgot about the fact that he was dead and returned to the idea that he lived far away and that he would soon come to visit. When he had been alive, *el negro* Robles visited them and took them on trips to the mountains in his Citroën, where they would make snowmen. I asked Andrea if that mountain was in Bariloche, and I told her that Forcás had taken me to see the snow in Bariloche, but what I didn't tell her was that he only took me once and then disappeared. She told me that it wasn't in Bariloche, but some mountain. What mountain? I don't know, Lorenza, I don't know what mountain, we didn't get into details. Andrea told me that it was the only time in her life that she'd seen snow, never again after that, even after she became an adult. Now that I think about it, *el negro* César took his kids to see the snow only once, like Ramón did with me. It's an important part of the story. And they were lucky because it snowed. Well, maybe he took his kids to the mountains several times, but it only snowed that one time.

"What I want to tell you about is that Andrea thought that her father's accident had been in the Citroën, and that a few days afterward had been very surprised when she saw the Citroën in perfect condition, not even a scratch on it. How was it possible that her father had died in the Citroën, and not a thing had happened to the car? But she didn't ask. Not at all. She said she didn't ask anything, didn't think anything, didn't come to any conclusions. Only later would she find out that he had been gunned down, and that the Citroën had nothing to do with it.

"Now Andrea knows exactly how everything happened and has filed a legal case against the murderers and she has to testify and give statements. But as a girl she knew nothing. She says that the death of her father seemed unreal because she was only eight when they killed him. She didn't understand what it meant to die, no one near her had ever died, and on top of that, during the funeral the coffin was closed and she never even suspected that he was in there.

"Andrea told me that she had loved him very much, and that her father had loved her in the same way. I asked her how she knew this, that is, how she was so sure that *el negro* Robles had loved her, and she said that he always brought her little presents, postcards and maps of the world. And some castanets. Andrea still had those castanets that *el negro* Robles had brought her once, surely from Spain. But she also knew that he loved her because when she was born, her father ran out and bought all the books by Piaget to understand what children were like and how to best educate them. Tell me, Lolé, did Ramón read all the books by Piaget after I was born, because if he did, they didn't do him much good.

"One day, Andrea had invited her father to a cafeteria to have a coffee. She told me that she was very small and that she had never in her life had a coffee because it probably tasted terrible, but because she saw *el negro* talking in cafés with his friends and they all drank coffee, she had wanted to do the same, and she tore into a long monologue on why he had to return to live with her mother.

"In any case, after they killed her father, Andrea Robles began to miss him like never before, that's what she told me. So she started to pretend that he wasn't dead but was traveling in Europe and that he would bring her back postcards and castanets. She also liked to imagine that he had lost his memory, a blow to the head or something like that, and since he didn't remember anything, he couldn't look for her or call her. It was funny when Andrea told me that, Lolé, because once I also relied on that story that Ramón had lost his memory. I asked Andrea Robles if she ever imagined that her father had been imprisoned, and now it was her turn to laugh, probably because she had thought up that excuse as well.

"Andrea Robles continued to make up stories for herself until one day she picked up the newspaper and saw a picture of her father riddled with bullets. It was on the anniversary of his death, or something like that. Andrea said that it had been a horrible blow, although she was already eighteen, a horrible blow to see the picture of your own father's body riddled with bullets. Imagine that, Lolé, it must have been quite the surprise. Of course it helped her, what I mean is that, in the end, finding that picture was a good thing for Andrea Robles, because it forced her to finally accept the fact that *el negro* Robles had died. And she also realized that he had been a brave man and that he had died fighting against injustices and for the poor, and she became such a fan of her father that now she wants to emulate him in everything. But what about that photo? He was bullet-ridden, Lolé, how fucking crazy, to all of a sudden come upon a picture of your own father riddled with bullets. Did I tell her I was named César in honor of her father? No, but I think she already knew."

⁂

One day at noontime, Lorenza had agreed to meet Forcás at a place called Banchero, on the way to Primera Junta. They had set aside barely an hour to be together and he had invited her to that pizzeria, where she had never been, because they made a top-notch *fugazza* that she had to try. But she was late, she had gotten the streets wrong and in haste had walked past the place and had to turn back, convinced that she would not arrive on time. Forcás would get up and go as it had to be. The ten-minute waiting period had just about come and gone when she saw him, at an instant when and in a place where she had not expected to see him. But it was him, it was Forcás; there he was seated at a table, in a white shirt, at a restaurant that had not been the one they agreed upon. Aurelia looked up and saw the name of the spot; it said Banchero. Then it must be the place, Banchero, she thought, look no further. Just a little while before she had passed right in front of it and kept on going.

He looked very handsome in his white shirt, but he was in a bad mood, maybe due to her lateness, or because he had asked for two very cold Quime beers and by the time she got there they weren't that cold anymore; and besides, Aurelia told him that she would rather have a Pepsi because she didn't drink beer and to make things worse, she didn't want the *fugazza* that he had wanted her to taste and instead ordered a small pizza *à la calabresa*, who knows why. So the truth was that their encounter had not been going as well as their previous ones. There was in fact a noted unpleasantness as their allotted hour slowly wound down, and so she did her best to try and fix things. But Forcás wasn't saying much and he couldn't take his eyes from a television screen in the corner, which the owners had put there so that the clientele could watch the World Cup, which that year was played in Argentina.

The local team consisted of players of the caliber of Kempes, Passarella, Fillol, and Ardiles, and the whole country was celebrating their goals with wild street parties. But the dictators were also celebrating ostentatiously, congratulating themselves, that was the fucking thing, coming out on their balconies to greet the crowds after each game, proud as peacocks, paternal and populist, as if the victories on the soccer field were something owed to their government. With the World Cup, the military junta was scoring its greatest goal: thanks to *fútbol*, it washed its face in an Olympic gesture and showed itself to the world recently shaved, spotless, free of dirt and straw, and cleansed of blood. If there were international doubts or causes for concern about what was happening in Argentina, now everyone could relax before the spectacle of a euphoric populace out in the streets celebrating the victories of the phenomenal team, side by side with the military. The generals had managed to get in their pockets a specific type of local, who boiled over with patriotic fervor, and some foreign correspondents, who praised the friendly climate and the feeling of good sportsmanship that reigned in the country. The collective enthusiasm even gave the impression that on that very day, at that very hour and moment, the dictatorship was reaching its zenith, its summit, its consecration, and its historic justification.

"These sons of bitches want to cover up the dead with goals," Forcás cursed in a low voice, and sucked furiously on his Particulares. "They've made even *fútbol* into a bitter topic." As part of its face-cleaning, the regime had decided to attack the deep-seated Argentinean tradition of throwing confetti on the field during games. With the argument that it was low class and damaged the image of the country, the regime had mounted a systematic campaign to intimidate the crowds and stop them from throwing the confetti. But every day Clemente, an irreverent and demented bird who was the central character in a comic strip, incited disobedience from the pages of *Clarín*, poking out from the frame of his little story to throw confetti on the reader. And it so happened that Forcás had not finished his *fugazza* nor Aurelia her *calabresa* when they saw on the television what looked like a torrential downpour of tens of millions of little pieces of white paper that began to fall over the field, slow and uncontrollable, inundating the stadium and bursting forth on the screen. Big win by Clemente, they had wanted to scream if they could have. The people had dared to throw confetti, to openly defy the regime, however innocently and spontaneously—more festive than anything, in truth, not a big deal. But during those days of panic and subjugation, maybe that had been a sign, a minute and somewhat imperceptible initial indication that upon reaching its highest point, the pendulum had begun to swing back. Or at least that's what both of them must have intuited, because in that fantastic confetti cloud they enthusiastically embraced, as if wanting to celebrate something.

Soon after that, they stopped seeing each other. Just like that, at the entrance of a theater. In a sudden crossfire of words, they went from the clouds to the mud, from eternal love to nothing, *rien de rien*, *c'est fini*, see you later, game's over. He admitted that he had another love, a relationship that was more than five years old, and she told him that she had left behind a boyfriend in Madrid. There was nothing they could do, no breaking the impasse, neither of them willing to break it off with the former party, so there were months, when they didn't see each other, of absence and anxious agony. Of stabbing aches in the gut, in the heart, in the head, the immeasurable punishment of breaking up, that small death.

⁂

THERE'S AN ALLEYWAY at the back of the well-known Mercado del Progreso on Primera Junta, in the Caballito section. Called Pasaje Coronda, it is the drop-off point for trucks bringing food to the market, and could well be one of the least memorable spots in Buenos Aires.

Number 121 in that alleyway is a type of small old convent where several families lived. A big and precarious one-story building, it is train-like, with a narrow façade and nine separate rooms lined up in the back, all facing a common hallway. At one time, Forcás rented the first of those rooms, the only one with a window facing the street, and his brother, Miche, the adjacent one.

Forcás's room had a door out to a small patio, a half bath, and a sort of corner kitchen. And since Miche's was only a room, Forcás had given him a key to his side, so he would use it whenever he needed to. And, of course, Miche needed to, coming in and out at all hours of the day and night.

"Do you want to come with me to Coronda, Mateo, to see the place?" Lorenza asked, and Mateo, who was in a better mood since talking to the daughter of *el negro* Robles, allowed himself to be convinced after a period of haggling.

"What an ugly spot," he said after they arrived, and his mother took it as an offense.

"Ugly? I wouldn't say that. Really, you think it's ugly? Well, I was happy here."

"It's still pretty ugly." Mateo patted her on the back, to make up for his comment.

"I always found it charming, from the day I arrived here with my suitcase to come live with Forcás. Before that, I had never come. I had no idea where in the city his hideout cave was."

"But didn't we just leave it that the two of you were breaking up, never to see each other again?"

"About a month and a half after that, we made up. He had looked me up to tell me that he had broken it off with his old love. I broke it off with mine with a long phone call from a public telephone, and a few days later we had already decided to live together. I said goodbye to Sandrita and the apartment on Deán Funes, packed my suitcase, and showed up knocking at his door, 121. It was the same exact door you see now, metal, with this same oxidized mustard color. I rang the bell. Very emotional as you can imagine, startled, really, not really knowing where I was and what I was doing."

Her worries vanished as soon as Forcás opened the door. He was in an undershirt and sandals and was drinking a maté, and she liked that. He looked like a neighborhood kid. He didn't smell like sheep's wool, nor like Drakkar Noir, but like that instead, an everyday kid, wearing sandals and drinking a maté in his neighborhood. It was the first time that she had seen him like that. Before, she had always seen him in some role, as a resistance fighter, or as director, or the handsome one, or an Argentinean, or a boyfriend. But now it was just the face of an ordinary young man, who smiled as he opened the door of an ordinary house in an ordinary barrio, who took her suitcase and asked her to come in. She sensed that the moment was important. It was something like landing in a normal life, or as much of a normal life as could have existed amid the general horror. It was also like stepping into the real Buenos Aires. For Aurelia, Coronda was the doorway into the city.

"It's not the same being in a city as stepping into it, Mateo. For example, you and I, in our hotel, we're in Buenos Aires, but we are not. At the apartment on Deán Funes I was in Buenos Aires, but not fully. But in Coronda it was different; Coronda was the real Buenos Aires, the city within the city, the heart. And it's not really a metaphor. Caballito is in the middle of Buenos Aires and Coronda is in the heart of Caballito. Or who knows, that's what they say. What is definite is that Coronda was my citizenship papers; as soon as I stepped into that house, I stopped being a foreigner."

Forcás introduced her to his two cats, Abra and Cadabra, a pair of ashen little things, barely alive, blade thin from hunger. A few days prior, he had found them in the vacant lot across from the convent, among the garbage from the market, where someone had abandoned them in a sack. They were half dead when he took them in.

"But they were already fine when you arrived?" Mateo noted with a touch of anxiety. He couldn't stand the thought of an animal suffering.

"They were starting to come back, thanks to some mineral water that Forcás fed them with a syringe. After he introduced me to his cats, he showed me the house."

"From now on it's our house," Forcas had told her. But he didn't tell her that it was also his brother Miche's, and his girlfriend Azucena's. That part Aurelia would find out that night.

The entrance to the room was through the small patio, which had a few potted plants, and Forcás showed her the washbasin and a rope ladder that led to the roof and that, he explained with hand signals, he had put there as a means of escape should it become necessary to do so. They ducked to go under the clothesline and Aurelia was shown the bathroom, a stream of water that came out of a piece of pipe and splashed on the floor, in a space so narrow that, she would find out the next day, on showering you had to watch that your back didn't graze the cold wall.

Aurelia wasn't exactly sure why, but she had the sensation of coming upon a cozy place. Or she did know why, the reason was clear as day: this was a real house, with potted plants and cats and clothes hanging on the line, something unexpected for someone like Forcás, who lived on the razor's edge. Before further exploring her new refuge, Aurelia locked herself in the bathroom, to be alone for a minute and think about what was happening to her.

"You didn't lock yourself in there to think, Lolé, but to pee, to mark your territory. That's what animals do when they take over a place."

Forcás later showed her the bedroom and she found it stupendous. There were a few books, those that could pass as innocent, Dickens, Kipling, and Stevenson, and a Ken Brown sound system, and a bunch of *rock nacional* records. The lone bed was simple, with a blanket of black-and-coffee-colored stripes. Forcás told her that it had been hand-knitted by the Aymaras and had been a present from some Bolivian comrades. This is my bed, he said to her, your bed now as well. She sat beside him and laughed, because it was really a narrow bed. A double bed would have been too big, for the room was no larger than thirty square meters. Aside from the bed, there was a table and four chairs, a stove in the corner, and a fridge whose door was held in place by a rope. Stacked against the wall were countless boxes with the name Yiwu YaChina on them. It would be much better without the boxes, she thought, but said nothing.

"Yiyu China?" Mateo asked.

"Yiwu YaChina. A wholesale Chinese jewelry. It was Forcás's minute. To the neighbors, he was the wholesaler for Yiwu YaChina."

"Boxes full of jewels! That must have cost a fortune . . ."

"They were Chinese jewels, kiddo, cheap fake stuff. The boxes were covered in dust, anybody would be able to tell that the merchandise wasn't moving. But it was his minute. As soon as your father took out a box, he replaced it with another one, and so he kept the neighbors from suspecting."

From outside on the street, Mateo wanted to look inside the window, hopping up, but he came up short.

So he brought over some bricks from the abandoned lot, stacked them, and stood on top of them, putting his hands on the sides of his face to block the reflection on the glass.

"What do you see?" Lorenza asked from below.

"It's empty. No one lives here." Mateo jumped down to the sidewalk.

"If you want, I can ring the bell, kiddo, see if we can talk with some of the neighbors, someone who knew your father. I can say that we lived here a long time ago. Maybe they have keys and we can go in the room, so what if it's empty. Or better yet, maybe it's for rent and they'll show it."

"You go ahead. I'm going to see what they have in the market."

"Let's go together. But tell me what you saw through the window, if the floor has greenish tiles like I remember—"

"I don't know, I couldn't tell."

"Wait for me here. I want to look." Lorenza went back to the window, added a few bricks to the stack, climbed up on top, and a few moments later was looking for Mateo in the market.

"The floor is green, kiddo!" she screamed at him when she saw him down an aisle. "A milky green, veined with white."

"Great news," he laughed. "Veined with white."

The day Lorenza had arrived for the first time, the floor tiles had recently been mopped with lavender water. The whole place smelled like lavender, because Forcás had just cleaned to welcome her. And he had cleared a couple of shelves above the records and told her she could put her clothes there as he helped her unpack. It was a whole big moving-in ceremony, and although they didn't mention it, it was clear that it was a solemn occasion for both of them.

"I saw the patio," Mateo said, checking out the slabs of meat on the counter. "You could see all the way out back. Small, smaller than I had imagined."

"We did everything on that tiny patio," Lorenza said. "Even roasted meat on Sundays during the summer. Miche had hung a mirror on the back wall, right between the potted plants that we used to comb our hair. And since there wasn't a sink inside, we washed pots, dishes, and clothes in the basin, as well as cleaned our hands and brushed our teeth. In the winter you had to be quick about it; funny to have to wear a coat to brush your teeth."

"Nice," Mateo smiled. "Everything in the open air, like farmers. In the middle of the city, Forcás lived like a farmer. I like that. Now I see how his name became him."

"In the summer things got ugly. Because the heat and humidity were so suffocating, you barely stepped outside the range of the fan before you began sweating buckets. But in the winter it was pleasant, that's the truth. I returned to the house each evening about eight or nine and I loved finding your father leaning back on a chair, sipping his maté, with the cats on his lap and his feet resting on the open oven door."

"His feet must have charred," Mateo said.

"He had his shoes on. It was a gas oven and since there wasn't any heating, we kept it on and open so that the place stayed warm. But in general, we wouldn't see each other during the day. We both left early to fulfill our tasks for the party, not having any idea where the other one was, and it was nice to come back at night and realize that the other one had returned unharmed. I swear, Mateo, the reunion each night was a gift. When you go fearing the worst, it's a relief to find out that nothing has happened. And so we passed the time, day by day, very much in love, not knowing about what was going to happen the next day, not guessing too much either."

"Were you scared?"

"When I remained alone in the house."

Sometimes Aurelia had to stay alone for the night in Coronda, because Miche, who ran a collective, had the night shift, Azucena wasn't home yet, and Forcás was traveling. She locked the door securely and bundled herself up in the Aymara blanket, Abra and Cadabra curled up by her feet, and began to feel as if the panic that spread throughout the neighborhood outside seeped in through the cracks in the wall and flooded the room. She couldn't fall asleep for thinking of the basements where people bled to death in the dark, their fingernails ripped off; of the pregnant woman from the neighborhood who had disappeared the week before; or of a comrade who had turned up cut to pieces in the gutter. When she heard the sound of a lone motor outside, she stood on the bed to look out the window and her blood went cold if it was a green Ford Falcon without plates, the fed cars, the true vehicles of death, which now and then parked in the empty lot across the street. Fortunately, around four, the trucks began to arrive to unload and that was the saving grace, life returning with all its noise to frighten off the ghosts, and then finally Aurelia could sleep, lulled by the voices of the truck drivers, which in the coldness of dawn offered each other some maté, or a Faso. It was a sign that the night had been left behind and that she was safe, and she slept soundly until six, when Miche, who returned from his shift, came into the room without knocking, with the day's newspaper in one hand and bags of the night's business in the other, to talk about the news and ask if she wanted breakfast. It was an issue trying to convince him that he had to knock before coming in; she never finally succeeded. He argued, convincingly, that no one should have to ask permission to go into his own bathroom. Besides, the kitchen was his domain; he was the one who generally cooked for everyone, and it was pretty tasty, especially his *milanesas* with puree and salad. Before working in the collective he had been a butcher, and in his room he still kept a hair-raising collection of cleavers and Swiss knives that he had once used for his profession.

"So they treated you pretty well," Mateo said.

"Yes, always. Forcás did whatever he could so that I felt at home. But not always. I do remember a specific case . . ."

Aurelia had bought a Japanese lantern, one of those round ones with rice paper that you see everywhere. She hung it from a string over the table, connected the electric wire, and was happy with it. She thought that it added a nice ambiance to the room. It was the first thing, aside from her clothes, that she had brought into Coronda. That night, Miche began to ridicule her immediately for putting up such a thing, and began to jab it as if it were a punching bag, quickly destroying it.

"Forcás watched him and did nothing to stop him. He let Miche destroy the lantern," Lorenza said.

"That's not unusual," Mateo said. "The house had belonged to the two brothers before you arrived."

"But that was really the only time they made me feel like an intruder."

"Maybe it was some sort of initiation ritual, a baptism of blood."

"Well, of paper in this case. But after that night, Coronda was as much mine as theirs, and Azucena's, of course."

"And what about Ramón when he eventually came to live in your place in Bogotá, did he feel the same?"

"It wasn't my house. I didn't have a house. We rented an apartment together, and with you, who had already been born. On the wall of your room, I put up a huge poster of wild horses, and you liked it when—"

"Wait, wait," Mateo interrupted her, "what I want to know is if Ramón was as content in that place in Bogotá as you were in Coronda."

"No. He was miserable. We had left Argentina at my request, distancing ourselves from the party. You were going to be two, we had gone through three tyrants, one after the other and each with his blood spilling—the generals Videla, Viola, and Galtieri. I couldn't take it anymore. The anguish over the fact that something might happen to us before four in the afternoon, and that no one could pick you up from the sitter, was killing me. That was the worst part of the fear, that it would be four o'clock and no one would be there to pick you up at the sitter.

"For your safety and for my peace of mind, Ramón agreed to move to Bogotá and distance himself from everything that was his, the party, his comrades, what he liked to eat, and the only job he knew how to do. And in Bogotá, I forgot about him and left him very alone and isolated. For some reason, I remember with an almost photographic memory each of the objects that we had in Coronda and not even one of the objects we put up in the apartment in Bogotá; except for the poster in your room, I don't remember any of them."

One of the lines in that letter from Ramón that she did not read, the one that he left for her during the dark episode, said "exiled from everything, even your love." And, "I'm taking the boy, the only thing that is mine."

"Then you did read the letter."

"No, only those lines."

"I need a screwcork to pull information out of you."

"Corkscrew."

"Yeah, that. You know, there are times I would like to forgive him."

"Wanting to forgive is already a form of forgiving, I suppose."

"But no, no, he was a bullshitter, I wasn't the only thing that he took with him. He also took that money that wasn't his."

⁂

AURELIA HAD BEEN in Coronda for only a brief while when Forcás announced that the leadership of the party wanted to meet with her. Aside from Forcás himself, Águeda and Ana would be there, two of the party's historic directors. They were known to be powerful and mysterious, and spent most of the time outside of the country, from where they pulled strings, and their methods were known to be relentless.

"It was very rare that they would attend a meeting," Lorenza told her son. "To meet Águeda and Ana was quite an opportunity. Ninety percent of the party membership had likely never seen them in person, only in photographs."

"So it was like meeting Brad Pitt and Johnny Depp at the same time, huh?" Mateo asked.

"I couldn't even begin to imagine what task I would be assigned or where they would want to send me. On the day of the meeting, Forcás accompanied me to the place, but didn't divulge anything. Apparently he already knew how I was needed, but he didn't want to tell me anything. I kept my eyes lowered, looking at the ground so as not to figure out the exact whereabouts of the meeting, although this precaution was superfluous, since there was no way I could figure it out."

When she could look up again, she was inside a darkened house where someone had smoked a lot, the smell of cigarettes was the first thing she noticed. But it also smelled like garlic, so they must have been cooking. Forcás led her into the kitchen, which was unlike the other rooms, bathed in daylight coming in from a window that faced an inner courtyard, and the comrade who was cooking there said, "It's gnocchi with ham broth, *che*, I hope you like it."

Seated at a table, in front of an ashtray filled with butts, were the two women. The one who introduced herself as Águeda was older and wore her hair so short that her ears were completely visible, two gypsy-like monstrosities hanging from them. Ana, the quieter one, her lips painted red, had a face like an otter, but was good-looking nevertheless. Both rose to welcome her with a hug and immediately began to ask her questions about the political situation in Colombia and about the functioning of the solidarity with the Argentinean office in Madrid.

"And then I thought, That's what they want," Lorenza recounted to her son. "They want information on the international work, and it even occurred to me that they had wanted to meet with me to ask me to relocate, to return to Madrid. But no, it wasn't that."

"Listen, *piba*," Águeda had told her, and Aurelia had listened, and on hearing what they wanted had gone cold. Her mouth grew dry and she couldn't respond.

"I know what they wanted, you told me once," Mateo said. "They wanted you to turn over San Jacinto to the party."

"It's called *cotizar*, to give up for the general welfare."

"Yeah, *cotizar*, for you to give up San Jacinto for the general welfare."

"They had found out that I inherited a finca in Colombia and they had come into the country to talk to me about how in the party we all lived with what we needed and gave up the rest for the general welfare, the good of the party. They said that this was the Bolshevik and proletarian thing to do, 'the *bolche* and the *prole*,' and that Homero had offered his mother's apartment when she had passed away, and that La Gata had turned in the whole of her inheritance, and that Rafael, who was the owner of a factory, had given it to the party and now lived on a laborer's salary."

The *bolche* and *prole*, *prole* and *bolche*, and Aurelia before them mute. She hadn't said yes, or no, not even maybe; she couldn't say a thing. San Jacinto was the only thing she had left of her father. More than a finca, for her it was a collection of Sunday mornings, afternoons of hot chocolate and fritters, trips to the countryside, and whole nights by the fireplace. San Jacinto was a handful of animals with proper names and soft hair. How do you give up animals and memories for the national welfare?

"But most important, it was a finca, damn it," Lorenza told the boy, "good land that was worth a few million pesos, in the end my only inheritance. And I couldn't say a word. My ears were buzzing and their voices grew distant. I turned around to look at Forcás, as if begging him for help. Up to that moment, Forcás had remained silent, and when he opened his mouth it was to agree with them, the Bolshevik and the proletariat on one side and on the other the fucking petite bourgeoisie."

She knew she didn't want to, but she couldn't avoid it, she had to say yes, of course she would give up the finca for the general welfare, but the words got caught in her throat. The worst thing in the world was to be a petit bourgeois, and she wanted with all her heart to be *bolche* and *prole*, but she heard those voices as if they were an echo, that So-and-so turned in his car, Such-and-such her marriage ring, and she was unable to hear anything but her own inner turmoil, as if she were chomping on raw carrots. Where could she find the words to explain to them that Papaíto baked bread in the oven, that San Jacinto was where his pampered cows grazed, that she had never received the dress he sent to Madrid? How could she tell them that her mother had sent her Bally shoes, that she had used the box to hide some dollars, and that Forcás had never given them back, although she reminded him of it every day? These were the only arguments that came to her head in defense of San Jacinto, and something told her that they weren't going to sound very convincing to the ears of the two monuments carved from living rock who were sitting there, inheritors of the purest and hardest worker's code, Águeda and Ana.

"So what did you say?" Mateo asked.

"That first I would have to go to Colombia to take over the inheritance, because it had not yet been transferred to me and I couldn't do it from Argentina."

"And what did they say?"

"To think about it, that it didn't have to be right away. Then the comrade who had been cooking served the gnocchi with bread and red wine and sat down to eat with us, and they talked to me a long while about the difference between a dilettante and a professional militant. When they said goodbye, they told me that I had to decide whether I wanted to cross over, or that I had to burn some bridges, or something about bridges and crossings, one of those irrefutable metaphors."

Up to then, Lorenza had always thought that she would hold on in Argentina as long as she could, and when she couldn't take it anymore, well, back to where she came from. She would stop being Aurelia and return to Colombia and that would be that, her mission completed and duties fulfilled in the resistance. But after the meeting with Águeda and Ana, her whole stay in Buenos Aires didn't feel so much like theater or some adventure anymore. She left that kitchen feeling that she was now bound by a deep commitment and there would be no going back.

"It all makes sense, Lorenza," Mateo told her. "The turning over of one's inheritance is a test that any hero has to pass. Like Luke Skywalker in *Star Wars*, how can you not see these things? The hero has to renounce his former life and his blood ties in order to begin clean and pure on his quest, without prior ties to his new family, which is the secret society. And he has to give up his former name. It's so much like in the movies, that going from Lorenza to Aurelia, from Ramón to Forcás. . . Like Darth Vader, which is the name that the Sith give Anakin Skywalker when he joins them. You were fulfilling all the prerequisites, Mother, and you still don't even realize it; change of name, truncated identity, coded language, secret society, danger of death, superior ideals, the renunciation of the previous life. . . . Do you see any of this? You were fulfilling all the prerequisites of the initiation ritual."

"Ini-ti-a-tion."

"Right, that."

"But look at it from a more practical point of view," his mother proposed. "To go around doing what we did using your real name would have been pretty stupid. And as far as San Jacinto . . . how else do you think an unarmed resistance can survive, but by the voluntary donations of those who ran it and supported it? Right? So let's just leave it at that and say that the gnocchi was one damn expensive meal."

⁂

"DID YOU LIKE Azucena?" Mateo wanted to know.

"She smelled like cookies."

Azucena, Miche's girlfriend, worked at Bagley, a cookie and cracker factory south of the city, on Avenida Montes de Oca, near Barracas. Her job consisted of taking cookies out of the oven, tray after tray of cookies, exposed to high temperatures and sweating buckets, until the smell got into her skin and impregnated her hair. At the end of the shift, she showered at the factory with hot water, scrubbing herself with soap and shampoo, but she could not completely get rid of that sweet, penetrating smell.

"She arrived at the house smelling divine, of cinnamon and butter and flour."

Lorenza remembered her sitting on a stool on the patio, trying to paint her toenails a dark red, with balls of cotton between each toe, and frustrated because she couldn't hit the target precisely with the nail-polish brush.

"I should have helped her do it, who knows why I didn't," Lorenza said. "In fact, it wasn't that easy to approach her. She was always tense, her movements sudden bursts of electricity, as if there was some kind of short circuit inside her. Maybe her blood pressure was a little high after a whole day of toiling at the factory, or maybe her illness influenced her inability to hit her target with the nail-polish brush."

Azucena's personality had been a mystery to Aurelia until Miche secretly confessed that he bought her Epamin tablets to prevent seizures. Epilepsy? Miche said yes, a mild form of epilepsy.

"What were they like?" asked Mateo.

"What was what like?"

"The seizures."

"I never saw her have one. She was thin, a good body; I'd say pretty, if she didn't comb her hair to look a bit like Betty Boop, and her eyebrows were plucked so thoroughly that they had almost completely disappeared. But she was pretty, although she had a strange and feverish way of looking at you."

At first she said she didn't want to know anything about politics, but Azucena ended up introducing them to a pair of workers from the Bagley factory, and thus, in that way, began raising the political consciousness in the food industry. And even though Azucena eventually stepped aside, these two workers presented them to another, and then someone from Terrabusi and from Canale, the other two traditional cookie factories, and so they started to put a small group together. To avoid using their real names, they decided they'd use the name of the cookies they were responsible for on the production line. So one was Criollita, another Smile, the others Two Smiles, Temptation, Merengue, Rumba, Twin One, Twin Two, even Twin Three during their busiest seasons.

"Good noms de guerre," Mateo said. "I would have enjoyed being in a subversive cell with Smile, Rumba, and Merengue."

The girls took at least an hour between the whistle announcing the end of their shift and when they showed up in El Chino, a little hole-in-the-wall bar a few blocks from Bagley, where on Mondays and Thursdays Aurelia waited for them to arrive at the group's secret meeting.

They would appear there without aprons or gray plastic caps, freshly bathed, their hair brushed and blow-dried, meticulously made up, in tight jeans and high heels. The minute was that they were getting together to see *Amor gitano*, the soap opera that was the craze then. They took Aurelia to the rooms they shared in the tenements of Barracas.

"Creaking wooden floors, twin beds, flowery quilts, a stove, a good-size TV, and a large picture of Evita in the most prominent spot," Lorenza told Mateo. "Nothing more, nothing less, those were their treasures. You couldn't miss the picture of Evita, with plastic flowers and lit candles, or I should say the altar to Eva Perón, dead so long but still on her throne."

Aurelia began to understand whom these girls resembled, whom they dressed, moved, and talked like. Who else could it be but Evita, prim and shaken by the country, ready to become martyrs if such a thing was necessary. *If Evita had been a laborer* . . . for Evita, and under her protection, the girls from Bagley would go up against anything, they would dare to confront anyone who got in their way, starting with the cunt of your mother's dictatorship, as they said: those military bastards and those bitch mothers who gave birth to them.

"But you weren't a Peronista," said Mateo.

"I was a Trotskyite, and they accepted me as the leader in their get-togethers, but if I had made one peep about their Evita they would have slammed the door in my face. And all for what, we were supposed to stand united against the dictatorship, no?"

Already locked in the room, seated three to a bed, they passed around the maté and got the ball rolling by talking about the quality of different brands of panty hose, about the varicose veins they got from standing on their feet for so long, about creams for dry hands, the prices of things, dastardly men, the miracles of saints, and the delays in menstruation. But at the stroke of seven, as if by magic, they all went silent at the same time. In the tenement, in the neighborhood, apparently in all of Buenos Aires such silence was imposed, because that's when the soap opera started. A new episode of *Amor gitano*.

Criollita, Smile, Rumba, and Temptation affixed their eyes on the screen, madly in love with Renzo, the Gypsy, as handsome as he was masculine, with eyes so deep. Impulsive and courageous, he had been unjustly convicted of a crime he had not committed and thus deprived of the love of the beautiful Countess de Astolfi, herself a victim of an infamous tyranny in a realm from an indeterminate place and time—but much like present-day Argentina—a place dominated by cruel villains such as Count Farnesio and his vile lackey the hunchback Dino, perhaps even crueler, and scattered with dungeons and secret passages and forest ambushes, where young and green-eyed innocents like Renzo were locked up in inhumane Islands of the Damned.

During commercial breaks, the girls from Bagley forgot about Renzo, the time had come for plotting. They turned up the volume, lowered their voices to a whisper, and the clandestine meeting took place. Rumba, who belonged to the internal committee, reported that in the nineteenth century the "law of the chair" had been approved, which their employer no longer respected, but which they should start fighting for again: for every hour on their feet, they had a right to fifteen minutes of sitting.

Then Renzo and Adriana de Astolfi pledged to love each other forever through a Gypsy blood rite, and during the commercials that followed Aurelia had them read excerpts from the party newspaper and talked about the articles with them. You should have seen how those girls hurled curses and insults in low voices at the military junta, at the executioners of Triple A, at the federals of coordination, against the Marquis Farnesio and his abject hunchback. And you should have heard how they pledged their lives and swore to overthrow them, all of them, to restore freedom to Renzo and to all the missing and kidnapped. Because if Evita were alive, she would not have allowed these criminals to fuck with our lives like this. If Evita were alive, if Renzo the Gypsy, if the Countess de Astolfi really existed . . .

⁂

In the third room in Coronda, the one right next to Miche's, lived a paralyzed man.

"How paralyzed?"

"Very paralyzed. He got around in a wheelchair, never went out, and could barely fend for himself."

That man was married to a much younger woman named Gisella Sanchez, who helped him with everything and certainly also supported him, because he could not work at all and she did, as a florist. Gisella Sanchez left early in the morning and returned at night, and if her husband needed anything while he was alone, he banged the end of a broomstick on the ceiling, which could be heard in the brothers' rooms, so whoever was there dropped by to help him. Maybe he had dropped the paper, and they would pick it up for him, or he had finished the bottle of water or had run out of toilet paper, so they went to the market to get it for him. Sometimes the wind twisted the antenna of his television and Miche or Forcás would climb on the roof to straighten it. Gisella Sanchez was very grateful for everything they did, and would bring them back flowers from the shop as gifts.

Forcás had never talked openly about politics with her, and yet they had agreed upon a pact as a matter of survival. More than a pact, it was a favor, a risky one that she had agreed to do for them if there were ever any problems. Lorenza did not know whether the husband, the paralyzed man, was aware of the agreement.

"It was a piece of cardboard with big red letters announcing FORD TRUCK FOR SALE." Forcás had given it to Gisella to hang on the front door if there was ever any sign of strange things going on in the tenement or the neighborhood while they were out. Something strange—Forcás had not explained this further and she had not asked him to. She only said that she understood, and that he could count on her. Such things could be done because there was some complicity between people, a kind of understanding that was given to this or that, by sign or smell.

"What if you were wrong?"

"There was a margin of error, but it was difficult to go too far wrong. You could see in a person's face whether he was for or against the dictatorship. Chatting for five minutes with someone beyond *fútbol* and the weather was enough to more or less know where they stood."

"Did you live in Coronda when I came along?" Mateo wanted to know.

One spring afternoon, Aurelia had come running into the house in Coronda with a paper in hand, a certificate that she had just been given. She handed it to Ramón for him to read aloud: "Laboratory Clinical Analysis, Dr. Juan Manuel Rey, Immunological Test for Pregnancy: Positive."

"Ramón was thrilled, Mateo. He went off to cry and was very excited," said his mother.

"Really?"

"Really. What I saw that day was a man who was happy."

"Then who knows when it ran out for him."

In the months that followed, Coronda was populated with dreams, sometimes Aurelia dreamed, sometimes Forcás.

Some were pleasant and full of good omens, while others were stifling, and recounting them to Mateo, Lorenza asked herself how they dreamed in that room, when they could barely sleep from the excitement of the news of the pregnancy, on that narrow bed, the noise of the trucks and the comings and goings of Azucena, her slippers shuffling to the kitchen and from the kitchen to the bathroom, before leaving for the factory, and then to top everything off, Miche, who burst in offering breakfast. Not to mention the negligible noise of any night, which at that time could easily be confused with something more alarming.

"You can't really sleep when even the sound of a cat on the roof seems like a dire threat," Lorenza said. "And yet we dreamed, Mateo. We dreamed about you."

Ramón dreamed one night that the child was born while he was away and that on his return he could not find him. Crazed, he wandered here and there asking about their newborn, until someone told him that the woman who looked after him had carried him in her arms to the sanctuary of Luján. In the dream, Ramón, who had not yet seen his child and therefore didn't know what it looked like, had to search in a crowd of pilgrims walking on their knees to the shrine.

Some time later, it was Aurelia who awoke, shaken by a nightmare. Her child was born and had a serious and beautiful face; he didn't smile but his features were perfect, yet his body was elongated like that of a lizard. She wanted to hug him, to wrap him in a blanket so he would not be cold, but the baby-lizard wriggled away.

"I suspect that when sleeping, your father and I recognized what we could not even ask ourselves when we were awake. How were we to care for you, Mateo, if we had made a profession of not taking care of ourselves? How to defend your life without knowing how long our own would last? Your birth was to be a success against all evidence, an urgent reclamation of life from within the gears of death that surrounded us."

It had been three weeks since they had learned of the pregnancy. It was Saturday, about one in the afternoon. Azucena was not there, and Miche had left that day with the announcement that he'd return to prepare an eggplant lasagna for dinner, provided they buy the ingredients. Aurelia and Forcás went to the market to get what they needed: pasta, eggplant, tomatoes, mozzarella, Parmesan, garlic, and olive oil.

They did not return directly but wandered around the neighborhood as was their routine, a stop at the pharmacy, another in the deli to assemble the charcuterie, as Forcás said: black olives, salami, poultry, and mayonnaise. They lingered a moment, smelling the jasmine on Primera Junta, then bought and leafed through the newspaper and magazines at the newsstand, the whole trip and back about an hour long. Returning by Alberdi, they turned into Coronda and approached the house. Forcás was reading something in the newspaper when she caught sight of the sign on the door, FORD TRUCK FOR SALE. Her heart kicked in her chest. She grabbed Forcas's arm and instinctively tried to turn around, but he forced her to keep walking forward. Slowly, calmly, without fuss.

Do not run, Aurelia, the first thing to do is not to run.

Pale, with their hearts in their mouths, they passed in front of the house without even turning around to look at it and kept on going, reaching the back entrance of the market.

They hid in the aisles, weaving through the vegetable and meat counters until they reached the front entrance facing Rivadavia. From there they walked to the Primera Junta Station. Mixed in with all the other people, they waited for what seemed a century for the subway to arrive, they took it, making several line changes and then resurfacing somewhere that was unfamiliar to Aurelia. They would never return to Coronda.

⁂

"Do you know how long a person can go without sleep?" Lorenza asked Mateo. "Twenty days and nights. You're going to say that this is not possible, but I know that it is. I know from experience. Twenty days and nights I had not slept, and weighed ten kilos less, when the call from your father finally came."

"Just follow his lead," she'd been told by Dr. Haddad, an expert on kidnapping who knew how to handle a call from an enemy who has your loved one in his hands. "If he says he loves you, you tell him that you love him. If he says that he misses you, tell him that you miss him. If he cries, you cry. But if he's angry, do not get angry. Cry anyway, that always works. Tell him you're sorry, that you need both him and the boy badly. Don't forget that, both him and the child: don't skip him. Don't lay the blame on him, blame yourself. Lie consistently and without scruples and pretend that what matters here is that communication is not broken, which will be prolonged and narrowed, the thread that leads you to the child."

To Lorenza's ears, the voice of Ramón arrived both as a saving grace and improbably, like a miracle. The same drone voice, the same hurried pronunciation that, years later, Mateo was to hear recorded on the answering machine. Where was he talking from? Lorenza did not find out. Ramón did not say, and she did not ask him.

"I didn't want to pressure him or make him uncomfortable," she recounted to Mateo. Haddad had said it would be like dancing with a partner, she'd have to keep up with the beat and not fall too far behind or leap forward.

"And why didn't you do it like in *NYPD Blue*, install a tracking system that in three and a half minutes finds out where the call is coming from?"

"I did. But it was like in the movies, after three minutes, he hung up."

It seemed to her that Ramón was speaking from another world, that other world where her son was, a slippery world, almost unimaginable, almost nonexistent, which had been lost in space until the voice of Ramón told her, without telling her, that there was a specific point on the map where her son was. No longer in the nebula, or in a vacuum, or in death, but in a city or a village, in a hotel or a house where there was a physical point, a phone, and probably a table and a bed. A real place. It was terrible not to know where it was, but at least Lorenza knew that such a place existed. And if it existed, she could get there.

The call lasted three minutes and seven seconds, as Guadalupe timed it and recorded it. And then Lorenza hung up and she was able to master the shock. Together, they listened to the tape again and again, lest any data, hint, or nuance escape them. During the three minutes and seven seconds, Lorenza had not protested or insulted, had not said anything off script. During the first two minutes, she had simply asked how Mateo was.

"Very well," said the voice, and she thought she felt the presence of the child, believed to guess his breath, trying to quiet the noise of her own heart, which thundered in her ears, lest it prevented her from hearing the boy's heart, which would be beating on the other side.

"He's happy, eating well, sleeping well, has learned two new words and repeats them every hour. I'll put him on in a moment so that he can tell you what they are himself. But he's driving me crazy repeating them."

Ramón's voice sounded natural, almost festive, as if nothing had happened, as if it were simply the voice of a father who has taken his child to spend the weekend on a finca, like he was supposed to do, and was making a routine call to the mother to catch her up on things.

"Put him on," Lorenza implored, trying not to sound too much like she was begging, trying to attune her voice to Ramón's, trying to sound like him.

She was gleeful, almost happy, playing the same game,

following Ramón's lead like Haddad had indicated, as if nothing had happened, as if she had not dropped ten kilos, as if she had not remained awake for twenty days and nights, as if she were not a death in life, which only the presence of the son could resurrect, as if she were any mom who has packed the suitcase for her son, including his warm pants, a couple of toys, and teddy bear pajamas, because the son has gone with his father but only for the weekend.

"What words," she openly pleaded now, "tell me what words Mateo has learned."

"He's going to tell you himself," said Ramón, but he never put the boy on. "Just calling to tell you that Mateo is well and to ask how you yourself are."

"I've been through hell but I'm fine now that I have heard from you," said Lorenza, and wished she could insist that he put Mateo on. But Guadalupe was standing beside her, stop-watch in hand, making peremptory signs not to go there and putting before her eyes a paper with writing in big letters, the passage that they had calculated might precipitate the trip: Today, a man came looking for me demanding that I pay the money from a check. Tell me what to do, Ramón, that man is going to kill me if I don't pay the money back.

Lorenza read what was written on the paper, word for word, trying not to make it sound like a reproach, but a matter of great concern.

"It was the same for me with my notebook. You also wrote down what you had to tell Ramón over the phone," Mateo said.

"You see, you're not alone in trying to tame tigers with words on paper."

"That's good, to get in the tiger's cage and hit him over the head with a notebook. But go on, Lolé, what did the tiger say?"

"He said, tell him you'll pay him next week and don't get all heated up about it, this has all been well thought out."

"Well thought out?" repeated Mateo. "How about that, my dad, on top of everything, well thought out? That's his thing, trying to head a heist and ending up with a hit on the head. Did he say 'heated'? What is heated?"

"He said not to get heated up, not to worry about it. I looked at Guadalupe, indicating that, yes, we had touched some nerve."

"I see," said Mateo. "According to him, you would not have to worry about paying that money because you would no longer be in Colombia when the narco lost his shit. But I don't know, Lorenza, I think that Ramón's motives were a little more entangled. Was he going to bring you to Argentina so that the narco would not kill you, or was he taunting the narco so that he'd force you to flee to Argentina?"

"Whatever it was, I clasped on like a tick and told your father in my most forlorn voice: 'But that man is demanding that he be paid right away, Ramón, don't leave me alone in this—' "

"I'll call back tomorrow," he said, and hung up without waiting for an answer.

"Swear, swear that you'll call me tomorrow," she pleaded,

if only to the telephone because communication had already been cut.

She asked Guadalupe to leave her alone and began to weep like Mary Magdalene. Now you finally cry, enough to fill seas, praying, calling, cursing, crying, crying, crying, and choking on tears, burning her eyes with tears of salt, outside of any script and beyond any calculation, still stuck to the telephone as if to let it go were to let go of the three minutes and seven seconds of the Mateo she had recovered. After much weeping, she was finally able to fall asleep. She could get some sleep, because the prophecy of Haddad had begun to come true.

"And what were those two words I had learned?" asked Mateo.

"Ook, snu."

"Ook, snu?"

"Look at the snow. But to find that out, I had to wait another three days."

⁂

"GISELLA SÁNCHEZ THOUGHT he was a guerrilla fighter," Mateo told Lorenza during one of the musical teas offered after five under the glass dome of L'Orangerie, at the Alvear Palace Hotel, amid potted ferns, large vases filled with roses, and a quartet that played Brahms, watering it down to background music, and waiters in white gloves, coming and going as they deployed silverware, served finger sandwiches, warm scones, and mini gâteaux. Lorenza had dragged Mateo to this spot through the circuits of her nostalgia. She had stayed at the Alvear Palace as a girl and then as a teenager, when she visited Buenos Aires with her family.

"Who was a guerrilla?" she asked Mateo.

"Forcás, who else?"

"Forcás was not a guerrilla, who believes that?"

"I told you, Gisella Sánchez believes that."

"But why do you say that?"

"Because she told me."

"Who told you?"

"I told you, Gisella Sánchez, your Coronda neighbor. Today I went to talk to her."

"What?"

"Today I went to talk to her."

"What do you mean you went to talk to her?"

"Today. At lunchtime."

"What? Yesterday you didn't even let me ring the bell—"

"It's better without you, Lorenza," Mateo said, while searching among the tarts on the pâtisserie cart for one with no fruit. "I found out things. The paralyzed man was named Anselmo and has since died. I bet you didn't know that."

"And Gisella Sánchez?" she asked, still perplexed. She could not believe that Mateo, who only a few days ago had been paralyzed before the PlayStation, suddenly had decided to embark on a mission to track down his father. "Well, kiddo, good! You don't know how happy I am that you went . . . And Gisella, what did you find?"

"I was told she had remarried, but not another paralyzed man. This time it was a dentist. I found her at the florist, she still works there. I think she now owns the business. It's called Flowers and Gifts."

"And did you go that far, in what, a taxi?"

"Yes, a taxi." Mateo asked the waiter to bring him milk instead of tea. "Lie, I took the subway."

"How did you know where her flower shop was? I didn't even know that."

"I asked around. I got to the florist and a saleswoman thought I wanted to buy flowers. It was Gisella Sánchez."

"How did you know?"

"I said I was the son of Forcás and was looking for my father, but she kept with the flowers and said if they were for my father she would suggest some white roses, and began to pull them out. I tried to explain that I did not want flowers, that I was looking for my father. Then she asked what Forcás, she knew no one by that name. She reacted differently when I explained that Forcás was his nickname, his real name is Ramón Iribarren and he lived in Coronda. I told her that I was his son, Mateo Iribarren. From then on, she understood everything I was talking about."

"No more, what a great investigator, you've become a tiger, kiddo, and to think that yesterday you pretended ignorance. And how is she, describe her."

"She is a señora with the face of a señora."

"It must be her. But why did she think that Ramón was a guerrilla?"

"Because he listened to *rock argentino*, I guess. I explained that he had not been a guerrilla. I told her that he was a Trotskyite who was against the armed struggle and that during the dictatorship had been part of the underground but without weapons. It's good, right, Lolé? Did I tell it right? She told me that from the very beginning she knew that he was involved in something because revolutionary music came from his room. That's what she said. Then she suffocated me with kisses, and said, You, the son of Ramón, a spitting image."

"Did she ask about me?"

"I told her that I had come alone to Buenos Aires, looking for my father. She said that she had not seen him in years, but she'd seen Uncle Miche. Uncle Miche lived for a while longer in Coronda, with Azucena. Did you know that, Lolé?"

"How?"

"After the Ford Truck for Sale incident. She remembered the story of the sign, that part was the same. But you don't know half the story. When you saw the sign, Forcás and you went into hiding. So far the two versions match. What you don't know is that Miche did not leave. Ramón didn't tell you that. See? You know nothing, Lorenza. Not even that. You did not know what happened right there in the house of Forcás, but he knew that you had inherited a farm far away in another country."

Gisella Sánchez told Mateo that one Saturday at noon, she was walking home from the florist when she saw at the corner of Centenera and Guayaquil two guys who had seized Azucena, her neighbor, and were dragging her toward the house. Azucena looked very ill, pale, wilted, with blood dripping down her face and staining her shirt. Gisella Sánchez believed that it was two *cana* who had beaten her so that she would denounce the others, so she hurried to hang the sign on the door as she had agreed to do for Ramón."

"That could be," Lorenza told Mateo. "So we scrammed out of there and never came back. How could we?"

"Listen to what I'm saying, Mother: Miche returned. He continued living there. Those two guys were not *cana*, Lolé. They were just two ordinary types passing by, when they saw Azucena fall to the ground because she was an epileptic. They wanted to help, that was it. Two strangers. One put a handkerchief in her mouth so she did not swallow her tongue, and after the attack happened, she said she lived at 121 Coronda and they took her there. Gisella Sánchez had mentally created her own movie of the situation, believing that the men were *cana* and had beaten Azucena, so she got ahead of herself and put the sign up. When she realized her mistake it was too late; Forcás and you had seen it and had left. Miche arrived later, and there was no longer the sign up and he went in as usual. Inside he found Gisella Sánchez, who was caring for Azucena, who with the attack had fallen hard and had a wound on her forehead. That's the thing, Lorenza, and thus they continued to live there. Miche and Azucena adopted the cats. Gisella Sánchez says that some time later, Miche was able to contact Ramón to tell him that it had been a false alarm. They lived there until three years ago, do you see? And then moved to a place called Villa Gesell."

"In Buenos Aires?"

"No, outside Buenos Aires on the coast, it seems."

"Sounds nice, Villa Gesell."

"Yes, Villa Gesell. Not only that, Lorenza, from time to time Ramón would visit the place in Coronda, and bring food to the cats. I bet that he never told you that."

"It would have been after we broke up—"

"No, it was then. It was when you were pregnant, believing that Coronda had fallen and that you were on the run. Nothing had happened in Coronda and yet Ramón told you nothing."

"Well, he didn't really need to tell me, these were things I did not need to know—"

"Not even about the cats? Didn't you ever ask what happened to the cats?"

"I asked, of course, I asked him a thousand times. The worst part of losing Coronda was that Abra and Cadabra had been abandoned. For the second time in their lives, too. Clothes and things come and go, but those cats. He told me a few weeks later that he had been able to rescue them and your grandparents had them in Polvaredas."

"No, the cats remained in Coronda with Miche. The thing is, you don't know a thing about Ramón, nothing."

"But why would he hide such a thing from me, what would he gain by not telling me?"

"Maybe he didn't gain anything, there were just a lot of

things he didn't talk about. Or maybe the cats spent time with Miche in Coronda and then with my grandparents in Polvaredas. Who knows?"

"Besides, that doesn't end the story of Abra and Cadabra, kiddo. I had to face a very dramatic situation because of them later."

"Stop, stop. Guess what, Gisella Sánchez gave me Uncle Miche's phone number at Villa Gesing."

"Villa Gesell."

"Villa Gesell. Uncle Miche lives there now. And I'm going to call him," Mateo said, sounding confident. "I need to know. I have a lot of questions to ask him."

Lorenza stared at Mateo, sensing that he was not the same as the previous day. They say it's possible to hear how the grass grows, she thought, and you can also hear how a child grows.

"You know what, it's not true that I went alone to Coronda and to the florist," said Mateo, suddenly. "Lies."

"You didn't go?"

"Yes I did, but I was not alone."

"Then who—"

"Andrea took me."

"What Andrea."

"Andrea Robles, daughter of *el negro* Robles. She had told me that she would help me find my father."

"She picked you up at the hotel?"

"Yes. And we took the metro together to Caballito. She has been finding out a lot about her father on her own, and I told her I wanted to do the same with mine. So today she helped me, to show me how."

"And where is Andrea now? I would love to meet her. Do you want to invite her to have tea with us?"

"What are you thinking about, Mother, she's an adult, she works. So I took her out at noon, when she was free. She's back in her office now, and besides she wouldn't like this place. The truth is, I don't like it much."

"I think that what you like is Andrea—"

"Don't say that, I told you. She's an adult. But she's pretty, though. Her hair loose and earrings. Very pretty."

"And Villa Gesell, where your uncle Miche lives, are you also going there with her?"

"No, what do you think? I'll call him and if I find him, I'll see him alone. As Andrea says, there are things you have to do alone."

⁂

"Uncle Miche said it was true that he was a bus driver and that he covered the nighttime route 166, from the Third of February to Freedom. Look, Lolé, here on this napkin he jotted it down and told me to keep the data for when you wrote a book about those times, Line 166, from Third of February to Freedom," Mateo told Lorenza after his return from Villa Gesell, having traveled there on the 7:40 AM Expreso Alberino, to spend the day with his father's brother.

He had called the night before and they had agreed to

meet. Apparently Miche knew nothing about Ramón's whereabouts. They had quarreled a few years ago and had not seen each other or spoken since.

Uncle Miche was waiting at the bus terminal and Mateo had no problem recognizing him, first because nobody else was standing around, and second because he remained the same as he had been in the picture that Lorenza kept in an album: a rather tall man, thin but with a potbelly, a pinched nose, and Ray-Ban sunglasses with mirrored lenses, smiling politely and holding his nephew, who was only a few days old.

"You look the same, Uncle Miche," Mateo said. "You have not changed at all." He only took the sunglasses off for cooking.

"Eyewear of the professional bus driver," Lorenza said. "The same ones he used when he drove."

"But now he's a butcher again, and he still uses them. I think it's because of the sand. The wind was blowing and picked up the sand and it got in his eyes. There in the Villa Gesell, Miche has a butcher shop, and he lives in the back. The first thing he told me when I got off the bus was that he was going to prepare me one memorable steak, that he had set the best cut of meat aside, that it was the kind of beef we never had in Colombia, and to get ready because I was going to taste the best steak sausage of my life. That was the first thing he said when I arrived."

"So? Was it good, the steak sausage?" Lorenza wanted to know.

"Yeah, very good, but best were the French fries. He

made a mountain of fries and we gobbled them down. Miche left the assistant manager in charge of the butcher shop and took the day off to spend it with me. We talked a lot. He said my dad was a wretch, who had never gone looking for me because he was a coward. He also told me that it killed my grandparents."

"Then they are dead?"

"Yes, both. Pierre my grandfather died first, of a heart attack. He was living with Miche, and was in the middle of building a stone fence. Miche took me to see the fence, which was half done, just like it had been left by my grandfather, a few steps from the butcher shop. According to Miche, Grandfather worked until the last minute of his life. And then Grandmother died, Noëlle."

"Did he say how she died?"

"Sadly. He said that my grandmother never could deal with the sadness of losing her grandchild. I really liked Uncle Miche. I liked going to see him. He said that Villa Gesell was gray and desolate during the winter, but that I had to return. He invited me to spend the summer there. You'll see what beauties come out to the beach in thongs, he said, you have to make the most of the fact that you're single, kid. I guess he can't because he is married. The wife wasn't there, she had gone to Buenos Aires for a few days."

"Azucena?"

"No, not her. With Azucena he had no children. Now he has another woman and a two-year-old child. Roughly the age I was the last time he saw me, so he said, and he showed me the photo of the baby. He said the child was identical to me. I didn't see the resemblance, but I kept quiet. Guess what the baby's name is."

"What?"

"Guess."

"I don't know . . . Ramón . . . Pierre . . ."

"No, wrong. I'll give you another chance."

"Oh, kiddo. Let's see . . . His name is Ernesto, Che. No wait, Leon Trotsky."

"Nope."

"Then Miguel, like his father."

"His name is Mateo, like me. Mateo Iribarren. Just like me."

"I don't believe you."

"I swear. So I have a double. But it doesn't bother me. Uncle Miche told me that he hadn't named him that to replace me, but to not forget me. He said he did it for the sake of Grandmother, who was doing so badly because she had lost one Mateo, and Miche wanted to give her another to console her."

"Okay—"

"Yes, it's okay. It was a bit sad to see that little wall that Grandfather was building when he died. A very short little wall, you know, Lolé? It wasn't like my grandfather was making the Great Wall of China or anything. It was a low wall, nothing more. I thought, so this was the last thing my grandfather did, and I would have liked to have helped. I would have liked to hand him the rocks, which I could have done, even as a child, they were medium-size stones. *Mar del plata,*

Miche said that they were called, an unusual name for stones, sea of silver. In any case, I don't think they weighed much. I should have asked Uncle Miche what the wall was for, why Grandfather was building it right there. Maybe tomorrow I'll call and ask him."

Mateo liked the voice of his uncle, who seemed calm. He had a slow way of speaking and Mateo understood him well. He had also shown him the set of Swiss knives that he used in the butcher shop and said that they had cost a fortune and were his greatest pride.

"The brand is Swibo, Lorenza, can you imagine? Think of Swiss Army knives but for butchers, with yellow, ergonomic handles. He had at least twelve of these, all different sizes. There was one that looked like an ax, I swear. They were some impressive weapons."

"If you want, we can practice some target tossing," Uncle Miche proposed and pulled out another set of knives, specifically for throwing, and began to toss them against a board. Mateo told Lorenza that Miche almost always hit the bull's-eye.

"Me, on the other hand, I didn't hit it once. It's difficult to throw a knife. Have you ever tried it? You have to grab it by the blade, but like this, so as not to cut yourself, and wham, you chuck it. I was a sissy with that and Miche made fun of me. But in a good way, right? He didn't want to offend me with his ridicule, or make me feel bad. He also has a retractable rattan stick for Filipino kali, a scimitar, and a professional nunchaku. He let me play around with all of them for a while."

"Was Grandmother Noëlle also living there when she died?"

"No, she was somewhere else, with Ramón. She lived at Villa Gesell until my grandfather died and then she went to live with Ramón, I don't know where."

"Do you know why they fought, Miche and Ramón?"

"No."

"Did you ask?"

"Yes, but I think he didn't respond."

"Could it have been because of that story of the robbery and prison?"

"Maybe. Told me the same stuff about what we already knew, but in the James Bond style, you know, the hero mode. What was new was that he said that my father told him he wanted the money to organize a political party." Miche wanted his half to open the butcher shop, and Ramón wanted to continue the revolution. That was what Miche told him. "Then he asked me if I'd like to take a walk along the beach and we went, but we stopped at a tin shack on the shore, and he ordered a beer and treated me to a Coca-Cola. He said that if the sea settled down we could go out on the boat, and I liked the idea, but in the end the sea did not settle down."

"Was the beach pretty?"

"Not really. It was cold and there was garbage. Uncle Miche said that in summer it became spectacular."

"Coronda was a wonder in those days. The city bus your uncle Miche drove," Lorenza said, "it was decorated in black lights, with psychedelic motifs and red tasseled drapes that swayed at every stop and jolt. He had installed hundreds of bulbs, like on a Christmas tree, which turned on whenever he braked. Not to mention the sound equipment and a high-decibel collection of tapes he'd recorded, of whatever songs were popular then in the city."

"A magical traveling discotheque."

"Yes. And he succeeded, Miche, believe you me. He had his success with girls, who when getting on the bus were delighted to see him there, driving, a real lord of the night with his black tie, blue shirt, and sunglasses, cruising through the sleeping city in his fiery ship with black lights to the beat of some psychedelic romantic ballad. That's how he picked up Azucena. Then when they became a couple, she put up photos of them on the dashboard, on the outside, and made him paint her name in phosphorescent letters on the body of the bus. One out of every ten nights, Miche was off and then we would take the bus out. Your father equipped it with Campari, soda, olives, crackers, mayonnaise, pickles, and sausages, and we were off and running for the night through Buenos Aires in our own private traveling club. Those were good times, kiddo."

⁂

EVERYTHING THERE WAS bright, like in a dream. The sky was light blue and the world seemed soft and gentle under the snow. In the background loomed the formidable mountain range that was duplicated, in mirror image, on the lake, with a wisp of smoke rising from the chimney of the log cabin in the foreground. Behind it lay a pine forest stretching up toward the low hills, and down one of them, on an old horse, a man was approaching with a small child tucked in front of him. He held the child in place with his arms as he gripped the reins. Both were protected from the cold with hats, sweaters, and scarves, brightly colored, and the boy looked like a miniature reproduction of the man. As they approached, Lorenza perceived an absolute calm in the boy's expression. He was happy, she realized. He had been happy, the entire drama has not affected him at all, she thought, and a sense of relief allowed a smile to appear on her face for the first time in a long while. Ramón made the boy turn his eyes to where she was.

It took a few moments for Mateo to recognize her and then the boy stirred with joy, shocked by the surprise. He began yelling at her to look at the snow, and the horse, and the snow, and was determined to point them out to her as she ran to meet him, the boy still in the arms of his father, and then embraced him, holding him against her chest with all the strength of her soul, falling to her knees in the cold snow.

Two days earlier, in Bogotá, Ramón's second and final phone call had come in, and this time they had talked at length. Not about the child, which was the only thing that interested her, she had to bite her tongue again and follow the thread without interrupting the conversation to ask him about the boy. They spoke instead about reconciliation. Ramón raised the possibility and took the initiative and

Lorenza echoed it, saying only what she believed he wanted to hear. To everything she responded with a positive, she asked for forgiveness, granted forgiveness, told him she was very sad over the breakup of the relationship, agreed that in Bogotá things had gone very wrong, recognized the infinite class arrogance of herself and her family, agreed to try again, to start over, to love each other like before, she'd return to Argentina, they'd raise their child there, watching him grow up together, making a fresh start, betting on happiness.

"Sad, that you had to tell so many lies," Mateo said to Lorenza.

"I didn't tell them, Tranzor Z did."

"That's one fucked-up robot."

"One who's been stripped of her child and didn't care about anything except getting him back."

"Poor Ramón, it was some cowardly shit he came up with to shake you down."

The call was made from a public phone, somewhere in Argentina, but impossible to identify where exactly. But it wasn't necessary; Ramón announced that within a few hours he would be sending a prepaid airline ticket. She claimed the ticket, and saw that it was one-way for the next morning at ten thirty, from Bogotá to Buenos Aires.

For her, it was very clear that this journey had but one goal: to recover Mateo and return with him. Against Ramón's will. Despite all the precautions that Ramón would take to stop her from doing so. She discussed with her family whether she should be accompanied, and everyone volunteered to travel if necessary. But that would be a declaration of war, and in this conflict she was the one who stood to lose the most. From then on, she would have to figure things out on her own.

She left on that plane alone, already aloft on anxiety and expectation, alone again to Buenos Aires, once again with dollars hidden and false passports, as if Argentina were a magnetic field, a place that would require her maximum effort and put her to the test, once more, as if the cycle had begun again in perfect symmetry. But it was a perverse symmetry, distorted, because this time the war would be over, and her enemy would be someone who had once been her closest ally. She wanted to ask herself when and how things began to turn into this, but she did not. She would dismiss any thought that opened the door to confusion. She could not give accommodation to anything not having direct bearing on what she should do, how she should act, when.

She arrived at Ezeiza International Airport overcome with longing, certain that Mateo would be there waiting for her. She would open her eyes and see him, as if waking from a nightmare. Within minutes she would be holding him and whatever happened afterward, she would never let go. She went through the military checkpoints knowing that she would not fail, could not fail this time. It would have been a terrible trick of fate to be brought down this time, when this trip had nothing to do with politics, and Mateo was waiting on the other side. Moreover, unlike her first arrival, now she had a minute that the soldiers would find more than respectable: her press card and a document under which the purpose of the trip was stated as a series of features for *La Crónica* on the most beautiful Argentine ranches.

Immigration and customs went smoothly, but her soul dropped to the floor when she realized that no one was waiting for her. Not only was Mateo not there but Ramón was not, either. In that crowded airport, she did not know a soul; and apart from the destination of Buenos Aires printed on the ticket, Ramón had not given her any information. Mistake, mistake, mistake! Lorenza wanted to bang her head against the wall, disastrous mistake, not to have realized that Ramón would have suspected a counteroffensive and would not be so careless as to show up at the airport, much less bring the child. She should have demanded a telephone number or directions to go somewhere, some reference point, a hotel, even a café, where they could reestablish contact, in the event of the misfortune that was indeed happening.

She waited five minutes, ten, twelve. Nothing, nobody. Again the black hole, the daily first sensation of paralysis, again that chasm between her and her child. In the haste of planning, she had not anticipated this. The possibility that Ramón wouldn't come to pick her up but would leave her there, stranded in a void, had not even occurred to her. She had considered a thousand other adverse contingencies, but not that one. Again she felt aimless and without a possible plan of action, again at zero, in pure anguish. Blood drained to her feet and her ears buzzed. She breathed deeply so as not to collapse, and then saw Miche walking toward her. Ramón had commissioned his brother to receive her, and he had been running late.

"Miche helped me with the suitcase and we took a taxi to the Avenida la Plata Station together," Lorenza told Mateo. "From there we took the metro to Plaza de Mayo, changed to line A and rode to Castro Barros, where we got off and took a taxi back, with Miche always looking back, checking and counterchecking to verify that we were not being followed."

"Followed by whom?" Mateo asked.

"My people, I suppose. Now that my people were the enemy. Suddenly everything we did made both the Iribarren brothers and me seem very pathetic. One of the strangest games. And ridiculous on top of that, for when Miche had arrived late to the airport, or rather from the beginning had blown the operation, the very first thing he said to me was not to tell Ramón that he had arrived late because Ramón would give him shit for it. How not to think of Marx, who said that the events in history happen the first time as tragedy and the second time as comedy. What was happening to us now was ridiculous and at the same time terrifying, because you were involved."

"And you complain of Wei-Wulong on my PlayStation."

"Wei-Wulong is a naïve child compared with these full-metal warriors that we had become, kicking each other in the groin."

"Why are we going around in circles?" Lorenza said to Miche. "Nobody's following us, I came alone, I swear. I'm not the enemy, Miche, I am just a poor woman who wants to see her son. I'm tired, come on, save me the fares."

"I have nothing to do with this, *che*," Miche replied. "I follow orders."

"We finally arrived at a building in Palermo," Lorenza told Mateo. "And don't ask me how, with my terrible sense of direction, I managed to record in my head every turn, every block, every traffic light, to the point that I could repeat today the labyrinthine journey we undertook that night. From the moment I landed at Ezeiza, and until I had you with me safely back in Bogotá, I made it my business to know exactly where I was standing."

Lorenza asked Miche how Mateo was and he said that he was enjoying himself, those were his exact words, and she didn't know whether to interpret them as naïve or sarcastic.

She did her best not to get agitated. She couldn't afford to lose control. Foremost, she needed a cool head, every step and every word had to be calculated, so she shut her mouth and walked in silence, amid tension you could slice with a knife, until they reached a furnished apartment, apparently uninhabited, at the building in Palermo, and Miche told her to take the bedroom, he'd sleep on the sofa in the living room. Then he ordered a pizza that they ate in silence, or rather that he ate almost entirely on his own because she hardly ate, either out of courtesy or hypocrisy.

It was all very strange. To Lorenza it was surreal to be there in that impersonal place, a sort of anteroom or limbo, on the journey to Mateo, with Uncle Miche acting as her jailer, but at the same time her guide, the one who would take her to her son. After they ate, Miche asked her if she wanted to watch TV for a while and she said maybe not, and he also asked if she wanted to shower, since the trip had been so long, and she accepted, said it would do her some good, so he struggled for a long time to light the boiler but in the end failed, and said it was better this way, better to go to sleep, because the next day they'd have to leave no later than six in the morning, and she was infinitely glad they'd start early and she asked where they'd be going, but he repeated that she had to have patience.

"What are we playing, Miche?" Lorenza confronted him.

"Don't ask me. I don't understand anything, I do what I am told and ciao, this dump stands between Ramón and you."

"You've always been a good guy," she said, or rather begged.

"Why don't you sleep a little, *piba*, you're exhausted."

Miche seemed to understand her appeal and took her hands for a moment. "Mateo is fine and you're going to see him tomorrow. As sure as my name is Miguel, you'll be with him tomorrow, I swear by my mother."

The bedroom had a double bed but she couldn't lie down. She paced from one side of the room to the other so as not to explode with impatience, six steps from one wall to the other, back and forth, back and forth, just as she'd done the night before the birth, in the Hospital Ramón Sardá, in Parque Patricios, the very popular Maternidad Sardá, when she refused painkillers and refused to go to bed, while Ramón, his mother, the internists, and the nurses tried to convince her to rest, but she just wanted to be left alone to walk through the halls, up and down, up and down. You'll be exhausted when the time comes, Ramón tried to reason with her. But she wouldn't stop, couldn't stop, walking and walking all night, stopping only when the contractions doubled her over and she realized she was early: the labor, expected for eight or nine in the morning, began at five. They were not able to get her doctor and she had to be attended by the internist, and they couldn't apply the epidural because the child was already on the way. She never even reached the delivery room and there on the couch, she realized that the moment had arrived and that she would have to make a brutal effort.

The cataclysm shook her, she felt her bones rattle and a pain so intense took possession of her that it was no longer pain, she thought, must have had some other name, since it was more like a force, and not only hers but a force of nature that zeroed in on her body and would intensify to an unbearable degree. And then came peace. She held on to the most serene creature she had ever seen, a little boy with delicate features and amazing, tiny, perfect hands, as comfortable in the world as he had been for nine months in her belly, gentle, like a gurgle of joy that so often announced itself with a slight kick, and that at the same time was a powerful presence, terrifying and overwhelming. And there he was, as close to her as before the birth but even more so, because now she could see him in the clear light of day, and maybe he saw it too, and perceived the intensity of that first blue morning of his existence.

Mamaíta, who as agreed upon the night before arrived at the hospital at six thirty, rested and ready and in flat shoes, so that she could remain by her side during the long, hard task of delivery, was caught by surprise by a nurse who was standing in a rectangle of sky against an open window, the baby wrapped in white cloth.

"It's a beautiful boy," she announced.

Now, two and a half years later, in that room in a half-empty apartment in the neighborhood of Palermo, Lorenza leaned back at last, around three in the morning. She did so with the deliberate purpose to rest awhile, to deal with what was waiting for her the next day, whatever it was, with her senses alert.

"From the other side of the door, I could hear the sound of the old movies your uncle Miche was watching on TV, one after the other," she told Mateo.

He couldn't sleep, either.

"Was he keeping an eye on you?"

"Maybe. The phone and the door were on his side, to make sure I remained incommunicado. I didn't care, hadn't really planned to communicate with anyone. Before seven in the morning, we were at Aeroparque Jorge Newbery and at eight were flying to San Carlos de Bariloche."

Bariloche, of course, thought Lorenza. You might have guessed it, where else would they be if not in Bariloche, Ramón's dream place, his refuge, his Utopia, but also a convenient spot for him and unfavorable for her, horribly difficult for executing any escape plan. Located in Andean Patagonia, near the tip of the continent, some two thousand kilometers from Tierra del Fuego and the antarctic circle, Bariloche was at that time a settlement area rather isolated from the rest of the world, a place she had never been and that he knew well from his work there as a guide for mountain excursions. During the flight, Miche kindly warned Lorenza that Mateo would not be at the airport, so she dampened any expectation and its consequent disappointment for this new landing.

Miche had in his pocket the keys to a white Chevrolet Impala that was there waiting for them. Without saying anything, they drove east, away from the town, which Lorenza inferred was a few kilometers from the Chilean border. She took advantage of the silence to engrave in her mind every name that appeared on the road: Lago Nahuel Huapi, Pioneers Road, Virgen de las Nieves, El Retorno Hostel.

Then they veered onto a road that led uphill to the cathedral, as indicated by the arrow at the crossing. The road narrowed and became steep without signs of any sort. About forty-five minutes after leaving the airport, they came upon a valley on the banks of another lake. Small log cabins peeked through the trees, a considerable distance from one another. If she had not been calculating how she was going to dash off to Chile, she would have had to acknowledge that this was one of the most beautiful corners of the planet. Miche stopped the Impala next to one of the huts. Lorenza got out and soon saw, approaching through the woods, coming down the mountain, riding an old horse, a man with a small child.

❋

"Is THAT OFFER to go skiing still valid?" asked Mateo, apropos of nothing.

"You said you didn't want to."

"I didn't want to before, I want to now."

"Then say no more," Lorenza replied, enthused. "Tomorrow is my last commitment. At noon, I'm free, and we'll be in Bariloche by nightfall. How nice you changed your mind, kiddo. This is the best news. Can you imagine? We can stay five or six days, and up to eight if we get a little cabin at a good price, or a couple of rooms in a pretty hostel, there must be one that's not too expensive, it's not yet high season. We can rent clothes and equipment there, so that'll be no problem."

"Not with you, Lolé," said Mateo gently, but it was as if someone had struck her on the head.

"Not with me?"

"I'd like to go, but without you."

"What do you mean, without me?"

"I really want to go. But without you."

"What about me? What do I do in the meantime?"

"You wait for me here in Buenos Aires."

Mateo must have been saturated with the constant presence of his mother, with the irremediable absence of his father, with adult stories, with claustrophobic days of Dynasty Warriors, so much anxiety and so much twirling the lock on his forehead with his forefinger, listening to dramas of times gone by during the resistance. It was only natural for him to be tired of roaming between ghosts, and he deserved to have a good time outdoors, in the present, with people his own age. Lorenza understood, why wouldn't she understand, it was perfectly understandable, and at the same time not so much. What happened to her eternal comrade? Why did he want to leave her behind? There was something there that was not entirely fair, and she too could use some air, some exercise. Mateo thought that her skiing was awful and he wasn't wrong, but she still loved it. And Mateo knew it, knew how happy she was coming down the mountain, even if she fell and had to get up ten times. Also, she very often dreamed of snow, had a veritable obsession with snow, maybe because she was born in the tropics and up until sixteen years ago, when she had flown to meet him, had to be content with wintry landscapes from pictures on boxes of cookies and Christmas cards.

But how could she keep her son from going alone, if only the day before she would have loved to have been rid of him, seen him as independent and active, passionate about something, instead of holed up in his room, his neurons electrocuted by the PlayStation. So why did she feel diminished now, as if she'd gone from high heels to barefoot, and why would she not be able to enjoy those five days without Mateo? It was only five days and she had so many people to see in Buenos Aires, so many things to do, why be sad if, after all, she had not fallen from a train, or been thrown out of a party. Though maybe she had, a bit.

She'd wait for him at Gabriela's house. She'd catch up with her old comrades, continuing to recover fragments of the old days. All right: she would stay and Mateo would go. And if the decision had been made, there was no time to lose, they had to find a winter camping site, or a ski school, so that he would be with a group and a good instructor.

"Then you're not going to call Ramón?" She hadn't wanted to say it, but she did, and was startled to realize she'd pulled one last trick out of her sleeve in order to keep him there.

Mateo ducked the question and did not respond. It was better that he didn't. It was only fair that they surrender in this first effort to find his father. They had done enough and could one day return to continue the search. For now his thoughts were aimed at other things. First of all, he wanted a new backpack; he felt that the suitcase he'd brought was no good, the others on the trip would have backpacks, and he did not want to be the only one with an old-man suitcase.

"Think about it, Lolé. It doesn't go with my personality."

They bought a red backpack with many straps and compartments, which Mateo felt was more in tune with his personality, and Lorenza was pleased to see him so happy, delighted to see him excited about his own plans. Then they fought about a new pair of boots. She insisted on getting some boots suited for the snow but he refused to go along. He claimed that there was no need and that he didn't even feel like trying them on, but she piled on her convincing arguments, so he gave up and they bought them. They went to several travel agencies to shop around and compare prices, made a second round, studied catalogs, looked at photos, and finally opted for a complete package, including airfare, accommodation, food, equipment rental, lessons, and a lift pass. They bought a pair of thermal gloves and again argued, this time about whether it would be necessary to get a warmer scarf. He won, and they didn't buy a scarf. The next day, at eleven o'clock in the morning, they were at Aeroparque Jorge Newbery, looking for the place where Mateo was to meet his fellow travelers.

Life biting its own tail. There she was, saying goodbye to Mateo at exactly the place where years earlier she had taken the plane to Bariloche to go looking for him. She thought about telling him, to make him aware of the coincidences, the tricks of time as it pursues itself and reconnects, closing cycles and opening new ones. But she said nothing, obviously this was not the time.

Mateo had on a new face. He was illuminated, as if he had opened some door to the world and a stream of light had poured over him. He was going back to Bariloche, a teenager, wearing the *Bridges to Babylon* shirt he had bought at the Rolling Stones concert, a little skittish but radiant by the time he approached the other boys and girls going on the trip, sixteen in total, with a couple of ski instructors, two polite, athletic women, at home in their roles as those responsible for the group, who gave Mateo an effusive welcome and introduced him to the others in the group, some new, like him, but most veterans of several winters, making the same trip with the same people. They called for their plane to board over the PA and Mateo ran after the crowd, lugging his red backpack and without saying goodbye. He was so excited that he didn't even realize he hadn't said goodbye to his mother, and she had to simply wave with her hand, in case he turned to look at her.

"I stood there like an idiot, and I swear I had to make an effort not to cry," she told her friend Gabriela a few hours later.

"The orphan of your son," replied Gabriela. "I know that sad figure well."

Lorenza headed for the window to look at the runway, to make sure that Mateo boarded the right plane, when someone shoved her from behind and almost made her fall.

"Goodbye, Lolé, I love you very much." It was Mateo, who rushed to hug her and ran back to catch up with the others.

She had accepted the invitation to spend the week in Gabriela's apartment, at 6000 Zelada Street, in the Mataderos neighborhood on the outskirts of Buenos Aires.

"It's full of fuzz," said Gabriela, passing her hand over a table, which was covered in gray dust. "My lungs must be full of lint. It's because of my job, I embroider here at home, and the fabric and threads shed lint."

"You embroider?"

"Yes. Sheets, towels, linens, baby clothes, trousseaus—"

"By hand?"

"My old lady embroidered by hand, what beautiful things she made; not me, I work with machines."

"So that's why you gave me those dozen little embroidered shirts when Mateo was born."

"You haven't forgotten," said Gabriela while making the bed on the living-room sofa, after picking up and piling on the floor against the walls the dozens of bundles the sofa had been buried under.

"What are they?" asked Lorenza, who had once again become Aurelia, because that's how Gabriela knew her and what she still called her.

"Sheets. One hundred twenty-seven sets of sheets, which I need to have embroidered, ironed, and ready to go by Monday. Monograms in blue, look: like this, RCH, Rochester Classic Hotel, the place the order is for."

Her workshop was right there in the apartment, so they had all the time they wanted to talk, as long as Aurelia let her work and helped if she wanted, steam ironing, pressing the sheets and pillowcases after they'd been embroidered, so that the delivery could be made on time.

They used to meet in the Basilica of San José de Flores, when they were both active in the front lines of the resistance. According to the minute they had agreed upon, they met in the alcove behind the altar, overseen from the vault by a young Christ Pantocrator who inspired them with confidence. There, they knelt with rosary in hand and pretended to pray as a duo. Hail Mary full of grace, and interspersed their Hail Marys with party information, blessed art thou among women, planning the activities of the week; and since both were pregnant, before leaving they sprinkled their bellies with holy water, to protect the children.

"Holy water, what nonsense," said Gabriela.

"If it didn't do any good, at least it caused no harm."

"Modesto Zupichín."

"Lucil Lucifora."

"Lomolino Lomo."

"Abramo Lomazo."

They recalled the list of names for their babies which they had found in the pages of the Buenos Aires telephone book, betting to see who could find the most absurd one, Dora Lota, Lubli Lea, Tufik Salame, Delfor Malanga.

"Delfor Malanga, flower name," said Gabriela. "And to think that you ended up naming the kid Mateo."

"And you, Mary, maybe because of the many rosaries that we prayed in San José de Flores."

"Can you handle the iron?"

"I am a tigress with the iron, *mi papito lindo* had a seamstress's shop."

"In the days of your *papito lindo* there were no steam irons."

"I am a tigress with the steam iron."

"You know who I still see occasionally, Tina, do you remember Tina?"

"Tina, the one from the elevator, how could I not remember. How is Tina?"

"She has two grown sons, both college graduates. She is now retired from teaching. She was a teacher."

"She must have been older than us. Five or six years older. Have you ever asked her about it?"

"About that? She told me without my asking. She said she had felt a sense of relief."

"Relief?"

"Yes, relief."

"*Madre mía*."

"She said that when she saw that the *cana* was behind her and got into the elevator, she thought he'd been following her and that it would be her fault that her comrades in the floor above, waiting for her to begin the meeting, got nabbed. She says that at the time she wanted to die, and therefore when the guy raped her, then got out of the elevator and ran away from the building, among everything else that she felt was that: relief. She had been raped but she was alive, and the ones who were waiting for her were still alive, had not disappeared, had not been murdered. And she felt relief."

"You think so?"

"It's what she told me."

"Could it be—"

"Do you remember Tebas, the one who always came to the meetings with a younger brother, Nandito, who was severely retarded?"

"Tebas was disappeared, that I heard."

"He was the last disappeared one of the party, at the time the military junta was about to fall. I don't know if you know about Nandito. They grabbed him with Tebas and disappeared him as well."

"Bastards. He must have been the most innocent of all the victims. He had such a sweet expression, Nandito."

"Sweet, yes, but he masturbated in front of people."

"Hush, what?"

"I swear, you don't know what a fuss it caused during the meetings when he started up with that. Tebas suffered tremendously, but what could he do, he couldn't very well bind his hands."

"As if that would warrant it."

"Crazy, right?"

"And Felicitas, do you remember her? The lawyer I introduced to you once."

"Yes, quite the number that one, from Barrio Norte, she was wearing a red fox coat that one time we saw her, imposing with her Gucci handbag and suede boots."

"Yes, that one. We became good friends. But just friends, no politics, friends to go to the movies with, talk about books and such. And last week I was with her and guess what, she told me that during that time she defended money launderers. I would never have suspected it, would swear she had nothing to do with anything, until recently, when she told me."

"Just look at her—"

"That's exactly what I told her. I told her that she looked

so elegant in her aristocratic office, I wouldn't dare open my mouth around her. She told me that she'd never been left wing and wasn't part of the resistance, but that on becoming a lawyer she had sworn to uphold elementary principles, as old as the French Revolution, and could not stand idly by before farcical trials and arbitrary sentences."

"Who'd believe it, with that red fox coat?"

"Well, look, that famous red fox coat was her lifeline, her bulletproof vest. She told me that thanks to the red fox she went in and out of the superior court of the armed forces without arousing suspicion of being a lefty."

"She, since she's tall, white, thin as a sigh; if I put that thing on I would be stopped right there for being a fox and a red."

"She said she did suspect that I was involved in something, that it was strange that I had no phone, never specified exactly where I lived, that if she wanted to invite me to something, she could never find me. That had seemed weird, but she didn't dare ask or bring up the topic."

"Nobody dared, that's the truth. We all knew everything but pretended not to know, even to those we considered close. Those who say they were unaware in fact did not want to know, because no one went without an acquaintance or relative who disappeared. For me, the first rattling was the disappearance of Mariana, my best friend from childhood, just because her name was in the address book of a militant. We were all witnesses. We knew that others knew, but never said anything. I had to do militant things hidden from my husband, and that should tell you everything." Gabriela confessed that she was now separated from the bank employee.

"He sympathized with the junta, your husband?"

"Not at all, but he was fucking scared."

Fear: another thing that no one dared mention. No militant ever said he or she was afraid, ever. As if simply by not naming it, you could escape it.

Lorenza told Gabriela about the days with her mother, who had come to Buenos Aires to be with her for childbirth, and her life with Mateo as a newborn and beyond, Mateo taking his first steps, and then confessed that, at that stage in her life, she had felt afraid. To be able to continue their work in the resistance, she and Ramón had decided to enroll Mateo in day care from the time he was three months old, the Jardín Pelusa on Avenida Santa Fe, and every afternoon, took turns picking him up at four o'clock.

"That was the face of fear for me," she confessed. "I became obsessed with the idea that if something happened to us one day, to Ramón or me, that four in the afternoon would come around and there'd be no one to pick up Mateo."

She had taken to thinking about it all the time and, as much as she tried, could not get the idea out of her head. She began to panic and picked up Mateo from the crib, to hug him, and then he'd wake up and she had to put him to sleep again. "Until then I hadn't known what anxiety was." Not the time that she had to escape from her house through the roof, nor when she'd granted San Jacinto to the party, signing the notarized papers and saying goodbye to her only inheritance.

She didn't remember having been afraid during the twenty-four hours she had been detained at a police station in Icho Cruz, convinced that she would not walk out alive. Shock, yes, and adrenaline by the bucketful, also heart palpitations and vertigo at the adventure, all that. But not fear. Fear, what is really called fear, that shadow of the enemy that invades you and defeats you little by little from within. That she had never experienced. Until Mateo was born.

Thereafter, the image of the abandoned child at the Jardín Pelusa, of the hundreds of children who were taken from prisoners and given up for adoption to military families, the possibility that something similar could happen to Mateo, gradually became a terror that sapped her strength. She bore it as well as she could, without a word, until Mateo was two years old and on the day when the boy blew out his pair of candles, she announced to Ramón her decision to take him away for a while. Much to her surprise, Ramón agreed. Not only did he not argue, nor reprimand her, or call her weak, or insult her, but he told her that he would go with them. For Mateo. For Mateo to grow up far away from the circle of death and breathe air that was free of threats. A month later, the three set off for Colombia, having made the decision to leave the party and to stay away at least a few months.

Amid clouds of steam and fuzz, the sputtering steam iron, and the hum of the sewing machine, they continued their chat laden with secrets that had never been revealed and indeed would never be mentioned again. The sheets, embroidered and ironed, piled up, and they had to be sorted into sets—fitted sheets, flat sheets, and pillowcases—then wrapped in tissue paper and placed carefully in a box. And it was there in Gabriela's apartment where Lorenza thought she finally had found the tone that would allow her to write, now, yes, that chapter in their history. She needed to put into words this story that had been so far marked by silence. She had always known that sooner or later the task would have to be taken up, there was no way around it, because the past that has not been tamed with words is not memory, only a sort of spying.

The problem had been how to tell it, and now she thought she had figured it out: simple, intimate as a conversation between two women reminiscing behind closed doors. No heroes, no adjectives, no slogans. In a minor key. Without delving minutely into major events, keeping just the echo, to wrap it in tissue paper, like the sheets, to see if it finally stopped beating and, little by little, began to yellow. Yes, wrapped in the silky tissue paper, maybe that's exactly what was needed: for the chatter, the laughter, the interweaving of moments and pains, the small confessions—these would smoothly envelop the old fear, reducing it to the realm of everyday gossip.

⁂

"I GET OUT of the car in the middle of the snowy mountains that I knew only through Ramón's dreams, a place that for me was not part of any map, but from the stories and songs he improvised as nursery rhymes for Mateo," Lorenza tells

Gabriela. "And suddenly out of nowhere there comes a horse, and on that horse is Ramón, and Ramón has my child. And he gives me the child. I swear, not even when he was born did I feel such a commotion, as if I was giving birth again, but after a much more difficult labor. There he was with me, my baby Mateo. I kissed him and hugged him; poor little one, he must have been suffocating from so much squeezing, but I couldn't stop, I had to be convinced that this was real."

It was the only real thing in that landscape of an imaginary postcard holiday, where snow bleached everything and settled everywhere, hiding the face of things. But there was her son. Everything else faded around her, like during a dizzy spell or a hallucination. But Mateo was laughing, he had learned to say new words, and was wearing a red cap: he was amazingly real. Fortunately real.

"I kissed his nose, his eyes, his hair, his hands, his laughing strawberry mouth, his soft skin. I planted kisses even on the yellow boots he wore."

"Mateo has been waiting for you," came the voice of Ramón.

"I couldn't look at him, Gabriela. At Ramón. I couldn't do it."

"How you must have hated him."

"That wasn't the problem, hatred in the end can be handled. But it wasn't pure, it was mixed with gratitude, even reverence, that ruinous gratitude, the odious veneration that you bear your abuser when you pardon him. That's why I didn't want to look at him."

"I explained to Mateo that we were on vacation, him and me," Ramón's voice said, "and that you would take some days to catch up with us because you had a lot of work, but that you were coming."

"I realized then that Mateo didn't know," Lorenza told Gabriela, "and I felt a huge relief. If the boy was happy it was because he didn't know about the drama and behaved as if he were on vacation, fascinated with the snow and the horse, with the fire in the hearth and the water of the lake. Ramón told me things. He told me that Mateo was in love with the horse, that the first night he had wanted to bring the horse into the cabin so that he would not be cold, and that he had no choice but to go out and show him the stable where the horse was asleep. The stable at the neighbor's place, from whom they rented the horse. I noted the fact, neighbors nearby, I might ask them for help. And there were horses. They might not be Bucephaluses, but they had four working legs. If I couldn't get hold of a car, I would flee with the boy on the horse."

"Great," said Gabriela, "with your eyelashes frozen like in *Doctor Zhivago*."

"It was cold as shit, and very dark," Ramón's voice kept saying, "you couldn't see a thing, and Mateo and I at midnight, with the flashlight, looking for the stable."

There was a flashlight, Lorenza registered; she had to figure out where he kept it. She looked around and saw no electrical wires. Doing all this while making efforts to look at Ramón, to say something nice.

"Something nice? With how you were feeling?" said Gabriela.

"Anything, that I had missed him, or that the scenery was beautiful, whatever, but nothing came out. I had come to play in the cold and I wasn't succeeding. I had to overcome it, to make him think that I was glad to see him."

"But what could he expect of you? He couldn't really believe that everything would be as before."

"I knew exactly what I expected of him: nothing. I had gone there to get my son, period. Now what he expected from me, I don't know, I'd have to guess at it."

"Did he believe that this was really a reconciliation?"

"Difficult to say, Ramón is anything but naïve. Oh yes, maybe he was acting in good faith. Like I said, I was a little out of it. I needed time to devise a way to take Mateo with me, and meanwhile I had to remain on good terms with Ramón. On good terms, by his lights, of course, that is, in tune with this love story that I was supposedly starting over.

"It was all very strange, Gabriela. My head was a mess. How could I make sense of the fact that the boor, who a month before had taken my child and put me in grave danger by stealing money from the Mafia, was this loving father, this Prince Charming who came out to meet me like in a fairy tale. What logic was there in that? And while he looked at me, I felt that he couldn't take his eyes off me, and that he was in the same situation, with horrible doubts about me. We both tried to appear spontaneous but we were walking on eggshells. He didn't have a full advantage, either. I relaxed a little when I realized that."

"You can rest easy," the voice said. "Mateo didn't have a single bad moment, all that was missing was his mother, and here she is."

It must have been true, she saw no signs of anxiety or discomfort in Mateo. He looked as radiant as ever. He seemed very proud of his wool pullover, red with green-and-blue dolls and a matching cap, clothes that she had never seen, which the father must have bought. It was clear that of all the marvels in Mateo's unexpected paradise, the father was by far his favorite. And now also her, the mother, who came without his ever suspecting that she might not have made it there.

She had to remain lucid, have a clear picture of the place, and make decisions quickly. But it was hard to think. Her head sent her contradictory messages, as if Mateo's unexpected joy cast a light on the dark episode. Because if things had not been, after all, as atrocious as she had imagined, she could well have made up the whole nightmare.

"You're skinny," Ramón said, shattering the illusion. He had dropped the phrase as if it were not his fault, as if every kilo lost was not a result of the agony of waiting.

"He asked if I wanted to eat," she tells Gabriela. "He said he was going to pop open some burgundy to celebrate my arrival. Impudence, I finally saw it in his face as he spoke. I told him I'd rather unpack first."

"Great."

"It was really something. And he said: Come, I'll show you the cabin, you'll see, it's like the house of Hansel and Gretel.

"And he takes my suitcase out of the Impala along with the briefcase with the double bottom, false passports, and the Revlon cosmetics bag with those lethal drops. My blood half froze, but my bag did not give me away, I told you it was a *vaina* for professionals. Now, the cabin was beautiful, tiny and cozy with the fireplace going, something out of *Robinson Crusoe*. Ramón's comparison maybe had not been well thought out; in the story of Hansel and Gretel, the sweet little house turns out to be a place of terror."

Lorenza felt that everything there was fictitious, someone putting on a show. She had just spent twenty days and nights preparing for war, had come resolved to confront her enemy, and her enemy was playing the fool.

He received her with open arms as if the matter were forgiven—even worse, as if there wasn't anything to forgive.

"And here I was, coming prepared to poison him."

"Did you really think about the possibility of poison, with the drops?" Gabriela asked.

"Well, no. Not poison him, but leave him dazed. Or in as deep a slumber as Sleeping Beauty, at least. Wouldn't you kill for your Mary?"

"Ah, yes, I would, but I'm crazier than you."

Lorenza sat by the fire, still clutching the child to her chest, thinking of how to break free and carry him away from there. She soon realized that Miche and the white Impala were gone.

"Bad start," said Gabriela.

"Very bad. I wanted to show Mateo what I had learned from my gringa girlfriends in the Washington winter, that if you throw yourself back on the snow and move your arms up and down, you leave behind the stamped figure of an angel with big wings. The first time I saw that I was dazzled, not that I really thought it was an angel. Mateo did not grasp the subtlety of it, however, and thought it was about wallowing in the snow and that seemed fine to him."

"Where's Miche?" Lorenza asked as they walked in, and Ramón replied to forget about Miche, that he'd told him they wanted to be alone, this wasn't Coronda with him coming and going as he pleased. Finally, they had the whole house to themselves.

"Idyllic," says Gabriela.

If there was no Miche, then no Impala, Lorenza thought. It was going to be crazy, the *Escape from Alcatraz* on the frail, old horse. Another thing: she did not see a phone, but dared not ask, since the purpose would have been all too obvious.

"Then he immediately told me, no phone, and his voice no longer sounded so friendly, as if he had read my thoughts and was offended. Or maybe not, maybe he wasn't offended, because he came and went, placing the food on the table. It was exhausting to be trying to even minimally gauge all his signals."

There was bread, ham, lamb, goat cheese, and something which he said was traditional winter pears with raspberry sauce. Ramón went to fetch wood from the huge pile outside, then crouched to stoke the fire, and next went looking for wineglasses. She was helping him, but meanwhile she measured his steps and movements, and scrutinized every corner of the house.

"That place was a prison, so coldly polite and calculating," she says to Gabriela. "A prison with doors that led nowhere. But we ate well, all three of us, and I did what I never do, I had two glasses of wine."

"You don't drink wine?"

"Not red, it gives me a headache. But that day I did, and we even toasted."

"Hard to imagine, that toast. I hope it was for happiness."

"Fortunately, no. We toasted Mateo, and we both left it at that."

The cottage had a kerosene stove on the lower level, the table where they ate and a couple of chairs facing the fireplace, and an attic-like loft that was reached by a ladder, where there was a double bed and another small one, toward the back. Ramón had placed the small one there, against the wall, and the double perpendicular to it, blocking it. So that Mateo did not go headfirst over the railing if he got up in the middle of the night and wanted to go looking for the horse, he said, adding that he would have to pass over them.

"There's sawdust, there must be termites in the beams," said Lorenza, shaking the blankets, but she was thinking that she too would have to pass over Ramón if she tried to take the child at night. Even with that, he was calculating. Zero chance of not waking him during the operation, unless she used the Revlon needle. The best thing would be to keep the briefcase with the cosmetic bag beside the bed. All of her instruments within reach. But he was quite sturdy, Ramón, she had forgotten just how sturdy. If she decided on the Revlon, she would have to do it viciously, she thought, or else it wouldn't even tickle him. "So I would sleep in the double bed, as well. Apparently it had already been decided."

Did Ramón not remember, would not remember, that they were separated, that they no longer lived together, no longer slept together? Lorenza chose not to protest. She too would play dumb, as long as it was necessary.

"At that instant, Mateo appeared with a package bigger than himself. I unwrapped it and it was a pullover for me. Handwoven by village women, said Ramón. Lovely, really. Open in front, a deep black, with blue-and-white trinkets."

"If it was open it wasn't a pullover."

"A sweater?"

"Nope."

"Then I don't know what the hell it was."

"A cardigan. It must have been a Scandinavian cardigan, back stitch. In Bariloche they make divine ones. I have some from there. Look at this scarf. It's made with Scandinavian backstitch. For the front to come out right, you have to hold the thread through the back. It's really not that complicated."

"But they also gave me a black cap, which I used for many years, who knows where I lost it, and snow boots, furlined. Well chosen, wouldn't you know, just my size. My heart melted to see Mateo's enthusiasm, the jumps and hops when he saw the three of us with our outfits on, looking like forest gnomes. I hugged them. Both of them. They had caught me by surprise with this generosity, Gabriela, how was I not going to celebrate it."

"I see where this is leading. He was always a charmer, that Forcás."

Hikes were still possible because winter had not yet descended on the region, and that same afternoon they went out to make a brief trek around the property. A short one, Ramón had decided, not going too far, just to warm up, with the kid riding on the horse, held by his leg from below to prevent him from falling. Although Lorenza was determined not to be impressed by anything that would muddle her resolve, the beauty of those snowy heights left her agape and it took her breath away when they contemplated from a peak the entire universe spread at their feet. But she also noticed how deserted the surroundings were. They were alone at the end of the world, and it was neither metaphor nor reassurance. They started to come down the mountainside in the afternoon. Mateo dozed, as if enraptured with the rocking of the horse, and the last rays of the sun spread golden streaks on the locks that escaped from under Ramón's cap. You can't deny it, she thought, the son of a bitch has very pretty hair.

With no electricity, the fireplace was the only source of heat they had. The chimney rose on the wall against the headboards, warming the loft space. It was night, the first one the three of them would spend together in the cabin. Lorenza put pajamas on the boy, who failed to drink his milk before he fell asleep, and she set him down in the small bed. She lay down, wrapped in blankets and without taking off all of her clothes, on the side of the bed nearest Mateo, keeping near the edge, as close as possible to the child, to feel in the darkness his sweet breath. Ramón remained downstairs.

"I didn't want to fall asleep," Lorenza tells Gabriela. "Mateo was with me and I wanted that long-yearned-for moment to last forever. I didn't want to fall asleep, but eventually I did."

The mixture of absolute fatigue and a restored sense of calm made her let her guard down. At least for this night, they would not escape, not even in her dreams could she take Mateo from that heated refuge into the frozen night and across the snowy field to fly through the curtains of sleep on an old horse or in a white car. At some point, she was awakened by the cold.

The fire must have died out. She felt Ramón's body stretched out beside her, facing away. Mateo had crawled to the big bed, leaving the three huddled tight like in a den, with her in the middle.

"And I felt good, Gabriela. What a difference from those tormented sleepless nights that I had spent alone. In times like that I forgot the monstrous things that Ramón had done. Well, and also the monstrous things I'd done to him as well in Bogotá."

But soon enough she remembered the disaster she was in and began plotting an escape. In the end, that cabin was just a trap, a baseless illusion, an untenable, extravagant situation that Ramón had pulled out of his hat to mend things. She would have to raise an invisible barbed-wire fence between them. But she felt his body against hers, and appreciated its warmth.

"Wait a minute," Gabriela said. "I still don't understand what had happened in Bogotá. What do you mean when you say that you were guilty of monstrous things as well? Which ones?"

"Ignoring him, leaving him alone, tossing him to the side when I should have supported him, as he had done with me in Buenos Aires, like he was trying to do again in Bariloche."

"But the measure of the two wrongs is so different. Come on! Taking a child from his mother! Even though it is his own father doing it, it's a brutal tactic that bears some resemblance—*some*, right?—to what the enemy did. I don't understand how you didn't throw it in his face. If it was me, the first thing I would have done was beat him senseless. I'd smash his teeth, shit. You didn't even reproach him for the money?"

"I've told you, it would have screwed everything up. Words were dangerous, Gabriela. I had to avoid them. He did too, he knew the settling of accounts would have ended the game. We talked about other things. About Mateo, mainly; about the cuteness that made Mateo Mateo. The two of us were crazy about the child and there we had no disagreement. And politics, of course. That was during the Falklands War. And we were up there, stuck with our drama and listening to the little battery-powered radio about the godforsaken mess developing below. Our ears glued to that little radio, keeping up with the news, we talked all day long, the two of us alone but like at a party meeting, arguing about whether we should support the Argentinean army in its just claim of a piece of national land. But how could we support such patriotic bluster from the junta, which was only looking to tame the domestic crisis; we shit on the junta but also the imperial vigor with which Thatcher mobilizes the Royal Navy, its Gurkhas, and task forces to continue their dominion over a few coin-size islands that were not theirs and were an ocean away."

Fearful of having to deal with personal issues, they busied themselves with hiking, mountain climbing, chopping firewood, clearing the snow from the road with a shovel, walking beside Mateo on the horse, rowing on the lake: anything that used their muscles, until they collapsed from fatigue. It was the only way they could be together, their busy bodies then less likely to turn aggressive or vengeful, more likely to go with the flow. Ramón, who knew all the ins and outs of those mountains, took them to visit places that had become legendary, since she'd previously heard of them from him, the cave where Slovenian nuns hid, the glacier called Black Snowdrift, the slopes of Cerro Catedral, which led into the waters of Lago Gutiérrez, the peak of Cerro Otto, where they witnessed cosmic sunsets with a cup of hot chocolate in hand. When their excursions brought them to steep cliffs, they'd leave the horse behind and Ramón would carry Mateo on his shoulders.

They paused to dig a crib in the snow, which they lined

with fur, so that the child could drink his milk and take a nap. This crowned their eight- or ten-hour crossing, from sunrise until reaching the refuge of the high mountains, which remained open to every traveler seeking shelter, firewood, and blankets at night. From peak to peak and cliff to cliff, they skirted the depths, like a devil's nose, standing on huge black rocks looking over the void. With one little push, Lorenza thought when she saw Ramón nearing the edge, just a little push and that would be the end of their problem. But he thwarted the initiative as his eyes countered hers, seeming frightened and strange, as if he were plotting exactly the same.

The days succeeded each other, pleasant against all expectation. Not since Coronda had a house welcomed them as this cottage made of tree trunks, where they could shut themselves in while the world turned on the outside. At times Lorenza thought that she was with the handsome and confident Forcás of earlier times, so different from that other grim, jealous, moody one she'd had to deal with in Bogotá. A honeymoon, she thought, somewhat amazed, it's as if we are honeymooning. Who would have thought?

"A somewhat macabre honeymoon. Moreover, there's no honeymoon without sex," says Gabriela.

"There was sex, of course. Not at first, but a bit later, there was. Yes. Good sex."

"I couldn't have done it. In that kind of situation, forget it."

"We never talked about the sex, and even in bed the silences were killing us. But the rest worked, perhaps because I was always outside the physical battlefield. I remember one occasion in particular. We had eaten dinner and we were listening to the radio transmitting these madly triumphant communiqués, which only confirmed that we were losing the war."

The people, who had originally celebrated the recovery of the islands with enthusiasm, now cried out against the slaughter of hundreds of teenage conscripts, poorly trained, badly fed, and dying from the cold, whom the inept bureaucratic superiors abandoned to their fate when the British moved in with all their firepower. The Argentinean patriotic fever became a wave of disappointment and anger in the streets. Rage against deception, against the inefficiency and bravado of those who behaved as butchers domestically but like lambs when facing a foreign army. The media, which just the week before had been bound by censorship, began to ridicule General Menéndez, the military governor of the Falklands, who had just signed the surrender to Moore, commander of the British troops.

"We were there, listening in," Lorenza told Gabriela, when the voice of a Uruguayan journalist from Buenos Aires reaches us, claiming to be on the corner of Diagonal Norte and Florida, where a group of people had taken a policeman's hat and began playing with it, putting it on their heads, passing it from hand to hand. No more fear, we said. And we hugged. Now the dictatorship will go down because the people are not afraid. Buenos Aires had become the burning

Troy. People screaming toward Plaza de Mayo. The police responded timidly, not dispersing the crowd or locking anyone up. General Leopoldo Fortunato Galtieri, head of the junta at the time, who besides being the ideologue of the defeat was an alcoholic, came out drunk on the balcony of Government House, responding to the claims of the crowd with a delirious speech. 'Those who fell are alive and will be sculpted in bronze,' he shouted, and assured them 'that we will be complete masters of our entire destiny total and will light torches as the highest values.'"

"Just that week I had been hospitalized for a stomach ulcer," Gabriela says. "But my sister Alina was out on the streets, even though she didn't understand anything about politics, nothing, and she came to visit very agitated to tell me that something was happening. She was startled, feeling that things were out of control. Suddenly we heard a ruckus outside and I asked Alina to open the window. *Madre mía*, we heard, it's over, it's over, the dictatorship is over."

"In Plaza de Mayo, the drunkard Galtieri was haranguing his nonsense while the people in the street were screaming in his face that it was over. It was almost over, Gabriela, and we were so far away, with those shitty little radios, full of interference and static, so that we couldn't quite hear. Or maybe yes, maybe what we heard was the roar of the collapse."

The war was lost, the dictatorship was being overthrown, and Lorenza and Ramón were gripped by bittersweet feelings—gripped, on one hand, by the euphoria at the ridiculous manner in which the tyrants had perished, on the other, by regret over the conscripts who had been sent to die. On the one hand, victory: the Falklands had overthrown Argentina's military junta. On the other, defeat: it had assured Thatcher's re-election.

"This was turning into a porn movie," Gabriela reminded her, "and now you're telling me a war story."

"Sorry, now for the porn, but it's going to be much shorter. No, nothing; just that we made love that night, how would you say, intensely but with great melancholy, as if that encounter would be our farewell. Ramón knew, that night I realized that he also knew. End of movie."

In keeping with the performance they were each giving, Ramón played his role as lover and father flawlessly. But it was clear that he could not trust her. He never closed his eyes. Miche began to visit often, bringing bottles of water and other provisions, helping with whatever was needed, and during his visits, the Impala was parked out in front of the cabin. But the keys always disappeared. Lorenza had noted that when Miche left them on the table, not five minutes would pass before Ramón put them in his pocket.

When they went down to the town, Lorenza managed to get a few minutes and would memorize street signs and gather information, sometimes she was even able to ask questions, checking bus stops and timetables, car rentals, nearby hotels, maps and roads. Chile had become her secret obsession. If they could only cross the border, they'd be outside his scope.

But during these brief breaks, she was never alone with Mateo. Ramón never left them alone, not in the cabin, or walking, or on the street.

At the cabin, Lorenza played for hours with Mateo, told him stories, doing housework, sitting and reading by the fire. Without feeling any urgency, given this contrived but, after all, placid stagnation of time. Time. Let time run by. After much reflection on the possibilities of escape, she had come to understand that the only thing playing in his favor was the weather. With Mateo already by her side, she would be happy to wait. The magazine had given her an indefinite leave from work. She could wait. Another week, two more weeks, a month. Sooner or later, Ramón would become neglectful. I have been isolated, she thought, but not defeated. If space is your tool, the weather will be mine. And let the hours run, always waiting for the right moment.

Now and then she was surprised to wake up and the father had already dressed the child and fed him breakfast, or taken him out for a ride. One of those mornings, she heard male voices down below the loft. A neighbor had come to ask for help, some repair in his cabin. Lorenza opened her eyes and saw the thick sky through the window. Strange thing, it always dawned clear, but a little later the sky always seemed lower, woolly, heavy. Heaven's donkey belly, she thought, that's what they call this kind of sky in Lima. Ramón came up. "Here's Mateo. Keep an eye on the baby, I'm leaving him here with you," he said.

"Are you going to see about the neighbor?"

"No, Miche is going to help him. I put cookies on the table, apples and tea, go down to breakfast anytime."

"Donkey belly, donkey belly," she tickled Mateo on the tummy.

Getting out from under the cold blankets, she felt how cold the house was. The fire must have died out. Strange, Ramón always kept it going.

"Ramón?" she called to him several times, and getting no answer, threw a blanket over her shoulders and went down with the child to stir up the fire.

"It went out," Mateo said, and it was true.

Ramón was not in the house, but he had to be around. She left the child on the carpet, entertaining himself with his old serpets, and looked out the window, feeling strange about the silence. The snow that had fallen during the night had erased the line between sky and land, leaving everything in a single confused vagueness. Large footprints, of three pairs of feet, moved away from the house and were lost to the left. Lorenza went out to examine them closely. These were Ramón's, she was sure, recognizing the zigzag marks they left with their imprint and the little circle with the make in the center. There was no mistaking it. Unless Miche was wearing them . . . and then where was Ramón? Lorenza looked around the cabin and did not see him.

But the Impala was parked here, dappled with mud, blending into the landscape. She went for a closer look. On the floor of the front seat, in the rear. There was nothing, why would there be? She returned to the cabin and saw the keys.

There, without much ado, on the table. The keys to the car. Like in a dream. So obvious that it seemed strange that she hadn't noticed them before. Then she picked up Mateo and climbed to the attic, slowly, so as not to trip with her eagerness, step by step, ceremoniously.

"Donkey belly, donkey belly, Mateo," and she tickled him with one hand, while with the other she struggled to put his coat on him and switch the yellow slippers to boots. She dressed with what was near at hand and grabbed the money and passports, which she had hidden behind one of the shutters, in case Ramón became suspicious of the old suitcase.

"It had been quite a task hiding it, loosening the boards of the shutter and then readjusting them."

"And the Revlon?" Gabriela asks. "I have to know, the Revlon?"

"I had buried it days before. Away from the cabin. Fearing Mateo would inadvertently find it and begin to play with it."

She went down the stairs with the child in her arms, pausing again at each step, as if life depended on the slowness of her movements. She did not ask herself if she wanted to or had to do what she was doing; she acted like one obeying a command. She put the apples, the package of crackers, and a pacifier for Mateo into the bag. She looked around, peered out the windows, and saw that the world was motionless. No one approached. Then she did it, she took the keys, which as if by magic were still there on the table, waiting for her. Heroes or buffoons, she said as she was leaving the cabin, and taking Mateo by the hand, she walked toward the Impala. She took the time that was necessary to remove frost from the windshield, buckled Mateo in the backseat, put the briefcase next to him, and when she shut the door was startled at the possibility that the noise would have betrayed them. She looked around again. The footprints of Ramón and the other men were being erased by the snow that was beginning to fall. The entire universe seemed calm.

She sat at the wheel with the parsimony that comes with any inevitable decision, releasing the emergency brake, shifting the gear into neutral, and then the immense Impala of its own volition, as if it knew exactly what was expected of it, gently rolled down the slope, gently complicit, mute as the snow, invisible in the falling snow, lovely as the mantle of snow that gave them camouflage. Twenty minutes later, the Impala pulled up to the road crossing. She had not expected much traffic, but when she saw a Volkswagen headed toward the village, she got out of the Impala and made some hand signals. The woman driving stopped immediately and offered them a ride, asking if the car had broken down, and thus saving Lorenza the need to make up excuses. Without looking back, knowing instinctively that no one had come after them and acting as if the day belonged to her, Lorenza left the keys in the Impala and the window half closed, so that Miche and Ramón wouldn't have any problems when they found it. She got into the Volkswagen with the child and the bag. On the way, the women spoke about the dangers of winter driving on such a bumpy road, and she thanked her when she left them in the central square of San Carlos de Bariloche, in front of the town hall.

Until then everything had been suspiciously easy, but suddenly Mateo began to cry, a rare thing for him, who until recently had done so little, but just at that moment he unleashed a fit of disconsolate and uncontrollable weeping, as if leaving a path of tears that Ramón could follow until he found him. He didn't stop crying when they stopped to pet a sweet dog who waited for its owner at the entrance to a shop, or when Lorenza bought a cupcake decorated with yellow-and-pink icing, or when she sat him by the window of the bus that would take them along Lago Nahuel Huapi and through ancient forests to Puyehue, at the Chilean border, where authorities would let them pass after stamping the false documentation that Lorenza would give them. Mateo only calmed down and stopped whimpering when his mother pointed to a herd of deer on the shores of the lake, searching for something to graze on under the snow.

⁂

EVERY NIGHT, FROM Gabriela's apartment, Lorenza called Mateo at the hostel where he was staying with his group. She wanted to know if Bariloche brought back memories for her son, if the mountains seemed familiar to him, but he was kept very busy and nostalgia wasn't his thing. Sometimes he didn't answer the phone because he'd gone dancing with the others at a nightclub, or there was such a racket in his room that he couldn't hear a thing, or he was already nodding off to sleep after a long day of skiing, or he was in a hurry because they were waiting for him to go ice-skating.

When they finally spoke, during the brief minutes when they could talk, Mateo told her how he'd gone down the red runs without a problem, but not so much the black-diamond one, although he had dared to try a short but terrifying stretch of the black-diamond run.

"A crazy cliff, Lolé, you know, I said to myself, heroes or buffoons, and threw myself behind others to see what the hell would happen. And nothing happened to me, I swear, on that mother of black runs I was a hero. Well, I did lose a glove, so there was a little bit of the buffoon, too, sorry. Lolé, what crap, I lost one of the great thermal gloves that you bought me, but I went on skiing and by the afternoon, my hand was numb and all purple."

"How can you ski without gloves, Mateo, why didn't you tell the instructor that you lost it?"

"Do you think Ulrica goes around with a bag of spare gloves?"

"Ulrica?"

"My instructor. She's an Olympic champion, Lorenza, what do you think? Well not anymore, now she teaches, but when she was younger, she was on the Argentinean team and competed in the Winter Olympics. Don't worry, tomorrow I'll see what I can do."

"Buy another pair, Mateo, promise me not to go skiing

without gloves. It's crazy, your fingers will freeze off, no one can ski without gloves."

"I'm not going to buy more gloves. They're very expensive here, I'm not going to waste money on that."

"Listen to me, Mateo, buy some gloves, don't start torturing me," she tried to tell him, but he said goodbye because they were calling him for dinner.

"Guess what, Lorenza?" he announced to her that night, when they finally managed to talk a little longer. "Can you believe it? I found a glove and fixed the problem."

"You found a glove? Incredible, kiddo, really incredible. And was it the right hand?"

"Yes, the right hand, and my size."

"Lucky Mateo, it only happens to you, now you can ski to your heart's—"

"No, you don't get it! I found my glove, the one I lost yesterday, but I hadn't lost it, it was stuffed in the bottom of my pocket and I didn't realize it."

Sunday came and the trips ended: Mateo's trip to Bariloche, and their joint trip to Argentina. Lorenza was upset because she couldn't get in touch with her son. They had to plan things well for the next day, carefully plot the moves from airport to airport, and meet up to take the plane together back to Bogotá.

"No use, that child is not answering," she complained to Gabriela, then the phone rang. It was Mateo.

"Good God, kiddo, you were scaring me, I couldn't get in touch with you and I had to—"

"Guess who's here."

"Who?"

"Guess."

"I can't, I don't know the names of your friends. Oh wait, I know. Ulrica."

"No."

"Come on, kiddo, tell me, I have things to do. I bet you haven't even packed yet."

"Ramón."

"What?"

"Ramón. He's downstairs. I called him the other night, that number in Buenos Aires."

"Can you repeat that for me?"

"Ramón. I called and he came. He drove down with his family."

"You're kidding—"

"I swear. You know what he says? That he let us go. That time, when we escaped from the cabin. He says he let us go. That he could have stopped it, but he didn't."

". . ."

"Lolé?"

"Huh?"

"Are you there?"

"Yes."

"Are you surprised?"

"No, not entirely."

"He's lying, right?"

"I don't know. Maybe it's true. It was too easy, wasn't it?"

"Aren't you angry? I am."

"I'm not. I took you with me. I'd gone to get you and I took you with me. The rest is not my business."

"But why would he let us go?"

"What did he tell you?"

"He didn't tell me anything. He cried. He said nothing."

"It could be for two reasons. At least that's what I've always thought."

"The first?"

"He realized that it was no use. Things were not going to fix themselves by force."

"That wouldn't have been too difficult to figure out. The second?"

"The second? He ran out of money."

"The Mafia money?"

"I imagine that he used it to pay for that."

"For what?"

"The whole operation in Bariloche. End of money, end of happiness. But you have him right there, you can ask him yourself."

"I don't know. He doesn't talk much. He just cries."

"Tell me what's going on, son. How are you holding up? Jesus Christ, what a reunion that must have been . . . So you called him, kiddo, who would have thought. You waited to get rid of me to call him, damn you. Did he just arrive?"

"Nah, he got here last night."

"How could you not have called me!"

"I called, I swear. I called your friend's house and no one answered."

"Oh damn, we were at the movies. But tell me, has he been nice to you? Does he look old?"

"He's got a belly. But it was true about the wide shoulders."

"How is it for you? Do you like your father?"

"For the moment, I like my sister. Yesterday, we went sledding."

"So you have a sister. How old is she? What's her name?"

"She's eleven. Her name is Eleonora. And there's a baby called Diego."

"There's also a baby?"

"Eighteen months old."

"Did you give your father the Basque beret?"

"No. I left it in Buenos Aires, in the black suitcase."

"What the hell, kiddo, how long have you had that gift . . . Don't worry, we'll find a way to get it to him later."

"No, he doesn't seem the kind of guy who wears a beret."

"Have you been able to talk to him, tell him things, like you imagined all this time?"

"Not much. There's no privacy."

"Oh."

"There's his wife and children. We haven't been able to talk one-on-one. I like his wife too. She says that in the kids' room there is a picture of me hanging on the wall. From when I was a baby. Lies, right? Last night, he and I did talk alone for a while, but about neoliberalism. He does not like it at all, neoliberalism."

"And you, what did you say?"

"Nothing, he didn't ask for my opinion. Just as well, I don't have an opinion about that. But I must tell you something, and then that's it, because I promised Eleonora that I would help her put the baby to sleep. It's her responsibility to put the baby to sleep every night."

"Wait, Mateo, wait. We have to coordinate everything, because tomorrow you and I have to move with the precision of a Swiss clock. You're coming to Buenos Aires, I'll wait for you at this airport, we take a taxi to the international airport, and from there we'll board the flight to Bogotá together. There is plenty of time, so don't worry, but we have to have our headlights on so there's not a hitch."

"That's why I called you, Lolé. You better go alone to Bogotá. Is it all right?"

"Is it all right? What are you talking about?"

"I'm staying with Ramón. Everything's taken care of."

"What!"

"The beret is for you. You can have it."

"Wait, Mateo, this is serious. What do you mean you're staying with Ramón, you can't just make that decision on your own, you know I— "

"It's only for two or three weeks, just until the end of my school vacation."

"But, Mateo—"

"Don't worry, I'm not two and a half years old anymore. If I smell a Ramónism, I'll take off running, and this Ramón will never catch me. I'm half his weight and a head taller. Trust me, Lorenza. I'll find out who this man is, and when I've figured it out, I'll come back."

A grant from the Guggenheim Foundation
helped to finance part of the writing of this novel.

a note about the author

Laura Restrepo is the bestselling author of several prizewinning novels published in more than twenty languages, including *Leopard in the Sun*, which won the Arzobispo Juan San Clemente Prize; *The Angel of Galilea*, which won the Sor Juana Inés de la Cruz Prize in Mexico and the Prix France Culture in France; and *Delirium*, for which she was awarded the 2004 Alfaguara Prize, with a jury headed by Nobel laureate José Saramago, and the 2006 Grinzane Cavour Prize in Italy. Recipient of a Guggenheim Fellowship for 2007, Restrepo currently divides her time between Bogotá and Mexico City.

a note about the type

The text of this book is set in Goudy, a typeface based on Goudy Old Style, which was designed by the American type designer Frederic W. Goudy in 1915 for American Type Founders. Versatile enough as both text and display, it is one of the most popular typefaces ever produced, frequently used for packaging and advertising. Its open letterforms make it a highly legible and friendly text face.